# the colour of water

**By the same author**

Cassandra's Disk

Angela Green

# the colour of water

**Peter Owen**
London and Chester Springs

Peter Owen Publishers
73 Kenway Road, London SW5 0RE

Peter Owen books are distributed in the USA by
Dufour Editions Inc., Chester Springs, PA 19425-0007

First published in Great Britain 2003 by Peter Owen Publishers


ISBN 0 7206 1204 7

A catalogue record for this book is available from
the British Library

Printed and bound by
Zrinski SA, Croatia

# Ackowledgements

My grateful thanks to Åse and Oddleif Nilsen for their kind hospitality in the Lofotens, and to Oddleif for taking me out to the Maelstrom on a calm day. The Norwegian Fishing Village Museum in Å also provided fascinating detail on the lives, history and legends of Lofoten fishermen.

Although the Lofoten locations in the story are real, all characters and incidents are entirely fictional.

*For Harriet and George*

Moskenes, the Lofoten Islands,

northern Norway,

February 1964

# One

She lives now on an island at the northern rim of the world in a place called, simply, Å.

Her house is of the type they call a *rorbu*: a fisherman's cabin, red-walled, square-set and gabled, built out on a timber platform over the arctic waters of the Vestfjord at the end of the island's only road. Downstairs there is a single large living space lined with smoke-darkened wood. Above are two sleeping spaces: one is hers; the other is empty.

On the island they know her as Anna Larssen. Sigrid Berg, who runs the tiny general-store-cum-telegraph-post-and-harbourmaster's office, and so hears all Lofoten gossip, knows that, although she lived in France for many years and the islanders call her the French Widow, she was born in Oslo. Since she arrived, boats have come and gone as usual, but the French Widow has had no visitors and receives no mail except for a few bulky parcels, all of which have been posted in New York.

This is her second winter on Moskenes and, although the dark polar days have begun to lengthen, she is still wary. Her one extravagance is fuel for the stove: she keeps the log stack high, for without warm fingers she can't type, and if she can't type she can't work on the translations that pay for the fuel. The villagers shake their heads as the boat unloads its weekly consignment of wood, but Sigrid's brother Leif quietly loads Anna's share on to his trailer and brings it along the rutted track to the cabin, upending it with a curt nod at the foot of the steps. Once he's gone, Anna pulls on thick gloves and stacks the logs neatly and quickly under the pitch of the low-sloping outhouse roof. Then she stands and stretches, pressing her hands to the aching small of her back.

Today the wind is from the north, trailing cloud in tattered banners from the high Lofoten peaks. The air is harsh and smells of cold metal, and the sea has thickened to icy meal among the stones. As Anna scans the horizon the first white flakes melt against her lashes and the gale buffets her ears with the distant roar of the Maelstrom. The noise fascinates her: over the months she has come to see the great tidal vortex as a warning against the dangers of allowing oneself to drift. As she did, all her life before coming here; drifted for years in the wake of one man and the dream of another, until she awoke and found herself clinging to wreckage.

Briskly, she turns back towards the warmth of the cabin.

This *rorbu* belonged to her father, who was not a fisherman, and to his father and grandfather before him, who were. Anna herself came to the island only once as a child, yet she never forgot that long sunlit summer of her twelfth year when for some reason her parents relaxed their careful hold on her and let her roam and climb and swim to her heart's content. Back again in Oslo everything in the family's tall townhouse had seemed fussy and cramped by comparison. She wandered dejectedly through rooms cluttered with pastel-coloured painted furniture, embroidered lace tablecloths, fragile china and the sad, slow boredom of clocks.

And for years afterwards she dreamed of the Lofotens: dreams in which she skimmed like a gull above the waves or stepped off the high peaks on to a thousand feet of giddy, buoyant air. But she never went back there – not until it was the furthest, remotest place she could think of. Then she arrived sick at heart, alone on the boat from Bodø, and waited for the bus that would take her down the winding coast to the place where the road ran out.

The polite, incurious Lofoteners did not ask her why she had come, and in any case she was in no state to explain. She left the heavy trunk to be brought on later and, carrying only a small, battered suitcase she toiled up the high track out of Å, slithering over wet rocks and squelching through the little peaty bogs, until she reached the last red house of all. The *rorbu* sat in the late September sunlight, perched in its own little fold of the cliff, jaunty and defiant, a survivor of storms and years of neglect. She unlocked the door with the rusty key and stepped inside.

The place was cold, with a smell of old woodsmoke and faint traces of fish oil. For many years it had been let out to fishermen in the winter cod-fishing season and to occasional holidaying families in the summer. The tiny rental income, which not even Vincent had known about, had accrued year after year in an Oslo bank account that she had cleared and closed on her way north. Now, setting the suitcase down by the door, she took off her coat, rolled up her sleeves and puzzled over and eventually lit the ancient iron stove. Then she found a cobwebbed broom and swept and dusted the handful of rooms. On a beam above the stove were two deep-carved initials, AL, which matched those she had been born with but were in fact, she supposed, those of her grandfather Andreas.

As early dusk fell, the carrier brought the sea-chest, and Anna unpacked the typewriter and the other few things she had brought with her, piling her dictionaries in neat stacks at the side of the table. On a low wooden dresser she placed a single photograph, of her mother and father, taken some thirty years ago on the Oslo waterfront: Gustav bear-like and sober-suited; Marguérite slender and pliant against the bulwark of her husband's torso, a figurehead on a galleon.

When all was clean, calm and orderly, Anna made a meal from the items bought in the general store and sat for a while, listening to the slow pull of the sea and the silence of the mountains beyond. At eleven she climbed the stairs to the little bedroom with the sloping wooden roof.

Even made up with crisp new linen, the little bunk tucked into the space between the roof-slope and the flue looked uncomfortably short, but by now she was too weary to care and merely drew her knees up and curved her neck down and fitted herself as best she could into the small, wood-walled compartment.

To her surprise she slept well, better than she had in months.

It was probably, she thought, waking late the next morning, because there was no ghost-filled empty space beside her. But weeks afterwards Sigrid told her that *rorbu* beds were short because Lofoten fishermen believed if they slept straight instead of curled their souls would slip away from their bodies in the night. She preferred this explanation, and each night after that she smiled as her body assumed its protective nautilus curl beneath the sloping cabin roof.

*

Once she was Anna Galland and lived with her husband Vincent in a bigger house than this.

La Verrerie was a low, yellow-stuccoed villa in the countryside some fifty miles north-west of Paris. They bought it in the early fifties, when even Vincent appeared to grow weary of their rootless post-war existence and announced himself ready to settle down. The villa had been empty for a number of years, but at least it was sound and free from damp. Its garden consisted of a broad stone terrace and a lawn with a vast copper beech tree at its centre. Beyond the high enclosing hedge a pleasant water meadow ran down to the wide, slow-flowing river.

Like an exhausted migratory bird Anna set about making La Verrerie a home for herself and her famous husband. Students, political colleagues, writers and journalists came and went, and for seven years her existence in Saint-Aubain-les-Eaux flowed past with all the surface smoothness of the river itself.

Even when, late in 1958, Vincent disappeared, for a while the life itself remained intact, like light from a distant star that has long since vanished. It was only later, long after her husband's body had been found on a lonely Breton beach, long after the telephone call and the arrival of the mysterious young American, that, to the astonishment of those who thought they knew her, Anna Galland abruptly sold the house and everything in it and left Saint-Aubain-les-Eaux for ever.

Respectful as an undertaker, Yves Dufour, director of the auction house Laforêt Dufour, entered the salon where his new client was awaiting his arrival.

Madame Galland stood at the window looking down the garden, her grey dress clinging in graceful folds about her thin body. Although she had to be in her early forties there was, thought Dufour, a gamine quality about her, something which aroused both protectiveness and desire. He brushed back his smooth hair. A professional, well used to dealing with the sensitivities of the recently bereaved, he coughed discreetly behind his hand as he moved forward into the light.

'Dufour. A tragedy, madame. My belated condolences.'

He clasped her hand in his and wagged his long, intelligent head.

Anna Galland nodded briefly.

'Thank you. Shall we begin?'

Hiding his surprise at such abruptness Dufour followed his new client around her house, murmuring appreciation of its fine furniture, gently lifting down pictures from the walls and exclaiming over them.

His skilled gaze registered and filed the tiny Chagall sketch of lovers, the matched Jacobean hearthside chairs, the books with their impressive fly-leaf dedications from the great and the good. He measured by eye the polished length of the dining-table and the width of the carved rose-wood bed. But Madame Galland said little or nothing, and in the face of her unnerving silence Dufour's chatter gradually dried. He didn't speak again until, in the last room, Monsieur Galland's study, he hesitated over a small group of objects on the desk. Piled carelessly in a small cardboard box lay Vincent Galland's war medals, his Croix de Guerre, the ribbon of the Légion d'Honneur. Beside them stood framed honorary doctorates and photographs showing the great man with international dignitaries of both Western and communist states.

'Madame? Forgive me, Madame Galland, but these objects are obviously items of great sentimental attachment.'

There was another silence. The woman stared at him for a moment and then gazed once more out of the window as if he hadn't spoken. Gamely Dufour persisted.

'With such a man as Monsieur Galland,' he said, 'where does one begin? Hero of the Resistance, man of letters, *homme du peuple* – in so many ways renowned – certain items will doubtless be preserved for posterity. Naturally these honours', he held up the medals, their ribbed silk bright in the sunlight, 'are not destined for the sale?'

Madame Galland turned slowly and, as she did, her eyes, great and saucer-shaped in her thin face, passed in and out of the light, so suddenly he could not tell whether they were blue as he had originally thought, or grey or even a pale leaf green. When she spoke her voice was so low and mild that he strained to hear.

'Naturally.'

Then, louder, 'If you will study the document I gave you at the outset, monsieur, you will find that those particular items do not appear on the sale inventory. My husband's sister, Mademoiselle Galland, will collect them . . .' she moved to the desk and pointed to a paragraph on the last typewritten sheet, 'on Friday.'

Dufour blushed. 'Ah, excellent, of course. Nevertheless . . .'

Softly, Madame Galland cut across him. 'I think you will find that everything you need is there, monsieur,' she said. 'Please let me know when you're ready.'

To leave, she meant. In a slow swirl of grey wool she turned and was gone. Curious woman. Dufour shook his head and scanned the list. It was, he had to admit, conscientiously detailed.

Upstairs Anna leaned against the landing banister until her breathing slowed. *Homme du peuple.* Lately she had found herself swept by great surges of anger that made even the most ordinary social contact difficult to sustain.

When, two weeks later, the last lorry from Laforêt Dufour rumbled away down the drive, Anna Galland shut the door on the echoing house and walked down the path to the waiting taxi. She travelled north by train with just two pieces of luggage: her grandfather's vast old sea-chest and a battered cardboard suitcase she had had as a girl.

*

Her pale hair grew untrimmed through that first Lofoten winter, and when spring came she scraped it back from her face and tied it back with a careless length of twine. There was no mirror in the cabin, and by then she felt no need of one. As the days began to lengthen she started to explore the island, setting off alone in the early morning light. Growing stronger and bolder she followed the steeper tracks, climbing further and further up into the rocky interior until she reached places where eagles flew in descending circles over silent tarns green as ice caves.

Alone in these remote sweeps she sat and watched the shadows of clouds pass over the peaks, while within her a new self gradually accreted over the old, like slow-growing coral over a fragile reef.

# Two

Now it is winter again in Moskenes.

In her cabin Anna Galland hangs her padded jacket on a hook and sits in the old wooden chair facing the scrubbed pine desk. Her calm gaze travels around the room taking in its details. Over the year she has grown into a comfortable solidarity with the objects around her – the blue enamel jug on the stove, the thick felt boots drying before the hearth – as if she and they have together taken on substance, acquired solidity and colour. Slowly, she stretches muscles stiff from stacking wood, savouring the warmth of returning circulation as she rests her fingers on the round metal keys of the typewriter.

She has been a translator for over twenty years, having had all her life what some people, her husband among them, disdainfully called a 'facility with languages'. She speaks four fluently – English, French, Swedish and her native Norwegian – and has a fair command of Italian and German. Originally, translation provided her with a means of making money from her one and only talent, and she set about it with quiet industriousness, but now it has become a deeply enjoyable activity for which she is fortunate enough to be paid. On the shelves of the *rorbu* are books in Norwegian by many famous foreign writers. Their names are printed in large, bold type on the dust-jackets or gold-embossed on the spines; her own appears only as a small note on the title page, with no accompanying photograph or biography – she has never been, never dared to be, anything more than the invisible lens through which writer and reader may understand one another.

Tonight, as usual, she inserts a sheet of paper behind the platen and rolls it through to receive the first line of type. When it is in position instinctively she looks down to her left where the author's source text normally sits annotated and waiting. But the table is bare.

She has been dreading this moment, avoiding it, for months.

Yet now it is here she finds herself ready, even strangely eager, to swim down to the lost banks of memory, where the fact and fiction and sense of her life lie closely entangled, like drowned men caught in weed.

She already knows where she will begin: with the day she met her husband, Vincent Galland. As she sinks back down through the years she can see it clearly: already the words are forming in her mind.

But suddenly, unbidden, another image intrudes. Brilliant. Insolent. Unforgettable.

Her hands drop from the keys; she brushes away the sand of intervening time and holds the fragment of memory up to the light.

Sunshine glints into the changeable eyes of a young woman and gilds her pale, straight hair. Believing herself a widow, Anna Galland sits on a park bench in the gardens of the Palais Royal, beneath budding trees. She is twenty-one.

As she watches the pigeons scrabbling in the dust a shadow falls over her.

*Hi, kid.*

'No.' She has spoken aloud in the silence of the cabin.

'No,' she says again. Not yet.

*

She was nineteen when she met Vincent Galland.

Her father had been dead a year.

Gustav Larssen, professor of architecture, had been explaining to his students the intricate harmonies of the Golden Mean, when a single cataclysmic seizure exploded his ordered mind into a hurtling diapason of light, and he crumpled to the floor of the lecture theatre.

Her father was a big man. His coffin lay on the table in the front parlour, filling the room. Anna and her mother followed it to the cemetery in Oslo. Afterwards, when they returned home, the house felt vacant and unfamiliar, a space now awaiting redefinition by stronger personalities than theirs.

And without her Norwegian husband Marguérite Larssen soon became uncomfortably aware of her foreignness. She yearned for the comforting familiarity of France, and French food, and the elegance of her mother tongue. Nine months after her husband's death she took her daughter back to Paris, rented them a small attic apartment in

Montparnasse and with a certain quiet astonishment found herself living the life she had known twenty years earlier. While she scraped a living teaching English and making dresses for *petit bourgeois* ladies of the locality, her daughter started work as a junior clerk at the Norwegian Embassy.

Anna's manager, an irritable, sandy-haired attaché from Oslo, found the new girl intelligent enough but disastrously lacking in self-confidence. The first time he criticized her typing she shook so much that she spilled a cup of coffee on his blotter. Irate, he ordered her to bring drinks in on a tray in future, which only made her nervousness worse. Every morning as she walked across the large expanse of floor to his desk, milk jug, cup, saucer and spoon clattered noisily against each other.

The three older clerks felt sorry for her and decided to take the poor girl under their wing. Hjordis took her to a hairdresser, Vibeke lent her scarves to update her few dresses, and Grethe introduced her to her French friends. At lunchtimes they took her out with them to sample the *plat du jour* at one of a dozen small bistros in the *quartier*, while senior diplomats lunched in more luxurious surroundings on the Champs-Elysées or near the Bourse, allaying rumours of war with *foie gras*, *filet de bœuf aux truffes* and cheeses of great ripeness and pungency, washed down with increasingly optimistic quantities of burgundy.

Anna left the embassy at six every evening. In cold weather she pulled her woollen hat down over her ears, wound a scarf around her throat and headed for the warm, tired air of the Métro. When she reached her local shops she bought bread and when she could afford it a pre-cooked dish of *cassoulet* or *lentilles* from the *traiteur*. The shopkeepers smiled and complimented her on her French, which was already fluent and almost accent-free. Often, with a wink, they slipped an extra spoonful into the container, and as Anna stepped back out into the street clutching the warm, aromatic parcel she had the sensation that, at last, life was a door slowly swinging open before her.

Then, one evening in March, as she stood with Vibeke on the fringes of a diplomatic reception, a tall, slim, smartly dressed man shouldered his way through the crowd towards her.

'Mademoiselle Larssen?' His sleek hair shone under the glittering chandelier.

Anna blushed, keenly aware that in the beige crêpe-de-Chine dress her mother had sewn for her she lacked the Parisian chic of most of the other women in the room.

The tall man bowed. Then, to her astonishment, he reached for her hand, lifted it to his lips and kissed it. At her side Vibeke giggled and moved away.

The man smiled. Hazel eyes, flecked with gold, gleamed at her.

'Forgive me for swooping down on you, but I saw you from the other side of the room, and Myles Pilkington told me your name.' He gave a slight bow. 'I am Vincent Galland, Frenchman, Czech, journalist, diplomat and, for the last three weeks, an exile from my home in German-occupied Prague.'

There was a sudden burst of conversation beside them, and he shook his head.

'Impossible to talk here.'

He took her elbow, and she let herself be steered through to the ballroom. An orchestra was playing, but as yet there were only a few couples on the dance floor, turning in slow, measured circles.

'Shall we?'

Supported at waist and hand, she let herself be led forward on to the dance floor. He waited for the beat, then drew her into the waltz. He was confident, sure, relaxed. After a moment, she heard his voice close to her ear, 'So, Mademoiselle Larssen, what is your opinion of the Nazis?'

She wasn't used to being asked her opinion. For a moment she hesitated, fearing that anything she said would sound naïve or foolish. But the lengthening silence quickly became worse than talking. 'I don't know,' she murmured. 'They frighten me, I suppose.' She blushed.

Vincent Galland smiled down at her. 'Good,' he said. 'Some people find them amusing. They see a hundred thousand arms raised in homage to a small, odd man, and they smile. But I have seen those same Nazi troops march down the streets of my mother's home city, Mademoiselle Larssen, so I do not smile.'

He brought her arm close against his chest and whispered in her ear, 'They're already here in Paris, you know. For the present they still call themselves envoys and attachés, but, trust me, it's a matter of time, that's all.' He looked around the room. 'To resist successfully you need to know your enemy. Where is he tonight, do you think? Over there, perhaps?'

Anna turned her head slightly and looked where Galland directed her, conscious all the while of his arm at her waist, his cool palm against hers, the antiseptic smell of his cologne against her cheek.

'Do you mean those two thin men to the right of the orchestra?'

He looked and smiled. 'Ah no. They're Polish, poor chaps – see their worried frowns? They're frightened their country will go the same way as mine. Which it will, whenever the small, odd man wishes. No, that one.' She was positioned to view a brilliantined aristocratic figure. 'And those two vultures over there', he spun her around again, 'are trusted henchmen of the inestimable Führer of the Third Reich. *Sieg heil!*' He gave a mock salute in their direction and whirled her down the room like a doll, in a series of dizzying spirals.

The young English diplomat called Pilkington smiled cryptically when she mentioned Vincent's name in conversation a few days later.

'Ah, you've met the mysterious Vincent Galland. Janus, they call him here.'

'Janus?'

Always pleased to have an opportunity to educate, Myles Pilkington tapped a cigarette on a chased silver case. 'God of portals? Chiefly known for looking both ways at once? As does your young Galland apparently. French father, Czech mother; born in Prague, spent much of his life here in Paris. Has been a journalist, an agitator, a diplomat and a philosopher. Looks both political ways, too, they say. I've heard him described as a committed nationalist and wholehearted communist, which is quite a feat. Although perhaps now it's the other way round.' He smiled tolerantly at her. 'Anyway, it's probably not such a rarity as it sounds, if you come from Czecho. The place has always been a melting pot: Czechs, Slovaks, Moravians, Bohemians, Ruthenians – God knows how they ever held together in the first place, the whole country was always a sort of political high-wire act, and the Nazis went through them like a hot knife through butter last month. Apparently your friend was there. Yes, he got out just in time.'

He paused, and Anna asked quickly, 'And what is he doing here?'

Pilkington frowned 'No one quite knows. As I say, "journalist" is what he's been telling people, but I gather that if you ask him after a few vodkas he'll say he's a Resistant.'

'Resistant?'

Pilkington nodded sagely. 'Probably means he's out to stiffen governmental sinews here and in Britain, although I hear tell he's been back to Prague already: some derring-do operation, all undercover. Linking up with his friends in the Party, I should think. Strange man. But damned persuasive by all accounts.'

Anna nodded. She did not think she would tell Myles Pilkington that she had already spent several evenings listening to the strange and persuasive Vincent Galland. In the smoky cafés of Saint-Germain the air was close and damp. Vincent loosened his tie, rolled up the sleeves of his shirt and talked. His theme was constant: war was inevitable. And when other nations fell to the Nazis as his own had just done, people would accept that organized resistance was the only possible course of action. Mesmerized by his certainty, his passionate articulacy, Anna watched the sweat flow in rivulets from his hair, like a melting halo.

She had, of course, no one to compare him with. The few boys she had known in Oslo had been awkward or inarticulate or both. And when one of them was brave enough to call at her house her father sat him down in the study and interrogated him so fiercely on the subject of his studies and prospects that the young man panicked and left before she came down.

So Vincent's brilliance shone new into Anna's eyes, unclouded and dazzling.

A week later Vibeke and the other girls took Anna to one side.

'Are you sure you ought to be seeing so much of that man Galland?' said Grethe. 'He's got a reputation.'

'What do you mean?'

Hjordis leaned forward, 'You shouldn't trust him.' She wrinkled her long, thin nose. 'Anders thinks he's actually a communist agitator trying to whip up public opinion.' Hjordis was engaged to a Norwegian intelligence officer and had suddenly acquired informed and firm opinions on most aspects of Parisian diplomatic life.

Anna frowned and stirred her coffee. 'Well, he's been kind to me,' she said quietly. Several times now, late at night, Vincent had walked her home. She trotted beside him as he described with flattering intimacy his childhood in Prague, student days at the Lycée Condorcet and his months with the International Brigade in Spain. But by the time they reached her door he had usually steered the talk back to Germany and the present.

'They're coming, Anna,' he had said last night, turning to face her. 'I don't say it to scare you, but please don't believe those who say Hitler is a man you can trust. The Nazis had been in my country for years before they finally invaded. Espionage, assassinations – they got away with everything. And now it's happening here.'

'Are you in danger?' she asked.

'I assume so. But I take care. And it's not constant. Tonight, for example,' he looked up and down the empty boulevard, 'tonight, they are simply watching someone else.'

Anna had told herself that if war came she and her mother would simply run away to a safe place. When they first met she had tried to ask Vincent which country was best to hide in, but he told her that his own mother and sister were stranded in occupied Prague, and she didn't raise the subject again.

They had reached the end of her street. Nothing stirred beneath the branches of the overhanging limes. Vincent glanced around them.

'I'll say goodbye here,' he said, then took her briefly in his arms and touched his lips against hers. Anna blushed gratefully in the darkness and hugged him awkwardly.

'Until tomorrow, then,' he said, 'dear Anna.'

'Until tomorrow,' she said and watched him walk down the street and turn the corner. Anna pushed open the heavy wooden door into the courtyard. He had confided in her. He had kissed her. What joy. She ran up the curving stairs two at a time.

On the landing she slowed, drew breath and slipped the key quietly into the lock. Over the past few weeks Marguérite had developed a painful cough and, although she dismissed it as a *petite grippe*, she was exhausted by evening. Anna tiptoed over to the bedroom door, but as she reached for the handle there was a moan from the couch behind her.

'Maman?'

She turned on the light. Her mother was lying on the sofa, her brown hair plastered untidily against her scalp, her eyes wide and black. Anna dropped to her knees. Marguérite's forehead was burning; she moaned again, then coughed and winced, her hands fluttering at her throat.

'Gustav, Gustav, it's so hot. I can't breathe.'

Anna stroked her mother's arm. 'It's me, Maman, Anna. What's wrong?'

'Gustav!' Marguérite bent double as a fit of coughing seized her. When she wiped her mouth on the back of her hand there was bright blood on it.

By the time the doctor arrived Marguérite was calmer and dozing. He examined her carefully, tapping her thin back and listening intently to her chest. Afterwards he asked Anna where he might wash his hands and stood over the basin scrubbing furiously at his nails.

'How long has she been coughing like this?'

Anna thought. 'A few weeks. She said it was nothing – a cold.'

The doctor shook his head and unscrewed his fountain pen. 'One doesn't have a raging temperature or cough up blood when one has a simple cold, mademoiselle. Now, this will help reduce the fever.' He went on writing. 'Have you yourself lost weight recently or had any coughing fits? Pains in the chest?'

Anna shook her head. She felt shamefully healthy.

'Well that's good. But your mother must have complete rest. And you must notify me immediately if there is any change.'

On Saturday Vincent arrived with a parcel of expensive delicacies to tempt the invalid's appetite: fresh eggs, butter, milk and dark chocolate.

Marguérite whispered thanks. She tasted tiny morsels of food and pronounced it delicious. She would eat more later, she promised. For the moment she wasn't hungry, only thirsty. But Anna must eat, oh yes, indeed she must, and keep up her strength for both of them. She passed the chocolate to her daughter and, with a smile, picked up the glass of milk from the table, pretending to sip.

Anna watched her mother's fingers, bony as sticks, tremble with effort.

# Three

She has been working for hours. Anna pulls the last sheet from the typewriter and adds it to the others, shuffling them into an orderly block. Then, shoulders hunched together like folded wings, she reads it all through. Usually she tests each phrase, recognizing the flaws by their dull, hollow ring, then cutting and polishing until the words resonate in harmony with the original like struck crystal glasses.

But tonight is different.

Tonight the words and memories are hers, and she is free to choose, to change at will. Of course, as so many of her authors do, she has chosen to begin with a pivotal moment, heightening its colours with a little self-conscious description. As she rereads it she is pleased enough with the technical aspects: certainly the scene unreels largely as she remembers it.

She gets up, stretches and kneels to feed the stove, placing each log carefully within the cave of orange heat to build a strong, lasting fire. When it is glowing she shuts the door and sits back in her wooden chair, listening to the wavefall outside.

She enjoys, she thinks, a curiously positive view of solitude, for a woman once abandoned and twice widowed by the same man.

*

Death by drowning was the final verdict.

Vincent's funeral took place on a rainy Friday morning in November 1961. Followed by mourners Anna picked her way along the wet gravel paths behind the swaying coffin. She kept her head down, avoiding the sight of the box that contained the body, and watched the toes of her black polished shoes stepping out obediently below her. She had been afraid of sudden overwhelming grief, of collapsing, but in fact she felt detached from the scene, as if she were watching it from the topmost branches of the trees that bordered the cemetery on three sides, their last leaves sheltering the mourners from the worst of the autumn rain.

The pallbearers lowered the coffin, words were spoken, someone squeezed her arm. Then handfuls of soil were scattered, and apparently she was retracing her steps to the gate, and behind her there was the noise of earth falling on to something hollow.

That night she had lain awake. She was surprised by the continued absence of tears and even tried unsuccessfully to force them, only to stop immediately, feeling ashamed. Many people had wept at the funeral: Florence had been almost hysterical, and at one point Bertrand Delamain's wife, Astrid, had staggered, half fainting, and had to be supported by her husband. Yet for Anna herself the idea of Vincent's death, of what so many people called his suicide, was unreal. She had felt more truly widowed in 1940 when, although he was reported dead, Vincent had still been alive. At least then she had known how and why he had 'died'.

She threw back the tangled bedclothes and went downstairs.

The study door was open, as if Vincent had just stepped outside for a moment. The room smelt of his cigarettes, of woodsmoke from old fires. On the desk were the familiar ranks of silver framed photographs: the two of them in Central Park in the early spring of 1942. And this one, in pride of place, the picture from *Time* magazine in 1944: Vincent, wearing the Légion d'Honneur, in front of the Arc de Triomphe, surrounded by cheering crowds. She was there, too, at the left of the picture, in a pale dress, smiling and smiling. 'A Hero's Return,' the headline said. And it had been. Such unimaginable pride and happiness, they thought they would die of it.

She took the picture back upstairs with her and put it on the bedside table. But even when she looked at it the following morning, still no tears came.

In the months that followed Vincent's funeral, grief, if that was what it was, crept up on her slowly and oddly. The happiness she remembered gradually faded until all memory of it – the mornings of waking beside him, of discussing their plans for the day; their walks, their companionable meals, their familiar, undemanding lovemaking – had melted away. Now the rooms had an echo she had never heard when Vincent was there. In life, she realized, he had filled the house, had filled her existence. His likes and dislikes, his foibles and irritabilities, his enthusiasms and contradictions had absorbed all available space, and without him she was apparently . . . nothing.

One morning his absence, and her own intrusive presence, struck her so forcibly that she couldn't bear the clatter of her shoes on the floors and went barefoot. Later, numb with cold, she pulled on a pair of his thick woollen socks to cut out the rising chill from the flagstones. All day she glided with fitting silence through the house, like a ghost.

Florence, still openly mourning her employer, answered the door, thanked the callers for their sympathy and begged them to understand that madame was inconsolable following the death of her beloved husband and was incapable of receiving visitors. To Anna, sitting alone and directionless in her room, she seemed to be talking about a stranger.

The mayor and his Conseil Municipal had sent a formal black-edged note expressing their regret at the tragic loss and declaring that they proposed to erect a monument to her husband or as they called him, in an ambitious simplification, 'this great Resistance hero of the People'.

Maire Fanchon reiterated this promise when, a few weeks later, he came to call on Anna in person. 'One envisages something worthy of the memory of this commune's most illustrious adopted son, Madame Galland,' he murmured, smoothing his white moustache. 'I myself and the entire council would be honoured by your presence at its future unveiling.'

Anna nodded mutely.

The memorial plaque to Vincent was ready in March.

The morning was bright and clear, with a blue rime of frost on the square of grass at the centre of the Grande Place. A draped tricolour covered a stone plinth. Behind it a row of ancient limes had been subjected to a brutal *tondage* in Vincent's honour, and when, at a sign from the mayor, Anna stretched out her hand and drew the flag aside, new bronze gleamed in the sun, unshadowed by overhanging branches. The plaque itself had been sculpted by a local artist from a wartime photograph and bore Vincent's profile as a younger man – a likeness that captured the fine straight nose, the proud cast of his head as he stared into a clear bronze distance. Below the image was the name, date and a single, defiant, phrase: *Héro de la Résistance*.

Dry-eyed as the band began the 'Marseillaise', Anna stared at the pollarded tree. How strange, she thought, that the word 'hero', which described something Vincent had been for just a few years of his life, should now be his only epitaph.

'*Qu'un sang impur / Abreuve nos sillons*,' sang the mayor at her side, his breath billowing about his head.

The sun glinted on Vincent's metal cheekbone. Determined not to cry now, after so many tearless months, Anna forced her tongue up hard against her palate and stared fixedly at the plaque. At least here he had regained an official, unassailable reality.

The band was marching away. At a distance, the mayor and his colleagues were stamping their feet and rubbing their reddened hands, patiently waiting to leave. Anna smoothed her black glove over her wedding ring and tightened the woollen scarf at her throat. Then she constructed a grateful smile and went over to thank the councillors for their kindness.

The empty spring of 1962 passed into silent summer. That year of her second, real, widowhood there were few callers at the house in Saint-Aubain-les-Eaux. Some were deterred by the presence of the late Monsieur Galland's sister, the sharp-tongued Marie-Christine, who arrived for the memorial ceremony and contrived to stay on through the summer; others found the widow herself excessively reclusive or went further and in some way blamed her for Vincent's death.

In her heart she understood their reproachfulness. A good wife ought to have realized that her husband was distressed to the point of taking his own life, should have been able to comfort him, especially if, like Vincent Galland, that man was well respected and famous, with a heroic past and an untroubled future ahead of him. In her guilt she became aware of the sudden silences which fell whenever she entered the *boulangerie* or the *épicerie*. Her fingers fumbled for small coins. Sometimes in her haste she forgot her shopping altogether and only remembered the abandoned packages when she reached, panting and empty-handed, the safety of La Verrerie.

Gradually her world shrank back until it consisted only of the house and the garden.

She was a prisoner whose gaoler had disappeared, taking with him the only key.

And then, one afternoon in August, the telephone rang.

Beyond the terrace the garden swam in the humming heat. The blossom and flowers were luxuriant, their profusion another mark of absence, since Vincent had not been there to prune the old Albertine rose to within a bud of its woody life or demand that the lavender hedge and the box trees be clipped into strict compliance. Latterly, Anna had begun to take some small horticultural liberties. For instance, she'd let the clematis climb through the hawthorn and drift across into the tall branches of the apple tree. She'd allowed forget-me-nots of a particular blue to haze the herbaceous border. And, most subversively of all, she had bought five packets of Californian poppy seeds and torn off the tops as she went, sowing tiny black specks indiscriminately into the wind like some bountiful Ceres. Now the yellow and orange and red flags nodded at her from every corner of the garden, preening themselves, unashamedly bold, and clashing garishly and ironically with Vincent's collection of rare pinks.

Anna stretched out on an old white-painted garden seat and closed her eyes.

Sunlight flickered over her eyelids.

It was hot.

So hot. And she was a Californian poppy, spreading her diaphanous skirts towards the afternoon sun. Suddenly the sunlight vanished, and Marie-Christine Galland plopped a white canvas hat on her head.

'Anna, *ma chère,* you've been asleep in the sun for hours. Your face is burning.' Marie Christine had her brother's voice: cultivated, civilized, faintly supercilious.

Anna pushed up the brim of the hat and squinted at her sister-in-law.

'Was I? Am I?' She felt her cheek. 'Perhaps . . . a little.' She rallied, 'Oh, you look hot, too.' She reached for the filmed bottle of oil that lay beside the chair.

'No *produits chimiques,* thank you.' Marie-Christine's pitying smile was brief as a matchstrike. She retrieved the hat and sank down on to the chair opposite, fanning herself gently. 'There were six visitors at the graveside this afternoon. *Six!*'

Anna blinked. Since the unveiling of the memorial plaque in the square there had been many articles about Vincent in the paper, and now there was a small but steady stream to the cemetery.

'I introduced myself, naturally.'

Naturally, thought Anna. Sometimes there was a ghoulishness in Marie-Christine's pride. 'Were they French?' she asked, trying to show interest.

'Two were. The others were *Américains*.'

Anna thought they were probably English, but it was impossible to tell: for Marie-Christine all Anglo-Saxons were Americans.

'Anyway,' she added, 'they found the plaque impressive. And, of course, they said how brave Vincent had been. And how handsome.'

Ah yes. Anna sat perfectly still, resting her arms on the warm wood of the chair. Throughout his life, and especially in his middle years, women had been drawn to Vincent: journalists, young comrades, left-wing students. And now, even after death, they were still fluttering around him. Sometimes she imagined Vincent lying back, mysterious and heroic, in the splendour of his white, silk-lined coffin, secretly luxuriating in their adoration, like a monarch at a levee.

She shook her head. Except there would be no rising to the occasion this particular afternoon. Or on any other.

Irritated by the lack of reaction to her news, Marie-Christine rose to her feet, smoothed her sleek grey hair back from her face. She would prepare a pitcher of iced *thé russe,* she announced.

Anna nodded thankfully. Oh yes, let her go off to the kitchen where her jangling busyness might be absorbed in the clacking of tea caddies and scoops, saucers and knives, lemons and tongs. Let her go, for pity's sake. She closed her eyes, red petals once more filtering the light.

Soon the sound of Marie-Christine's favourite atonal music was drifting through the kitchen window, vying with the bee-hum in the garden.

When the telephone rang Anna sat up immediately and before she knew it was on her feet and walking across the terrace. As she stepped, swaying, into the cool dimness of the hall, the ringing stopped.

'*C'est un Américain*,' said Vincent's sister triumphantly, holding out the receiver.

Anna took the telephone from her, put her hand over the mouthpiece and half turned away, so that even Marie-Christine could not help but see that she was now expected to leave.

When the kitchen door finally slammed at the far end of the corridor, Anna said quietly, 'This is Madame Galland.'

'Hello? Hello?'

An American voice crackled through space and time.

Anna gripped the phone to steady herself, her knuckles white as exposed spine.

*Harry.*

*Harry?*

Then, abruptly, the line cleared, and she realized the voice belonged to a stranger.

*

The cold outside is circling the cabin, squeezing it like ice floes shrinking around the hull of a ship. Anna shivers and goes over to the stove, wraps a cloth around the handle of the enamel jug and pours hot, perfumed coffee into a mug. As she bends forward, the initials AL stare back at her from the beam. Her grandfather must have stood here, leaned against this hearth, presiding over the crew of reeking unwashed fishermen. And the cabin would have been full of the smoke of their pipes and the buzz of their talk and their grateful laughter – grateful because without the shelter of the *rorbu* they would have slept as their ancestors did, huddled under an upturned boat on the beach, wrapped in a salt-stiffened sail.

Anna carries the mug over to the desk, the steam trailing behind her like incense from a censer. The ghosts of her past have been waiting patiently for her return: conjured by the memory of an American voice, they crowd around her as she sits. Black-and-white scenes whirr through her mind like film through a projector, flickering faster than her fingers can type.

In a hotel room a stoppered bottle glints in late sunlight and, tipped, drenches the air with the perfume of vanilla and carnations. There is a sound of distant guns. In Lisbon music fills a darkened apartment with yearning . . . *I hope that he / Turns out to be / Someone who'll watch over me* . . . and she is dancing her dream – dancing for the last time with Harry Quinn. His hips brush against hers – hardness against hollowness. Her head is bowed against the whiteness of his shirt, and his hand is at her nape, slowly caressing the long, taut tendons of her neck.

'I can help you leave me, Anna.' Harry Quinn whispers. 'If that's what you really want.'

His arms fold around her and she lets her feet drift between his.

*Harry.*

No.

Violently, Anna shakes the recollection out of her head. Tonight she mistrusts her memory. Tonight she is her father's daughter and mistrusts fiction and invention altogether. What she wants, what she craves, is a source text, a bedrock. In need of facts, she goes over to the old camphor-wood sea-chest by the chimney and lifts the heavy lid.

The room fills with the perfume of ancient forests.

At the back of the chest, wedged between a faded watercolour of Oslo and a tattered photograph album, are three slim notebooks bound in faded blue cloth. Each has a pasted slip on the spine with dates written in sepia ink. Anna takes out one marked 1941 and opens it, letting the brittle pages fan. They are brown-edged, fissured and smell of the past. Leafing slowly through it she carries it back to the captain's chair.

The writing inside the blue cloth cover of the journal is so neat and devoid of character that Anna scarcely recognizes it as her own. At first she is disappointed by the lack of resonance – after twenty years she has no memory of writing these words – but then, slowly, she becomes absorbed by their fluency, the sheer volume of forgotten detail, and reads until sleep overtakes her.

# Four

After three days of wind and cloud, the next day is a fresh and brilliant blue. The winter sunshine, although chilly, is too good to waste. Anna carries a table outside and places it in a sheltered corner of the platform. A large flat stone serves as a paperweight, and she sits muffled in scarf, hooded jacket and fingerless gloves, reading the journals and typing. From time to time she looks up from the past and breathes fresh salt air and watches the seagulls wheeling serenely between the snow-covered peaks.

It's past midday.

The wind is rising, riffling the pages on the table.

Lines of cloud are coming up from the south-west – on the horizon the island of Værøy is dark purple against a charcoal sky. The late winter afternoons are brief: soon the sunlight will be gone. She carries the table back inside, and the chair, and neatens the pile of typescript before adding it to the other on the desk. Lunch is a hunk of cheese and a few oat biscuits, followed by an apple. When it is finished she takes the canvas bag from the back of the chair and sets off to walk around the point to the village.

All the length of the shoreline there are long scribbles of sea-wrack and driftwood. She trudges between these undulating lines, making mental notes of kindling to pick up on the way back. Some mornings there are exotic finds to be made: a crate of salty oranges, a scarred shark carcass, a dead, beseeching starfish.

It takes her twenty minutes to reach the far side of the bay. It's the fishing season and the wooden racks are full of drying cod – the stockfish that has earned the Lofoteners their living for a thousand years. Today the boats are out at sea, grateful for a day's calm weather, and the village is peaceful; the only sound is metal striking metal from the smithy up on the hill.

As she climbs the steps to the store she collides with the massive form of Sigrid's brother Leif. In the half-sun half-shadow they do three brief sidesteps, successively blocking each other's path.

'Sorry,' says Anna hoarsely – the first word spoken aloud for days.

'Missus Larssen.' Pulling off his salt-stained cap, he steps back outside, waiting for her to pass.

For a moment she wonders why he is not out at sea with his crew and the other fishing boats, but then she remembers.

She had been standing outside the store one morning last summer. Sigrid, hefting cartons outside on the platform, had straightened to return her brother's farewell wave as he sailed out of the harbour, his big frame filling the boat's tiny cabin.

And Anna had said, impulsively, 'Do you think Leif would take me out to see the Maelstrom one day?'

'No,' said Sigrid quickly. 'Not him.'

Anna had watched the little boat reach the harbour mouth. Instead of turning south to the Maelstrom and the open sea, he turned left towards the calmer waters of the fjord.

'Why not?'

The big woman stood, red-cheeked from effort, and surveyed Anna as if trying to make up her mind about something. Then she sighed. 'Because he doesn't go out to sea any more.' She wiped her hands on her sweater and sighed again. 'Five years ago Leif had a proper trawler, one of the largest on Moskenes, with a crew of four, all men from here in Å. One day they were out fishing beyond Værøy when a sudden storm blew up. They were trying to beat their way back to harbour when they hit the Maelstrom, and the youngest lad, Harald Ringstadt's boy Lars, was washed overboard.'

She turned away, straightening cartons. 'Leif blamed himself for what happened. He sold the trawler and bought himself a smaller boat, one he could sail single-handed. He still fishes, sure, but he never goes out of the Vestfjord. And he always goes alone.'

Out in the sea fjord the little boat had disappeared.

A week later Sigrid's husband Gunnar called across to Anna from the back room of the store. 'If you want to visit the Maelstrom,' he said, 'I can take you, if you like.'

Anna said apologetically, 'I was curious, that's all. Last winter, in the storms, the vibrations came right up through the rock – the whole cabin shook with the roaring. I kept wondering what could do that, what it looked like.'

Gunnar's son Johan came to stand by his father's side. 'Let's show her, Papa. I'll come, too.'

Gunnar Berg shook his head. 'I'll take you both, but not today. It's a full moon, the tide's too big, and the wind's in the wrong direction. You don't take risks with the Maelstrom.'

The following day he'd also refused. 'Storm before dark, look.' Although the sky to the east was still cloudless blue, the sun was sinking in feeble yellow light, and behind the mountain was a massing pile of cloud.

It was not until several days later that the combination of wind, tide and weather appeared propitious enough to satisfy him. Then, to the boy fidgeting excitedly in the doorway, he said, 'The forecast is good, and they say on the radio that the wind's veering south-west, but I think we'd better consult the expert – what do you think, boy?'

Johan ran to the front door.

Moments later he was back.

'King Cod says south-west,' he said excitedly.

Anna looked at Gunnar, but he simply spread his hands and shrugged. 'If you want to survive you've got to watch the signs. Come see.'

Father and son led her around the side of the house. On a wooden rack a dry fish carcass hung twisting in the breeze.

'Every now and then we catch a fish like this, with a great bony crown on his head. He brings good luck – and he tells us whenever the wind's about to change.'

Anna stared at the king cod's empty eye-socket and shivered

'How does he know?'

Gunnar Berg rubbed his stubbled chin with one enormous hand. 'Well now, some say he knows the ways of nature, and some say the string he hangs from is affected by the moisture in the air.' He smiled. 'Anyway, today he says the wind's good for the Maelstrom. What do you think, Johan?'

'I think he's right,' said the boy solemnly.

The sea was pale blue and irreproachably calm. Anna sat in the middle of the boat, between the boxes of lines and weights, and watched father and son standing by the wheel in the tiny cabin. Gunnar kept his hand on the boy's shoulder as Johan steered. They wore matching grey-and-black sweaters, an intricate pattern knitted, Anna supposed, by the indefatigable Sigrid.

They were passing a steep-sided bay. A lone wooden house stood dwarfed by a thousand foot slope.

'That's Hell Cove,' called Gunnar over the sound of the diesel. 'Where Sigrid and Leif were born. There's a sheltered inlet, you can't see it from here, and just behind is a freshwater lake. The place is abandoned now; all the families moved to Å a couple of years ago.' He cuffed his son fondly. 'Johan doesn't believe his mama, but when the weather was too bad to sail around to the headland she and his Uncle Leif used to come over the mountains to school in Å.'

Anna looked at the narrow trail winding upwards from the sunlit bay into the shadow of the peak and imagined two stocky figures toiling up the mountainside and then thought of the children in Saint-Aubain-les-Eaux walking their few hundred yards to the village school.

Life was still harsh in these remote islands. And yet of all the places she had lived in the world, it had become, in so short a time, home.

'The Maelstrom,' called Gunnar, 'we're on it now. Look.'

They were passing the squat white lighthouse at the southernmost tip of Moskenes, and ahead of them as far as they could see the glassy blue water was suddenly ruffled, as if alive with a million fish. Waves raced in agitated circles, sending small clouds of salt foam bobbing, and in the centre of each vortex was an ominously swollen dome of smooth water.

Anna, who had read *Descent into the Maelstrom* and had envisioned Poe's 'huge, writhing wall' of ocean, was vaguely disappointed.

Gunnar cut the engine, and came down to stand beside her. 'It never gets calmer than this,' he said. 'Although even today the current is running at ten, twelve knots, and the big whirlpool is probably half a mile across. But when you're out here in a westerly gale, at full moon and with a flood tide running, you'll see the sun through the waves.'

He looked down at the fretted water. 'My grandfather drowned here, and Per's lad, Lars, from Leif's boat. They never found the bodies. The Maelstrom doesn't give back its dead.'

He glanced towards Johan, but the boy was out of earshot, leaning over the side of the boat, staring into the blue swirling water. 'Until now I've only brought him out here in the calm weather like this. Plenty of time for him to know how bad it can be.' He walked over and ruffled the boy's blond head, then climbed back into the wheelhouse to correct the drift.

Anna stands on the steps of the Sigrid's store and watches Leif Pedersen stroll down through the village to the quayside.

The windows of Sigrid's shop are running with condensation, but the rime on the steps and rails has melted in the lemony afternoon sunshine. Inside there are layered smells of fresh bread, paraffin, fish and coffee, and the wet footprints of visitors are all over the wooden floor.

When Anna shouts hello, Sigrid calls a greeting from the back kitchen and emerges with meaty forearms thick with flour to proffer her an elbow. Gunnar is at sea with the other fishermen, and Johan and his sister are at school.

'There's a parcel for you, Anna. Can I have the stamps after, for the boy?'

Anna likes the way Sigrid speaks: the big, nodding head keeping the rhythm of the words. As usual, she finds herself using the same sing-song intonation.

'Sure-ly.'

'It's on the side there.' Sigrid gestures towards the counter and Anna walks over to pick up the parcel. The familiar brown paper and string proclaim its origin as clearly as do the rows of George Washington stamps and the heading on the printed label: K. Kirchener, Translation and Typesetting Services, etc., New York.

Anna weighs the parcel in her hands. It's heavy – a month's work at least. Wood to take her through the last cold days of winter.

Vincent had never taken much interest in what she did, never talked to her about it, although late one night, slightly drunk at a dinner party in Saint-Aubain-les-Eaux, he had said loudly to the famous communist author sitting at his side, 'Ah yes, my wife writes, too, don't you know? Day after day, tap, tap, tap. But never a word of her own.' There was a thrill of polite, educated laughter around the table, and he went on, 'One day machines will do what Anna does. Or we'll all speak one common tongue, the international language of the brotherhood of man. And what will the translators do then, poor things?'

Anna had flushed but had joined in the laughter – Vincent was rarely cruel, and over the years they had both grown adept at avoiding unnecessary pain.

Now she puts the parcel down. 'Anything else?'

'Just the letter there.' Sigrid nods to the rack of pigeonholes where there is a single white envelope.

Anna draws it out carefully. The envelope is slightly creased from its long journey and bears red and white images of Marianne in one corner. A few lines of type have somehow brought it from Paris to the Arctic Circle. Uneasy, she turns it over in her hands, then, conscious of Sigrid's disappointed stare, she slips it unopened into her jacket pocket.

'Coffee?'

Anna turns in the doorway. With the writing she has spent many days on her own recently, perhaps too many. She smiles. 'Why not? Yes, please.'

Sigrid goes back into the kitchen and there is the sound of running water. When she emerges she is drying her hands on a blue gingham towel and pulling her vast floral pinafore over her head. Panting, she pins back straggles of damp reddish hair and leans over the stove to reach the coffee-pot.

She pours two cups, adding milk and three spoonfuls of sugar to hers, and lowers herself on to a wide pine bench.

'There was something I meant to tell you,' she says, eyeing Anna above the cup. 'Yes.' Her pale blue eyes are dancing with barely suppressed excitement. 'There was an odd call yesterday,' she says, blowing waves across the coffee.

'Oh, yes?' Anna gives her a mild, uncurious smile.

'From Oslo, he said, but he spoke in English. It was a terrible line, but he was asking questions.' She gulps hot coffee and swallows.

Anna senses they are getting to the nub of Sigrid's excitement and prepares herself for the usual diatribe on the wickedness of wholesaler margins, the complexity of fishing licences or the exorbitant cost of fuel. But for once the big woman says nothing, apparently happy to prolong the anticipation of gossip.

Anna sighs. 'Questions about what, Sigrid?'

'Ha, well, that's the thing, Anna, you see. About *you*.'

Anna's hand continues to move smoothly towards her mouth, and she manages a casual lift of the brows.

'Me? Are you sure, Sigrid? Nobody knows I'm here apart from these people.' She taps the parcel.

'And him,' says Sigrid, a bushy red eyebrow jerking towards the pocket where Anna has concealed the white envelope.

'Oh, that's probably a bill. For books.'

'It wasn't the bookman on the phone. I know *him,* and anyway this call was from Oslo, like I said.' Sigrid grinned, releasing the information drop by precious drop. 'He was shouting on account of the bad line and talking sort of simple and slow, as though he didn't expect me to understand him. "Is-there-a-Mrs-Galland-on-the-island?" Like that.'

'I see. And what did you say?'

Sigrid's mouth makes a small grin. 'I told him no. "Nobody of that name here," I said, loud, like him.'

Soberly, Anna puts down the cup. 'Well, sounds to me like you did the right thing there, Sigrid.'

'Eh, *ja*. Well, I thought so, too.' Sigrid grins happily, showing a double row of white molars in a jaw the size of a small shark. 'Want a loaf to take back?'

Anna swirls the last grainy dregs around in the bottom of the cup. They gradually still into a strange pattern: an eagle with outstretched wings and a single, vigilant eye. Quickly Anna gives the cup a little shake as she replaces it on the table and the picture dissolves. She looks up and finds Sigrid watching her curiously – the woman, she remembers, believes in all manner of signs, portents and probably even *tussen,* the ancient Norse house spirits.

'See something?' says Sigrid, thick-arched eyebrows raised.

'I never see anything but the grains,' says Anna firmly. 'I must get back now. Mail boat on Friday as usual?'

'Eh, *ja*, you can be sure, they never miss, those boys. I'm gonna get Leif to clear a good big space in the store-room. We've been running low on the basics and there's a big order coming.'

Anna tucks the cloth-wrapped bread inside her jacket and forces the zip up over the bulge.

Sigrid giggles, 'I think you'll be wanting Ada Molud sometime soon.'

Anna smiles back and pats her swollen front. 'No thanks, Sigrid. I think I can deliver a loaf myself.'

'Well, kid, don't forget to bear down!' Sigrid roars happily, as Anna sets off down the shore to the cabin.

Hey, kid, he had said

Anna leans against a rock to catch her breath and wait until the vision fades.

# Five

Back in the cabin she places the heavy parcel on the table and hangs her jacket on the hook behind the door.

For a moment she considers opening the package and even stands for a moment with the scissors in her hands. But over on the desk the journals are waiting for her. She sits and takes up where she left off.

Lisbon, 15 October 1941

Low cloud today and a fine, drizzling mist. Everything in the city is grey: the branches of the great cedars in the garden outside, the crooked rooftops, the river beyond.

At ten, we went again to the British and American embassies in search of visas and letters of transit. Because of Vincent, they see us promptly, but the outcome is always the same. In careful, diplomatic ways, they say, 'We shall do our best, Monsieur Galland, but you must understand in wartime such things take time.' We thank them, and they invite us to call again in a few days.

'Don't worry. They're only checking our story,' whispers Vincent in my ear, as the secretaries show him out with sympathetic smiles.

Ah yes, she remembers those embassies, those ambassadors, those secretaries. Her husband was in his early thirties then: a handsome man, tall and slender, with light brown hair and gold-flecked, hazel eyes. In the high-ceilinged embassies the secretaries' cheeks grew pink when he spoke to them – Nancy, Lucinda, Dorothy – he was always fastidious about remembering names. And of course his reputation as a Resistance hero had gone before him: as each woman opened the double doors through to her ambassador's presence, Vincent's eyes would hold hers, their hands would briefly brush. But the young Anna, even if she noticed, did not remark upon it, for there were other more serious worries in that black-and-white, wartime world.

When we step back out into the street we find the same two men watching us. They are probably Abwehr agents, Vincent says. He tells me we should ignore them, but I find their presence sinister and frightening. There is talk of people being thrown into Portuguese prisons or Nazi agents spiriting refugees out of the country.

These men are not afraid – they come so close that I can see their features clearly: a young one with a long, sheep-like face and an older, sallow colleague who keeps his chin tucked deep in the collar of his raincoat. Today they followed us from place to place, standing for hours beneath the dripping trees. At the American Embassy Vincent pointed them out to one of the attachés, but the man just shrugged. 'What do you expect? This is Lisbon.'

Lisbon, 21 October 1941

We sit in cafés and wait, and wait, often making a single cup of coffee last a whole afternoon.

They were not alone. In every hotel lounge, in every café, refugees clustered, exchanging anxious bulletins of news. Some had almost abandoned hope of escape. Richard Koppes, an elderly lawyer from Bruges, sat slumped and despondent at their table, fingering grey, frayed cuffs.

'Nine months, Monsieur Galland. Nine months here in the city. I have watched many people leave, and yet I do not begrudge them their good fortune – it helps me keep my own hopes alive. Most of us despair of the embassies. Everyone says our best chance is with the black marketeers. One does not want to trust them, but what else can one do?'

He lit a cigarette and, as he did so, beckoned to Vincent to bend closer. 'That is one of them, Monsieur Galland, a new one, only recently arrived. But we have high hopes of him, Claudine and I. There, you see him, over by the bar? An American. The dark-haired man in the grey suit. They say if you seek a way to leave Lisbon, he is the man you must ask: Monsieur Quinn.'

Vincent glanced briefly in the direction of the bar. 'Then I shall ask Senhor Quinn.'

And Anna sat, frozen with joy and terror, as Harry Quinn looked up and smiled enigmatically across the room.

*Hi, kid.*

No.

Anna closes the journal on the memory and turns back towards the parcel on the cabin table.

It is from Kurt himself. Anna recognizes the great looping tails on the address and on the capital L of Larssen. It's six months or more since she heard from him: he usually lets Mavis handle the manuscripts these days. Anna studies the note before reading it through and sees a slight unsteadiness in the lines – Mavis says the old man is trembling more and more.

'Not that it's made him any softer spoken or considerate,' she wrote in November. 'He still terrorizes every translator we have, except old Gurdinsky.'

The Russian professor of literature had worked for Kircheners when Anna was in New York more than twenty years earlier.

'Look at his stuff,' Kurt would say, waving a sheaf of handwritten pages in front of her, 'it's *magisterial.* I tell you, this is a new Chekhov we have here.' He scowled. 'Now all we gotta do is find a Russian proof-checker who can read the genius's writing.'

Kurt's note, clipped to the front of this latest manuscript, still reads like the man himself.

> To the Snow Maiden of the Lofotens, greetings!
>
> I trust the cod are spawning in plentiful numbers and that the stove is warding off frostbite.
>
> Your friends in New York say Hola, Bonjour, Guten Tag, Buenos Dias – it's the usual tower of Babel here. Mavis sends you her best, whatever that is. I send you a cheque, which is better.
>
> But to work.
>
> For some reason best known to them those little-known literary giants Manning and Blythe insist on having the enclosed opus translated into Norwegian – and by you. Now, as Geoff Chan would say, 'Shakespeare it ain't.' The style reads like a cross between Raymond Chandler and a rookie police report – but then what can I tell you – literature is dead. In fact, it was so bad I almost sent Messrs M&B elsewhere, but then something about the story struck a chord. So here it is, for what it's worth (which is a lot – these guys have more money than literary sense).

So, Snow Maiden, see what you can do. We need it back here first week in May.

Yrs ever, Kurt

There will be wood and food and warmth for months to come. Smiling, Anna puts the note and the manuscript to one side and puts the cheque in her jacket pocket. As she does so her fingers brush the white envelope from France. She sniffs it: it is odourless, anonymous. She taps it gently against the table, feeling the weight. Although she doesn't believe in omens or *tussen* or in very much at all, the envelope has a brooding, malevolent presence. Resisting the temptation to open it she props it against a jug on the table.

It is not until late, just before sleep, that she finally relents.

The knife blade makes a steady, neat incision along the top of the envelope, and a small square of pale blue paper slides out on to the quilt. It is creased. In fact it appears to have been folded and unfolded many, many times – it almost falls apart in her hands. She holds the letter delicately, like fragile lace, and breathes apart the folds. At first she simply turns the paper this way and that in the light, amazed that such a fragile piece of history has survived and ended up here in the far Lofotens.

At some time the note has been wet, for its surface is puckered and the ink is as blurred as a watercolour; but the writing between the folds is still legible and in a hand so young and anonymous that she scarcely recognizes it as her own.

'My darling Harry,' it begins, and ends abruptly, three lines below, 'Anna'

She reads it through again.

Then she picks up the anonymous, typewritten envelope and slowly covers her mouth with her hand.

She is forty-two and in all her life has only slept with two men.

Of course it is too few.

In these last solitary months she has often wondered what she might have gained from wider experience of love. (She calls it love, even though her translator's mind presents an entire thesaurus of alternatives: sex, desire, obsession, lust, 'the flesh'.) Would she have learned self-love from beautiful, callow youths? Courage from unprincipled, erotic women? Perhaps even wisdom from old men ripe with late-fruiting, tender lust. And as each tiny arc of experience touched her it would have defined and refined her in some way, bringing into sharper focus the nebulous, shimmering thing her father had called her soul. But instead, out of a sense of convention or guilt or fear, or all three, she clung to her marriage and the memory of a single, long-vanished lover.

And now it is too late. Yes, from now on, anything she learns of life will come to her not through physical experience but intellectually, theoretically, from the realm of the mind alone.

She fingers the slit white envelope.

The red Mariannes dance gaily across the surface, mocking her naïvety.

# Six

The brief afternoon is over. In the dark outside the wind is rising again. It keens under the door and whistles around the corners of the cabin. A few flakes of snow find their way down the chimney and fizzle on the hotplate of the stove. Anna feeds logs into the burner, adjusts dampers. When there is nothing else to be done she opens the blue journal and turns the pages.

The last Lisbon entry is a few shaky lines of abbreviated, coded Norwegian: 'V. is slnt. Bdies on tmb.'

Bodies on a tomb.

When she was ten, Gustav had sat beside her at the dining-table, his tweed suit smelling of pipe tobacco, his broad, square-cut nails tapping gently on the open page of her history book.

'See, Anna? Look closely now, here, at the knight's feet.'

She had leaned forward obediently, the tips of her plaits swinging over the picture, elongated limbs, elegant folds of drapery, stone hands tented in everlasting prayer.

'Oh, it's a dog, a little dog, fast asleep.'

'A dog, yes. And what does that tell us? That this great knight died peacefully at home and not in battle. Remember?'

She remembered.

In the winter of 1940, when she was in Paris and Vincent was away, already submerged in his own private war, she had wandered through ancient churches and, like a child counting plum stones, had made a superstitious tally of those warriors who had survived into old age and those who had met untimely, heroic deaths. And now another memory comes, rising unbidden before her like a hallucination.

A Lisbon hotel room. The ornate ceiling is streaked with grime, the chandelier lopsided and the rugs worn to bare string by a half a century of feet. The bed in the room is wide and draped with swags of dusty brocade, redolent of stale face powder and cigarette smoke. And on the bed, not touching, lie Vincent and Anna, husband and faithless wife, statues drifting silently through eternities of stone.

What symbols would a mason have carved for them, Anna wonders, if they had died that night in Lisbon, in their wide hotel bed? For Vincent, surely, there would have been a heroic profile beneath a knightly visor; vast granite gauntlets clasped around a two-edged sword.

And for me, she thinks, setting her cup down beside the waiting pile of paper, no faithful dog but a tiny child, curled trustingly against the soles of my feet.

But no.

For no one had known, then, about the child.

*

In the cool polished hall of La Verrerie Anna stood, straining to hear the young American voice across the crackling telephone line.

'Hello? Madame Galland, we haven't met. My name is Keen.'

'Oh,' she said and sat down abruptly.

'K-e-e-n. Did Edward Duras mention me to you already?'

A different name; a different time; a different man. Anna took a breath.

'No, Mr Keen, I'm afraid he didn't.' Vincent's lawyer had telephoned earlier in the week, but as usual she had put off returning his call. As she put off so many things, even now. There was a short pause.

'Ah well, that's a little awkward, Madame Galland, because I hoped to come and see you before I leave on Thursday?' His rising inflection made it a question.

'Leave?'

'Leave Paris? To go back to New York?'

She was beginning to wish she had talked to Edward after all. Covering her confusion with a little of Vincent's old incisiveness, she said abruptly, 'What is it you want of me, Mr Keen?'

The American didn't sound the least taken aback; obviously her briskness was unconvincing.

'Henson Press have asked me, and, well, I hope you will agree, now that a little time has passed . . .'

'Agree to what?'

There was a pause, then the American said quickly, 'They want me to write a book about Monsieur Galland, and an article for a magazine.'

'What magazine do you work for, Mr Keen?'

'Well, actually I'm a bit of a freelance. But *Time* have said they'd be interested . . .'

'Oh. I see.'

He cut across her. 'Is there any chance at *all* that you could see me on Tuesday, Madame Galland?'

Anna hesitated. 'Where are you staying, Mr Keen?'

'The Grand Hotel? In Paris? Near the Opéra?'

'Yes. It is in Paris, near the Opéra.' She found she was smiling into the telephone, and there was something urging her on now, a tiny tug of impulse and curiosity.

'Would eleven suit you?' she asked.

He said eagerly, 'Wonderful! Thank you. I appreciate this. So I'll see you in Saint-Aubain-les-Eaux on Tuesday, Madame Galland, at eleven?'

Oh, no. Anna waved a horrified hand at the phone, imagining an American journalist ensconced at La Verrerie interviewing her, with Marie-Christine scurrying in and out, ever mistrustful of what she might say. Marie-Christine, since Vincent's departure, was the self-appointed keeper of the Galland flame.

Suddenly decided, Anna said, 'No, Mr Keen, I prefer to come to Paris.'

There was a beat of disappointment before he collected himself. 'Of course. Yes. That would be . . . fine. Good. I'm truly grateful, Madame Galland. Until Tuesday then?'

'Tuesday. Yes.' Anna's voice sounded serene, but her heart sent rapid irregular judders through her chest. Replacing the receiver she stood for a moment, considering what she would say to Marie-Christine.

*

In the summer of 1939, in Paris as everywhere else in Europe, there was an awareness of normal life unravelling. Vincent's absences from the city lengthened and, although he told her little, Anna understood that he was embarked on some underground mission alongside his comrades in occupied Prague. She fretted about him while he was gone, and

Marguérite Larssen watched her daughter and worried, too.

One evening in late July they sat together in the stuffy apartment. Marguérite, thin and dark-eyed, sat propped against pillows. She was repairing a tear in Anna's blouse, the tiny needle moving with agonizing slowness in and out of the blue fabric. Anna sat by the window, hugging her knees and looking down into the street, pale hair swinging by her cheek.

Marguérite grimaced and let her hands drop to the quilt. After a moment she said softly, 'Vincent takes great risks, doesn't he, Anna, going backwards and forwards to Prague?' Without waiting for an answer, her head still bent, she went on, 'He does it partly for his principles of course, but also, I think, because it's in his nature.'

Anna looked up sharply, uncertain if her mother was being critical. 'No one else can do what he does, Maman – he has to take risks.'

With effort Marguérite lifted a tiny pair of scissors and briefly held them steady as she cut the thread. 'Is he a communist?'

Anna hesitated. Vincent's hard-line comrades called him a reactionary, while his nationalist friends found his enthusiasm for communist ideals naïve. But somehow, by sheer force of his personality, Vincent seemed able to hold both opposing views and ideas in a charmed circle.

Marguérite smoothed the silken material with her palm and sighed at the uneven stitching. 'You admire him, *chérie,* and that's natural, but can't you see that little by little he's involving you in whatever it is he does? Soon you'll be in danger, too.'

Anna jumped down from the windowsill. 'Maman, you don't know him. Vincent looks after me. He won't let me do anything dangerous. But, as he says, it's no good just sitting here thinking war won't come. It will. Prague fell so quickly – the same thing could easily happen here.'

Marguérite sagged back against the pillow, her lips grey-blue.

Anna knelt beside the bed and reached for her mother's hand. 'Maman, please. You said it yourself: Vincent takes all the risks. And he looks after me, after both of us, doesn't he?'

She picked up the mended blouse. 'It's good as new. Perfect. Thank you.' She kissed her mother's forehead and frowned. 'You feel hot. And you look worn out. Sleep now, and when you wake up I'll whisk an egg in milk, like you used to do for me when I was ill.'

She tucked the bedding around her mother's shoulders, trying not to look at the pale, fretting face. 'Everything will be fine. You'll see.'

Marguérite closed her eyes.

The day Vincent was due back from Prague Anna hurried around to his apartment, carrying the heavy bundle of newspapers that he had asked her to buy and save for him during his absence. She knocked on the door and there was a long silence. When finally he drew the bolts and opened the door she was shocked at his appearance: his face was gaunt, his hair was lank and he smelt bad, as if he'd been sleeping rough for days. As she stepped inside, he grabbed the papers, waved her aside and sat at the tiny kitchen-table, his head propped on his hands.

As quietly as she could she prepared the food she had brought: slicing bread and cheese, glancing across at him every so often. The corner of his mouth twitched as he read, although with tiredness or anger she couldn't tell.

At the embassy everyone had been on edge for weeks. To the north the German army was at the Polish border. War was imminent now, almost everyone said so. Even the optimistic Englishman Myles Pilkington no longer talked of appeasement.

Vincent had stopped turning pages and was sitting hunched over one of the newspapers. A cloth twisted in her hands Anna drew closer. The date was 23 August, the headline stark: Germans and Soviets Sign Non-Aggression Pact.

The Norwegian Vice-Consul had been stunned, then vitriolic. Back in Norway the NKP had immediately stated their support for the Soviet action, but in France disillusioned comrades had quit the PCF in their thousands.

Silence flowed out from Vincent like cold air from a glacier. Abruptly he scraped his chair back. Pushing her roughly aside he flung himself out of the apartment, and she heard his feet clattering and echoing in the stairwell.

Anna tidied the apartment, washed a pile of reeking clothes and settled in a corner to wait for him.

It was almost ten when he returned, swaying slightly, his bloodshot eyes glaring blearily around the room. 'Put the radio on,' he said, leaning against the wall. Anna obeyed, and the room filled with the sound of an accordion and Charles Trenet singing of Paris and lovers.

'For God's sake, not that rubbish. Here, let me.' Vincent reached across her, and she almost gagged at the smell of tobacco and whisky. With great concentration he turned the dial through a series of whines and whoops until he found what he wanted.

Over the crackling air a strained English voice informed the world that since, despite all assurances to the contrary, Germany had launched an unprovoked attack on Poland, accordingly Great Britain was now at war.

Vincent slumped back in his chair. 'Poland's done for. They're pouring in from both sides, the Germans from the West, the Russians from the East.' And then, brokenly, 'Filthy, lying bastards.'

She didn't ask him who he meant.

When, after a while, his head lolled against his shoulder and his breathing became regular, she let herself out of the flat and went home.

Vincent came to call for her early the following day. He was clean and tidied and, although his eyes were still red-rimmed from lack of sleep, his manner was serious and sober. He didn't mention his behaviour of the day before and clearly had his emotions back under control.

Side by side they walked down the boulevards towards the Louvre, crossed the river to the Ile de la Cîté and descended the steps to the quais, where the river flowed silently past them, muscled and slick in the grey light. They walked to the tiny park at the tip of the island where the river parted as if around the prow of a ship, and Vincent leaned on the railings, gazing down into the water.

Anna looked at his expressionless face and wondered what he was thinking, wondered if he would ever tell her, wondered if she would ever be able to guess. Suddenly, as if divining her thought, he turned towards her and with a strange, almost pleading look on his face placed his hands on her shoulders.

'Marry me, Anna.'

'Oh,' she said. And then, because in her astonishment and joy and pride, it was the only possible answer: 'Yes.'

Vincent held her chin and tilted her face up. She closed her eyes and hugged his shoulders through the thin folds of his jacket.

*

It's late.

Anna rubs her aching forehead, pulls the typed sheet from the machine.

At the sink she fills a glass with water and drinks deeply, feeling the cold drop into the pit of her stomach. As she washes her hands and face she listens to the storm. The sea sounds closer than usual, as if the ocean has tilted out of kilter. Trying not to imagine the black advancing waves she bolts the door, banks up the stove and with a last glance around the tidy room switches off the light.

The darkness is complete.

In her grandfather's time there was no electricity here. Those who could afford it had their own generator; those who couldn't burned paraffin; the oldest, poorest people lit iron train-oil lamps, as their ancestors had done for a thousand years. In this *rorbu,* as in all the others, every upright timber is striped with soot.

Anna climbs the few creaking stairs to her bunk. The warm air from the stove has risen to fill the space under the steeply pitched wooden roof. She undresses, brushes her hair in three careless strokes and lies down in the bed that she hopes is short enough to stop her soul from wandering tonight.

# Seven

The London plane had been standing in the mild Lisbon sunlight for most of the afternoon, and the air inside was tepid and smelt of sweating bodies. The passengers all seemed to be in couples, ten or fifteen of them, most of whom sat with clasped hands, their faces already radiant with happiness and relief. There was only one empty seat, in the last row, beside a man in a grey suit who was reading a newspaper. With his smooth hair and fine self-conscious profile he looked like a successful actor. He turned the pages rapidly, as if bored with waiting either for his missing companion or for the plane to depart or both.

Anna walked quickly down the aisle, slipped into the seat beside her husband and fastened the safety belt, her sweating fingers leaving damp prints on the warm metal. Outside the propellers began to turn, the engines whined, the plane shuddered and began to move. As it headed out on to the runway the sun slanted in through the windows, and she saw, silhouetted against the brilliant light, a handful of figures watching the departing plane.

*Harry*.

The aircraft picked up speed, bumping faster and faster over the tarmac, the engines screaming at full and deafening pitch. Then, abruptly, there was smoothness and gliding, and the ground fell away beneath them. Vincent turned to her.

'You cut it fine.'

'I'm sorry.'

He folded the newspaper and stowed it away in the pocket in front of him. For a moment she thought he was going to say something else, but he laid his head back against the white antimacassar and closed his eyes.

'I'll sleep for a while, I think. Will you see I'm not disturbed?'

'Of course.'

Towards the front of the aircraft the steward nudged his colleague, a brunette in a pale blue uniform. A few moments later the girl came swaying down the aisle towards them, carrying a cushion.

'Monsieur?' she whispered loudly. Anna smelt the girl's breath as she leaned across them: mint over something sour.

Vincent sighed and opened his eyes. He took the proffered pillow and settled it against the porthole. '*Merci*,' he said quietly.

'*Je vous en prie, monsieur*,' murmured the girl.

The plane dipped a wing and turned north towards England. At the top of their climb the engines slackened, and Anna slid a hand protectively across her belly, as if sensing, deep within its folds, the first fragile flutter of dividing cells.

Far below them now an empty ocean unravelled, striped with charcoal shadow-waves.

*

Anna Galland looks back sadly at her younger self.

Gustav Larssen's daughter had made her predictable choice. There she sits, loyally faithless at her sleeping husband's side, her shoulder a scrupulous inch away from his and her long thighs awkwardly aslant, doggedly telling herself that in time she will forget.

Why didn't she hear that prescient whisper telling her to resist, to think for herself?

Anna shakes her head. Perhaps such infinitesimally small sounds are only audible to the human ear when amplified across time and experience.

She bends once more over the keys.

*

It was not only the thought of escaping her cloistered, widow's life in Saint-Aubain-les-Eaux that had persuaded Anna to accept Mr Keen's invitation to meet him in Paris. Secretly she longed to be rid, if only for a while, of Marie-Christine Galland.

Is a sister-in-law still a sister after the death of the husband and brother who once linked them? Marie-Christine had hauled her worryingly large suitcases up to her room on the eve of the memorial's unveiling, then stalked through the house like a hunting heron, her long thin head swivelling left and right as she checked off an invisible inventory of Galland memorabilia. Anna had followed a few paces behind, quietly straightening photographs and restoring them to their accustomed positions.

The two women had never had an easy relationship. Marie-Christine had always made it clear that she felt her brother had married beneath himself both socially and intellectually and had made a point of spending almost every summer at La Verrerie, as if determined to ensure that Anna's grip on her brother never became too strong.

Unsurprisingly, it had taken Anna several days to pluck up the courage to ask Marie-Christine whether she thought Vincent had killed himself.

They were sitting at either end of the dining-table, the remains of an unappealing lunch uneaten in front of them.

'You have the verdict,' said Marie-Christine, in her clipped, Czech-accented French. She was peeling a pear with a knife and fork; a spiral of rind descended to the plate, exposing shoulders of sliced white flesh. 'What more do you want?'

Anna put down her water glass. 'But there wasn't any note. And he hadn't seemed depressed. Well, perhaps he was for a while, after Hungary, but not since then.'

Marie-Christine placed a last wafer of pear on her tongue, chewed it thoroughly and swallowed. 'I'm not sure you *ever* truly understood what Vincent was feeling, Anna.' She wiped her narrow lips on the fold of a napkin, then slid a cigarette from a packet and held it up between two long yellow-stained fingers. Anna sighed, soundlessly. The unique complexity of the Gallands was a favourite topic of conversation for her sister-in-law.

'You have to remember,' said Marie-Christine, 'Vincent was both an idealist and a pragmatist. For men of principle it creates a certain tension.'

Anna lifted her head at that. 'He never lived a lie,' she said. 'Even when he became a Gaullist after the war it was what he felt, what he believed at the time. And later, when he rejoined the Party, it was for the same reason.' It was how she had rationalized them to herself, the great *voltes faces*: Vincent had never been an ordinary man. He had been extraordinary. Unique.

Maddeningly, she felt her eyes filling with tears.

Marie-Christine opened her mouth, then shut it with an audible snap. For a moment she fiddled with the great rope of turquoises that hung across her flat chest, then she appeared to relent and went on, in the patient voice that so resembled her brother's.

'My dear Anna, the Party has always been good at ignoring what it doesn't want to see, but sometimes even they can't turn a blind eye to what is going on.'

Anna shook her head. 'I don't understand. What are you saying? That Vincent was insincere, that he wasn't really a Marxist?'

Marie-Christine looked around the yellow-and-grey dining-room with its silk-covered chairs and crystal chandelier and gave an ironic smile. 'Few of the comrades choose to live in solidarity on the proletarian breadline, do they? But no, that wasn't what I meant.'

From long experience Anna knew not to ask for an explanation before one was offered: sooner or later, out of sheer malicious glee, Marie-Christine would tell you what she meant, but it was always a delicate process. Anna frowned, uncharitably wishing her sister-in-law back in her dreary Left Bank apartment, with its heirloom bookcases, its smell of stale cake and, well-lit above the mantelpiece, its prize possession: the graduation portrait.

'Vincent and Marie-Christine Galland, 1924,' said the small gold caption. Those two long, intelligent profiles gazed out confidently towards their glorious future: he at twenty-two, home bearing *palmes* from the Sorbonne; she two years older and already a proven rarity in Czech society of her day, a woman doctor of philosophy. 'A double first,' Vincent had said, proudly, his hand gripping his sister's while her pale, prominent eyes shone into his.

The silence in the dining-room had lengthened. Marie-Christine sat staring into the middle distance, occasionally drawing on her cigarette. After a while Anna had stood, cleared the plates from the table on to a tray, and carried everything off to the kitchen.

Now, standing in the hall, Anna replaced the telephone receiver and wondered if Mr Keen's phone call might also provide a way to bring her sister-in-law's protracted visit to an end. Having briefly considered a number of possible untruths she walked into the kitchen and said that she had been called to attend a meeting in Paris to discuss the design of a national monument to the Resistance. It was very short notice, but at least this way she could give Marie-Christine a lift back to the city so that she wouldn't be obliged to carry her luggage on the train.

There was a long silence.

'Oh, I'll leave, if that's what you want,' said Marie-Christine sourly. And then, with the familiar half-smile, 'Are you sure you can drive all that way?'

'Of course,' said Anna. 'I'll take you right to your door.' With an outer show of calm she went to the study to look for the garage keys.

Throughout their married life Vincent had driven Anna everywhere she needed to go. Suddenly, driving herself to Paris seemed a vital rite of passage. Weeds had grown up through cracks in the concrete outside the garage door. Anna unlocked the padlock and pushed back the heavy wooden gates.

The police had found the Citroën parked on the headland in Quiberon. Bertrand Delamain had driven it back to Saint-Aubain-les-Eaux. She opened the door and slid into the driver's seat. The black leather squab was set back too far from the pedals, and she wrestled to slide it forward. This is where Vincent had sat that last afternoon, she thought, here in this seat, looking through this windscreen. She gripped the steering wheel, placing her hands at the ten-to-two position as she had been taught, and feeling the polished smoothness where Vincent's hands had rested. But nothing came to her, no thoughts, nor any trace of him. Closing her eyes she turned the key, and miraculously the great engine fired and the car rose gently on its suspension.

Early on Tuesday Marie-Christine seated herself in the car, poised and angular, the cynical pleat at the side of her mouth signifying that she was well aware that Anna was pleased to be rid of her company. They made their way towards Paris in silence broken only by Marie-Christine's occasional snorts of scorn at her sister-in-law's inexpert driving.

Anna felt a sense of liberation when she finally dropped the other woman outside her apartment in the rue Jacob. It was not merely relief that the journey was over without mishap but also a new, sly joy at finding herself once more alone. Going docilely with the light flow of traffic, she managed to find her way across the river and over to the Grand Hotel, where she parked the car in a nearby avenue, turned off the engine and sat with the windows down, resting her head on arms that were now shaking with the delayed strain of hours behind the wheel.

Gradually her body calmed and cooled. At eleven twenty-nine she unscrewed a tube of lipstick, brushed windswept hair into place, wound the windows almost up to the top and stepped from the car to go in search of Mr Keen

'Madame Galland?'

She stood on the threshold of the vast hotel lobby. Small knots of people were grouped around the reception desk, while others sat in the deep armchairs listening to a small group of musicians – piano, clarinet and guitar – playing softly in one corner.

'Madame Galland?'

He was very young, with a short, almost military haircut and earnest grey-blue eyes, and he smiled and shook her hand up and down with the enthusiasm of a puppy tussling over a stick. Even before they had sat down he was already launching into a rapid introduction to his project and himself.

Dazedly Anna listened, trying to take in the sense of what he was saying. She had forgotten how attractive an American accent could be.

A waiter bustled over, surveyed them both quickly and flashed her a pained look when the young man ordered coffee for them in execrable French. When the *garçon* had gone Mr Keen shook his head.

'As you can tell, I'm afraid I'm just another gauche American in Paris. I can actually *read* the language without a problem, but speaking it, especially here in France, is a different matter. Sorry if I embarrassed you.'

Anna smiled politely. She had lived in too many countries and spoken so many languages that she no longer even remembered which one she had dreamed in the night before.

'The accent comes with practice,' she told him, smiling. 'But perhaps you'd prefer to speak in English for now?'

'Actually, I'd prefer to persevere in French, if you don't mind,' he said. 'If I make mistakes, just correct me, would you? That way I'll learn faster.' He smiled briefly and glanced down at a notepad lying open on the table. Anna glimpsed a list of questions, neatly numbered.

Just as he was about to begin the coffee arrived. Deftly, Mr Keen unwrapped three cubes of sugar and dropped them into the small cup of espresso. Then he sat back in his chair and scrutinized Anna carefully. She found herself blushing. Vincent must have been used to this sort of thing. In the early fifties, before Hungary, many newspapers and magazines had come to interview him: a glamorous post-war existentialist hero; a thinker who was also a man of action and political conviction. Vincent would take the latest journalist into his study at Saint-Aubain-les-Eaux, and when she brought them drinks she usually interrupted animated discussion, and sometimes laughter.

She, on the other hand, after only a few minutes, had already decided that interviews were awkward, intrusive and unsettling.

'So, Mr Keen,' she said, striving to calm her nerves, 'you want to talk to me about my husband.'

'Yes, Madame Galland, I do. May I?' he said, suddenly leaning forward to pick up a packet of cigarettes.

Lucky Strike. Harry's brand.

'Do you?'

She shook her head.

The American flicked open a lighter, then drew on the lit cigarette just as Harry used to do, his narrowed eyes watching her through smoke whose scent was as familiar and evocative as perfume. After a moment he leaned close again, his hand hovering a few centimetres above her wrist, as if she was a precious relic he yearned yet feared to touch.

'May I tell you something, Madame Galland? I feel *destined* to write this book. Really. Vincent Galland was my boyhood hero. I remember seeing him on a newsreel at the cinema when he addressed the United Nations in 1954. I was fourteen. He was talking about world peace. I never forgot that speech. He was . . . inspirational.' He stopped, blushing.

'Yes,' she said. 'I was there.'

And yes, she had been there, although she had missed the first ten minutes of the address because she had been scanning the vast auditorium, vainly searching for the one American face she thought would be, *must* be at the UN to hear Vincent Galland talk about world peace. And yet all the time Vincent's words were reaching out to this earnest young man and changing his life, as so much in life could and did and had turned on a chance handful of words.

*'I can help you leave me, Anna,'* Harry Quinn whispered, *'if that's what you really want.'*

Keen was staring at her.

'Excuse me? Mrs Galland, are you OK? You've gone very pale. I'm sorry if I've upset you.'

The hotel lobby tilted like the deck of a sinking ship. Anna shivered. 'No. No. The drive. I'm not used to . . . I'm sorry.'

Patches of blackness swirled around her; blood hissed through her temples.

She slumped sideways, heard Keen, his French suddenly rapid and fluent, say, 'Waiter, a glass of water for madame, please. Quickly.' Gently he bent her head down to her knees and took her wrist.

When she came to she was sitting back in her chair. The American was leaning over her holding a glass to her lips, and she sipped the water, slowly, conscious that the giddy coldness was gradually being replaced by warmth.

Suddenly she felt ravenously hungry.

As if he read her mind Mr Keen smiled, 'You had a long journey and in the heat, too. Will you have lunch with me?' His diffidence seemed less marked, and this time the waiter hovered, watching the American's half-raised finger.

'Lunch?' she whispered, and then was mildly surprised to hear herself say, 'Yes, thank you, Mr Keen, I should like that.'

Despite its awkward beginning the meal turned out to be a more relaxed event than she had imagined. Perhaps it was the wine. (It had been so long since she had drunk champagne that she'd forgotten the wonderful exhilaration of it, the way its tiny bubbles burst against your face like minuscule kisses as you drank.) She gazed around the room, dazed and excited, and suddenly realized that she hadn't been listening. Apparently Mr Keen was half-way through a list of sources for his biography, and it was clear that he expected her to be impressed. He had already assembled a sizeable amount of archive material on Vincent, he said.

'Believe me, this book will be as accurate and true as I can make it.'

'Ah, yes?' she said and realized she'd used his own quizzical lilt.

'Yes indeed,' he replied, with the certainty of a man who has never experienced loss or even disappointment. 'Absolutely.' And then, perhaps seeing the doubt on her face, he stretched a hand across the table towards her. 'But I really can't do it without you, Madame Galland. Will you help me?'

She wondered if she could simply not answer, if she could let the question and the moment pass into oblivion, together with the murmur of conversation and the steady hum of traffic in the street outside. The musicians in the lobby were playing a melody she vaguely recognized. As the clarinet described a slow, melancholy arc, its words came back to her:

> There's a somebody
> I'm longing to see,
> I hope that he . . .
> Turns out to be . . .
> Someone who'll watch over me.

She took a breath. 'Yes, Mr Keen. I'll help you.'

He beamed with evident relief.

'Thank you, Madame Galland. I can't tell you . . . thank you so much. And please, will you call me Hal?' He paused for a second, 'It's short for Harry.'

She swallowed.

'I knew a Harry once.'

Suddenly he was watching her so intently that she had to knot her fingers together in front of her to stop them trembling. There was a long silence. After a moment he leaned back in his chair and gently stirred the conversation into life again, and by the end of the meal she seemed to have agreed that Mr Keen might spend two weeks at La Verrerie during his next trip to France in order to study Vincent's papers at first hand.

He thanked her effusively and called for the bill, counting new notes from a full wallet. Fanning them out, he said slowly, 'I read the reports in the paper. You know, about . . . Quiberon last year. Can I ask you, do you think he . . . you know, in the end? . . . that he . . . ?' He looked up.

Anna stared at him. Vincent's last evening at Saint-Aubain-les-Eaux had been unremarkable: the usual meal, the usual conversation, the usual bedtime routine – Vincent staying downstairs to read, she going upstairs to bed. And in the morning there had been nothing sinister and yet nothing the same: the sheets beside her unturned; the empty kitchen full of spring sunshine and the empty drive leading down to an open gate.

'I don't know,' she said. 'Really, I just don't know.'

# Eight

At three o' clock Anna and the young American said their goodbyes in the foyer of the Grand Hotel. Outside, the street was hot and dusty and the exhaust fumes made her head throb. Summer crowds flowed around her: men in shirt-sleeves and girls in bright, full-skirted dresses, their glossy hair piled elegantly high in the afternoon sun. For a moment she closed her eyes, breathing in the hot, dry air.

She wished now that she had something to draw her back to Saint-Aubain-les-Eaux that evening – manuscripts to type, a meal to cook, even a shirt to mend – but ironically, now that Marie-Christine had gone, she had no one to consider but herself.

Of course, if she chose, she could simply catch the Métro and cross the city beneath the August streets and emerge in the sunlit Montmartre of her past. Even though for almost twenty years she had avoided the place, from Les Abbesses she might even now, if she so chose, climb the steep stairways to the small hotel behind the Place du Tertre where the open window on the third floor probably still looked out south over the hazy rooftops of Paris to Montparnasse. If she chose, she might be so foolish.

She ran her hand back through her damp, warm hair, considering: a small licence after all these years.

It would even be wise, because Montmartre was one of the places that the engaging and conscientious Mr Keen would expect her to mention during their October conversations, when at some point he asked, as at some point he must, 'And you, Madame Galland, when you were in Paris in 1940, while your husband was in a concentration camp but widely believed to be dead, where were *you?*'

'Oh, I . . .' she would say, 'lived in Montmartre for a while until, on the day before the Germans arrived, news came that Vincent was alive but sick. Then I went to find him and we were together again. We stayed hidden in Paris for a while, and then we went south to Marseilles and from there to Oran and from there to Lisbon and the Free World.' Even as she rehearsed the familiar, easy words she discerned the old lies and omissions, like rocks beneath the surface.

But at least this afternoon, alone in Paris, there was no need to lie. Just as there was no reason not to remember the third-floor window of a small hotel behind the Place du Tertre, where on a June night long ago her lover's breath had been warm against the nape of her neck.

Suddenly she couldn't face the stifling car, the shimmering roads, the empty house and empty evening at Saint-Aubain-les-Eaux. Instead, striding out impulsively into the traffic, she crossed the road to the Opéra Métro station and descended into the darkness. An aromatic gust of sweet, stale air wafted up from the tunnels and swept her back across the years.

At Les Abbesses the sunlight was waiting for her and pounced as she stepped out into the street. In a dazzle of reflections from glass and metal she turned up the hill, aware that she was swaying slightly as if wading through deep water. Slowly. Up, up, up. Here, in this very place, where the handrail was rubbed bare, was where she used to stop and turn, gazing out over the slopes of Montmartre, drawing out the sense of anticipation, savouring the excitement that had so quickly and completely and shamefully replaced her grief.

Up, up, up towards the sun. Cobbles and flagstones radiated heat through the soles of her shoes. There was the familiar stench of drains, of a city gasping in drought. And then she was in the Place du Tertre, walking across the square towards the little side alley hardly visible to the casual passer-by (which she might have been but was not in the spring of 1940). And . . . it was still there: a tallish building, its slim balconies brilliant with geraniums, and to its left branches of green acacia spreading shade over a tiny pocket garden. Hotel de Fleurie: three floors of windows, the high ones open, as always in summer, to catch any trace of breeze. She stopped, stricken because it was the same, faithfully unchanged through the years as if waiting for her return.

She walked slowly past, afraid she was being watched, afraid that a long-ago voice would call her name from the third-floor window. She walked as far as the terrace wall and in the merciful dimness under the trees she leaned against the balustrade, pretending to admire the view.

Oh, Harry.

*

She had married Vincent Galland in secret in 1939, on an October morning so warm and golden that it hardly seemed possible that the world was at war. She was to tell no one about the marriage, he warned her, not even her mother. It would be safer for all of them that way. Anna wore her serviceable beige crêpe-de-Chine dress and a tiny cream-coloured hat. Vincent bought a rose from the flower seller and pinned it to her lapel. The ceremony itself was brief and impersonal: the mayor in his tricolour sash spoke in a rapid monotone, the witnesses were two strangers brought in at random from the street. When the formalities were complete Vincent bent to kiss her, lifting the minute wisp of veil, and it seemed to Anna that virtually no time passed before she found herself once again on the stone steps, blinking in the sunshine and fingering the plain gold ring on her left hand. She was Madame Vincent Galland; Anna Larssen, *épouse* Galland. The tall, handsome man at her side was her husband.

Their wedding breakfast was two cups of coffee at a grubby café opposite the Gare de l'Est. Couples strolled past arm in arm enjoying the unseasonable warmth, the girls' frocks fluttering like butterfly wings in the breeze. Anna watched them while Vincent studied a sheaf of documents.

The waiter cleared away the dirty cups. Vincent pushed the papers away and lit a cigarette, pinching fragments of tobacco from dry lips. She touched his sleeve.

'When will you come back?'

'Soon,' he said, with a brief smile. 'A couple of weeks, three at most.' He folded the papers and slid them into an oilcloth pouch.

'Anna?' he leaned forward and she closed her eyes for the kiss, but then she felt him slipping the bright new ring from her finger. He curled her palm over it. 'Keep this somewhere safe.' He gripped her fingers hard. 'I have to go now.'

He picked up his rucksack, kissed her softly on the cheek, and before she could say anything he was walking away from her, crossing the street to the great dark pillared entrance of the station, where he turned and waved.

Anna waved back. She wanted him to see that although she was young and naïve she was now a loyal wife for whom waiting was a small hardship – a duty she accepted and was proud to have.

He waved once more and was gone.

The Montparnasse apartment was quiet when she returned: there was no sound from her mother's room. Anna tidied and cleaned then changed her clothes. She hid the new wedding-ring in the pages of a poetry book, tying the volume shut with a ribbon. By now Vincent was miles from Paris, more distant every minute.

At five o'clock Anna set a pan of milk to warm. When it was ready she added a spoonful of sugar and cracked an egg into the cup. The room was dark when she entered.

'Maman, are you awake?' she called softly.

There was no answer.

She tiptoed through the room, put the milk on the bedside table and switched on the little yellow-shaded lamp.

Marguérite lay on the bed, her eyes sunk into brown hollows, skin stretched over oval pebble cheekbones, her breathing shallow and fast.

Anna knelt by the bed. Suddenly the world seemed to shrink down to this, the two of them, mother and daughter, motionless in amber light. Everything else – the coming war, the wedding, even Vincent himself – vanished, and she knelt by the bed, mesmerized by the coverlet's almost imperceptible rise and fall.

'Maman?'

Five days later, Marguérite Larssen, née Lejeune, died quietly in her bed.

The concierge, who had liked the young widow from Oslo, comforted the weeping daughter and then went to call upon another tenant, an employee of the local *pompes funèbres*, to make the necessary arrangements.

Only a few mourners stood in the wintry sunlight among the marble monuments: a big ponderous boy who had been one of her mother's pupils, an acquaintance from the building and the concierge and her husband. The first spadefuls of earth rattled down into the hole and bounced on the wood below. The concierge stifled loud sobs and the boy gaped at her stupidly. Beneath the borrowed black veil tears ran in cold lines down Anna's face. She was an orphan. Her soul was now in her own care and she wasn't ready, wasn't good or strong enough. One by one the mourners left. Anna shook gloved hands and mutely refused the few awkward offers of help.

When she was alone she unpinned the veil and walked back

towards the apartment, wandering through unfamiliar back streets and deserted squares. It was almost dark by the time she arrived. She reached for the banister rail and was suddenly startled by the sight of a tall, forked shadow hovering on the wall. It moved towards her. She gasped and stepped back, but even as she did so a strong arm came around her shoulders and held her tight. Anna turned and buried her face in Vincent's coat.

'My poor girl,' he murmured. 'My poor girl. Don't worry, I'm here now.'

Anna, leaning against his arm, felt as if she had stepped from a small, sinking boat to the decks of a great ocean-going liner.

They moved Anna's things into Vincent's apartment the following day. His studio was a large, spare attic room, lit by a row of skylights. A sagging sofa faced an empty grate, an iron bed was tucked in a corner, and a curtained doorway opposite led to a tiny bathroom. Vincent cleared space in the chest of drawers; sombrely Anna unpacked her few clothes and placed them neatly beside his.

'Are you hungry?' called Vincent.

Anna glanced around her. There was no sign of a kitchen nor any plates or glasses.

'I only ever eat at midday,' said Vincent, following her gaze, 'usually at Chez Basile. It's cheap.'

Anna hid her surprise. It now occurred to her that she had no idea how much money Vincent had or how he earned it. 'I-I'm not really hungry anyway,' she stammered.

Vincent was slipping papers into the rucksack, 'Look, I'm meeting Antoni and a few others at the Deux Magots at nine. Do you want to come? It might take your mind off things.'

Married or not, it was clear that she was only one of Vincent's many priorities and concerns. Uncomplainingly, she walked with him to the Boulevard Saint-Germain and slid in beside him on the banquette behind the door. The table soon filled up: Georges Pocquet, Antoni Nosek and Jean-Luc Calvet welcomed Vincent back, and soon discussion and argument was flowing around the table as if it were an evening like any other.

*Maman.*

Anna drank, quickly, the small glass of cognac Vincent had bought her and then, slowly, another.

Midnight came and half past midnight. The waiters were emptying ashtrays and collecting unpaid bills. Various people stood and put on coats. Antoni took Marie-Ange's hand. Finally, Vincent said awkwardly, 'I'll walk you home, Anna, if you like.'

'Thank you,' she said calmly.

People shook hands in the night air. Vincent and Anna walked back through the emptying streets, their hands close but still not touching. After all his earlier volubility Vincent was now silent and preoccupied. Only when he had closed the apartment door behind them did he speak. Leaning against the wall he yawned, then drew her to him and kissed her gently on the forehead.

'It's time for bed.'

She sat with her back to him, pretending to read, while he moved about in the little bathroom cubby-hole.

'Your turn.' His voice came from the direction of the bed.

'Thank you.'

Behind the curtained doorway Anna took off her skirt and blouse clothes and hung them up, then washed her face and hands and brushed her teeth and stood in her slip, her body silver and blue in the moonlight.

He called her name.

Taking a breath, Anna stepped through the curtain and ran lightly across the bare wooden floor like a diver to the end of the board. The sheets were cold, but Vincent's naked body was warm against hers and for a while they lay close and still, as if stunned by their sudden physical closeness.

'You know that I love you,' he said with quiet formality. It was a statement and a question.

'Yes, Vincent,' she said and laid her hand on his shoulder. Unhurriedly, he began to stroke her arm.

She shivered at his touch, her lungs filling and exhaling jerkily, as if they had forgotten how to breathe. For a long moment his fingers traced the line of her collarbone, moving to and fro, to and fro, across the hollow at the base of her throat. Gradually, his very restraint became a delicious torment: between her legs Anna felt a thick pulse of desire.

She turned her head and looked at the closed, handsome profile on the pillow. This was her husband. She was his *wife.* The word rang out in her mind, and in a single, instinctive movement she flung her arms around him and arched the whole of her naked body against his.

He recoiled immediately.

Anna fell back, her fist across her mouth. She had been brazen, shameless. This wasn't what good women did. What must he think of her? She must disgust him.

Terrible moments passed.

Then, at last, she felt him reach into her hair and take a hank of it in his hand. Slowly, deliberately, he twisted and tightened his grip. She winced in gratitude and felt his free hand burrow deep between her legs, forcing her thighs apart. Then suddenly, shockingly, his body rolled its entire weight on top of her, crushing the air from her lungs. She cried out, squirmed sideways, but with a single thrust of his thighs Vincent subdued her, parted her legs and drove himself fully inside her. Something deep in her belly stretched and tore. She screamed then, flailing her legs against him, but he was strong. Pinning her to the mattress, on each in-thrust he called her name.

Afterwards she lay beneath his body, conscious of warm liquid trickling down between her legs. She felt his heart thudding against her breast, smelt sharp sweat from his armpits. Tentatively, she folded her trembling arms around his back.

At her touch he turned his head, brushed her hair back from her face and kissed her slowly and tenderly on the lips. 'I hurt you, Anna. I'm sorry.'

The soft, kind voice. He still cared for her.

'It doesn't matter.'

He lay beside her once more, his head profiled in silver on the pillow. Almost immediately his breathing calmed and deepened to a soft, regular snore.

'Vincent?' she whispered.

After a while, she, too, slept.

When she awoke, chilled, the room was grey with dawn and Vincent was standing at the side of the bed fully dressed. When he saw she was awake he smiled, dropped to his heels by the bed and stroked her cheek.

'Good morning, *ma belle* Madame Galland.' The light voice was soft, caressing. 'You looked so peaceful lying there I didn't want to wake you.'

Anna raised herself on one elbow and saw the faded green rucksack by the door. Vincent followed her gaze.

'I know. A week, two at most. But if anything . . . look, this is the man you must contact. He's an ex-police inspector, and his wife is somewhere in Prague. He's working with us.'

She read the paper. 'Léon Carré, Les Deux Perroquets, rue de Navarin.'

'It's not his real name. And he knows you as Anaïs.' Vincent held her chin and shook it gently. 'You won't need it, you know. You'll be fine.'

Anna lowered her head, felt Vincent move on to the bed beside her. She hugged him, rocking gently against him. The buttons of his jacket scratched against her face as he gently pulled away.

When he'd gone she went into the tiny curtained alcove and sluiced her body down and stripped the bloodstained sheet from the bed and put it in the sink to soak. The view from the scullery window was down into a dark, inaccessible courtyard far below.

Vincent made two more trips into Slovakia that winter. In December he managed to get news of his mother and sister. They were living in his grandmother's house in the country. Although food was scarce they were in good health and did not appear to be in any immediate danger. Vincent had not wanted to put them at risk by trying to visit, and when his work was done he slipped out of the country as quietly as he had come.

In January he went back.

'Rallying support' was all he would tell her. 'Setting up cells. Recruiting couriers. Working out lines of communication.' She nodded, understanding little.

Each morning while he was away she went to the embassy as usual, but wary of saying more than she should she ate alone at midday and refused all invitations from the other girls to go out in the evenings. These she spent alone, quiet as a nun, waiting for Vincent's return. Sometimes, lying awake, hearing distant bell-towers chime, she wondered whether she would ever get used to this unsettling, elliptical existence of closeness and distance, anxiety and relief. She thought that when he came back she would ask him if she might be trained as a courier. Then at least, she told herself, she would have a better understanding of the work he did and could play some part in his hidden life.

The date of Vincent's return came and went, and there was no sign of him. A week dragged past. January became February. Anna hardly ate or slept, listening through the night for the sound of his step on the stair. On the tenth day, early, an envelope was pushed under her door. She raced out on to the landing and saw a small boy descending the stairs in great leaps. Before she could call him he was gone.

The envelope was blank.

She opened it. It contained an address and a brief message: 'Seven tonight, LC.'

Anna was early for the rendezvous with Léon Carré. Anxiously she walked up and down the *passage*, part of the maze of covered arcades south of the Bourse. Finally, when it was exactly seven, she went in. A black door with a curtain of yellowing lace opened on to a tiny room with a handful of dark-stained tables and chairs. At the back of the room a giant of a man sat reading a paper; his bulky presence seemed to fill the entire room. As Anna entered he nodded to the elderly woman behind the counter to bring them coffee and then waited until she had gone before he spoke.

Léon Carré folded his newspaper into a neat rectangle and slid it into his pocket.

'Anaïs.' It was a statement. He looked her up and down, taking in her black woollen coat and straight blonde hair. 'You're younger than I thought. There's news.'

He was peering intently at her face, as if trying to decipher her state of mind. Abruptly he said, 'And it's bad news, I'm afraid, *ma fille*. The worst, in fact.'

She stared at him, wide-eyed and silent, so he made it quick.

'The Germans arrested him as he was crossing the Czech border. They put him in gaol, but he managed to escape. We had people watching for him, just in case, and they saw him cross the street, but before he reached them the guards opened fire. He was hit several times, they said. The Germans came out and they dragged his body away.'

Anna closed her eyes. She felt Léon draw close, and his heavy hand came to rest around her shoulders.

'Don't know what I can say. I'm so sorry, kid.'

She forced her tongue hard against the roof of her mouth.

Léon glanced at his watch. The girl was sheet-white. 'What will you do? Is there anyone who can stay with you?'

She shook her head. 'I'm fine. Don't worry.'

Léon dropped coins on to the counter, turned at the door. 'If we hear . . .'

'Yes,' she said.

'Are you sure you'll be OK?'

She nodded, and with a gesture of helpless sympathy he left.

After a while Anna left the café and walked down through the echoing arcade and out into the rain-soaked night.

The spring of 1940 came slowly and unwillingly into the Paris streets.

At the embassy colleagues noted that Anna Larssen was even more quiet and subdued than usual. They assumed she was still grieving for her mother and did their best to help her recover her spirits, but the poor girl refused all offers of sympathy, all invitations, and gradually they stopped trying to persuade her to join them for outings or meals.

Anna herself performed her duties dully, mechanically, and was often surprised to find that the day had passed, that she was once again alone in the office and it was time to return to the empty apartment. But the weekends were interminable. Since she had little money she rarely went out and spent days in bed, watching the pale grey light move slowly around the sloping attic walls. The hum of the city barely filtered through into the room.

Sometimes she remembered to eat, sometimes she didn't.

It was not until April that she finally awoke.

On the morning of the 10th the Norwegian Ambassador called the entire staff into his office.

The Germans were in Oslo, he said. There was fighting in the streets. Reports said that the King was fleeing before the advancing German troops and still refusing demands for his surrender. But the situation was desperate, and so far the Allies had been strangely silent.

There was little doubt, he said sombrely, looking at the white, set faces of his staff, that in a few hours Norway would be overrun. When this happened, the embassy would close and every member of staff would have to decide where his or her future lay.

Anna sat silent amid the burst of frightened chatter that followed.

Many people spoke of going to London to enlist in the British forces and continue the fight. Some were for going south or east into Switzerland.

'What about you, Anna?' said Hjordis, struck by the young girl's blank face.

'I shall stay here,' she said quietly.

# Nine

She wakes, abruptly, in daylight. Someone is knocking at the cabin door.

Grabbing an overcoat from the peg by the door she wraps it around her shoulders and peers out of the front window. All that is visible is the corner of a heavy red plaid jacket and giant high-laced boots which she recognizes as belonging to Sigrid's brother.

She lifts the latch.

'Missus Larssen.' A bass voice and a face red-brown from weather; a smell of fish. Leif pulls off his cap and shaggy fair hair sticks out from his head at all angles; his eyes, netted by deep lines, are a startling sea-green.

'Sigrid said I should come over straight away.'

'You caught me by surprise. I don't always sleep so late.' She runs her hand through her own tangled hair. 'Will you put the coffee on while I get dressed?'

'Sure-ly.'

She feels his eyes on her bare legs as she scampers upstairs. As she hurriedly pulls on last night's smoky sweater and trousers she can hear him banging around in the kitchen.

By the time she comes downstairs again Leif is pouring hot coffee into two mugs. His hands are big and covered in fine white scars. He nods at her and sits down, ignoring the protesting creak of the old pine chair under his weight.

'There's a man come into Moskenes harbour,' he says, straight away, as if he's been practising his announcement. 'On the boat from Bodø yesterday.'

'What man?'

'Foreigner. American. He tells Jan Nilssen that he's come to study the birds. Got a big telescope in a carry case and a trailer-load of supplies. Jan took him up the road to the old Markusen place around the coast in Sørvågen.'

He's watching her closely; she keeps her face expressionless. 'Why did Sigrid think I should know?'

'Because this man asked if there was other outsiders on the island, and Jan told him there was only one, a Missus Larssen, the French Widow, over in Å. And the man says nothing, but then he gets Jan to show him where Å is on the map and tell him how far from Sørvågen. And Sigrid says you ought to know this.'

He takes a big swallow of coffee and wipes his lips on the back of his hand. 'He told Jan his name was . . . King. No, sorry, Quinn. You know this man, you think?'

'Yes,' she says, and now her breath is caught and fluttering against the bars of her ribcage. 'Yes, I think I do.'

*Hi, kid*, he had said the day he met her, twenty-four years ago.

Simply, wonderfully, *Hi, kid*.

*

That morning, weary of herself and of hopelessness, she had gone for a walk through Paris. Head down under light spring drizzle she made her way north to the river and crossed to the Right Bank. At first she was hardly aware of her surroundings, but little by little the fresh air and exercise lifted her spirits, and by the time she reached the colonnaded square of the Palais Royal the rain had gone and the sun was shining through banks of high, white cloud.

She brushed rainwater from a bench and sat beneath trees misted with tiny points of green. A breeze whisked across the gravel paths and brought with it an indefinable scent of something freshly minted: chlorophyll; morning? For a while she watched a group of children playing by the fountain. Bare-kneed boys dared each other to run in and out of the flying water, while girls squealed with terrified delight. It reminded her of childhood games in her garden in Oslo.

At that moment a shadow fell across her face and stayed there. A man was standing in front of her. He was silhouetted against the sun, but she could see he was wearing a raincoat and a hat tipped forward over his face.

Anna raised her arm to shade her eyes from the glare and as she did so he said, as if he knew her, 'Hi, kid.'

She blinked, and the man moved sideways into the light. She saw that he was of medium height, dark-haired, with a face that was long and thin and curiously immobile and dark-blue eyes that were not.

'May I?'

He sat beside her on the bench and bent forward, offering phantom crumbs to the grey pigeons scrabbling in the dust at his feet.

'Hungry little creatures, aren't they?'

He was American, not English. Anna kept her gaze fixed on the sinuous necks of the pigeons.

'D'you live round here?' He half turned and looked around the arcaded façade. 'Quite a place, eh? Imagine all those courtiers in fancy robes playing Chinese windows.'

She looked down at her long, ringless fingers, primly clasped on her lap.

The American pushed back his hat, 'Excuse me, but do you speak *at all?*'

Never to strangers; her father and Vincent had taught her that.

The stranger fumbled in his pocket, brought out a packet of American cigarettes, lit one and then belatedly offered her the pack.

'Speak English? *Parlez-vous français? ¿Habla usted español?*'

Anna nodded.

He grinned. 'Aha. Bit of a linguist, huh? OK, let's see now. I'd guess you're not French. Or English. And certainly not Spanish. Hmm.' He looked her up and down, and again she was struck at the contrast between the immobile face and the flickering eyes. 'Swedish? Maybe. Dutch? No, not Dutch. Czech?'

*Czech?*

'I don't like questions much,' she said in English.

'Norwegian,' he said, triumphantly, and the planes of his face shifted into a different configuration. 'Aren't you?'

Anna frowned. 'I told you, I don't like questions, and you've already asked a dozen or more.'

'Really, *have* I?' He pulled a face of mock horror, and looked so comical that she burst out laughing then immediately covered her mouth with her hand.

He continued unabashed. 'I apologize. Truly I do. My mother always said I was too inquisitive for my own good. But . . . well, now this is kind of awkward, because I wanted to invite you to have a cup of coffee with me on the terrace over there.' He pointed to where a few metal tables had been laid out under the trees. 'What to do . . . Hell. Look, if I promise not to ask you another question apart from this last one, will you join me?'

Anna hesitated and then said, a little wildly, 'Yes, I would like a coffee. Thank you.'

The American ordered coffee and called the elderly waiter by name and asked a question in fluent French. The old man brightened, '*Ah, oui, merci*, Monsieur Keen', and rattled off a bulletin of news.

'Robert's family is in Alsace. He's worried about them,' said the stranger as the *garçon* shuffled off into the café. 'And yes, before you ask, yes, I'm afraid I do come here that often.' His voice was light, cynical, sure of itself.

'Your name is Keen?' said Anna.

He raised a solemn finger. 'Well, you know, that's really a question, and we agreed there'd be no more of them, but then I guess I do owe you a few. No, that's just Robert's best attempt at English pronunciation. My name's actually Quinn. Harry Quinn. Originally from New York, lately from all over, and in Paris for the last three months. What's yours?'

Again, his eyes were flickering over her like lightning over grass.

'Anna.' And then, because it sounded too little, 'From Oslo.'

Harry Quinn grimaced. 'Ah, bad luck, kid. But at least it looks as though the British are finally doing something positive up there – maybe everything isn't lost, huh?' He shook his shoulders and glanced around the square. 'OK, back to Paris. Safer ground. I'd bet this is your favourite square. Am I right? No?' He put his hand to his forehead in mock distress. 'Oh dear, two more questions slipped in there. OK, even if it isn't your favourite, I bet I can guess your shortlist. No, don't laugh, I'm serious. Hmm, let's think now . . .' He looked her up and down as if reading her for clues, and all the while his face was immobile and his eyes were moving over her. 'Yes. Place de la Concorde, of course, you'll certainly have that, everyone does. Then you'd have that little gem on the Ile Saint-Louis – the Place Dauphine. Place Vendôme's too grand for the likes of you and me, and Bastille's too dull. So, no, I'd say your favourite is in the Marais – and I'll go for the Place des Vosges.' The rapid, amused voice paused, and blue eyes widened enquiringly.

She wilted under the torrent of words. Vincent had only ever spoken at such length to groups of people, never to her alone. And Vincent was gone. Anna replaced the tiny cup on its saucer.

'I'm sorry, I don't know what to . . .' she said softly, and then, her voice strengthening, 'You know the city very well. I mean, for someone who's only been here a few months.'

'Yeah, I guess I do.' He pushed his hat back and said lightly, 'Quite cosmopolitan – for a Yank, that is. Let's order another coffee and decide about bridges.'

A quarter of an hour later they had agreed on the best bridge, (Pont Neuf); best window (Notre Dame); the best view (from steps of the Sacré Cœur), and the coffee-cups were almost empty again.

Harry Quinn leaned back in his chair, suddenly serious. 'So, tell me, Miss Anna from Oslo, what do you think will happen to all those favourite places when the Germans come knocking at France's door?'

For the space of half an hour she hadn't thought about Vincent or her mother or Nazis marching through Norway. Now all three sadnesses enveloped her at once and she slumped back against the chair.

The American stretched out a hand. 'Hey, watch out, you nearly knocked the cup over. You're right, it's probably best not to think about it. In fact, why don't we cheer ourselves up with a small toast? Robert? *Deux verres de champagne s'il te plait.*'

When they came, he chinked his glass against hers. 'You and me and Paris, kid.'

She raised her glass and sipped in silence.

When the drinks were finished Quinn paid the bill and they stood to leave. Suddenly awkward, he reached for her hand. 'Look, Miss Anna whatever-your-name-is from Oslo, if you're free, I'd like it if you'd have dinner with me tonight,' he said. And then, quickly, 'That's a statement of fact, you'll notice, rather than a question.'

Anna looked at him. 'My name is Larssen . . .' She didn't know why this stranger was sweeping her along and had no idea why she was letting him do so. It certainly didn't seem right or fitting when she had been, and was still supposed to be, sad. In guilty panic she searched for some calm, adult part of her that would refuse with dignity. Yet the truth was that she was physically and emotionally exhilarated. She felt her mouth smile, heard herself say, 'Thank you, Mr Quinn. I would like that.'

'At eight, then,' he said. 'Over there. Le Grand Vefour, see?' A faded gilt sign hung over the arcade.

'At eight,' she said. 'Yes.'

And at five to eight Anna Larssen walked down the length of the vaulted arcade towards the brightly lit restaurant. She was wearing the same beige dress that she'd worn two years before, on the night she had met Vincent. Harry Quinn was leaning against a pillar, watching her coming towards him under the lamps. When she came level with him he pushed himself upright from the pillar, flicked his cigarette on to the flagstones and ground it out under his shoe.

'You're extremely punctual, Mademoiselle Larssen. It must be your tidy Norwegian soul. Come on in, I've ordered champagne.'

So at eight o'clock, on a spring evening two months before the fall of Paris, Anna and Harry Quinn entered the restaurant where once Bonaparte and Josephine had dined.

*

Anna is staring at Leif, but in her mind she sees not his broad frame hunched over the *rorbu* table but a shorter, wiry man, his eyes sparked by candlelight.

She loved Harry for all the ways he was different from Vincent: his humour, his brashness, his cynicism, his careless confidence; the way he tucked his arm under hers as they walked, so they huddled together like two children conspiring; the way he teased her and made her laugh; his gentle and earnest lovemaking.

*Now* he comes back. *Now*, a lifetime too late – when her feelings have at last diluted to the point of colourlessness – he comes back. And there is something malevolent, something over-intense in his sustained pursuit. Since yesterday, since the letter with its dancing Mariannes, she has been frightened.

Puzzled by her silence Leif frowns and runs a paw through the chaos of his hair.

'You want to take a look, Missus Larssen? See this man before he sees you, maybe? I got the boat and a good pair of field glasses, if you'd like to go.'

She is about to refuse, to say, warily, that she knows he always sails alone. But, as if anticipating her he shakes his head and shrugs. And it is as if he has seen her thoughts swimming through her mind in panicky shoals, as he must sense fish moving far below the surface of the sea.

'Yes,' she says.

'Best we go now, then, while it's good light,' says Leif with a glance to the window. 'The tide is right,' he stands, jams his cap on his head. 'And in case you don't know it, Missus Larssen, it's well past ten already.'

She stands, running her damp palms down her sides, and reaches for the felt boots on the stove rail.

# Ten

It's sunny and achingly cold outside. Overnight the mountains have received a fresh powdering of snow, and the sea is a pale blue mirror. Anna climbs into Leif's log-trailer, and he drives back down between the stockfish-racks, along the track to the village. He stops at his cabin, a *rorbu* like hers, and picks up a jerrycan of fuel from the porch. Then he whistles up his black-and-white dog from her kennel. As they walk past the post office on their way to the jetty Sigrid comes out on to the steps.

'Going to take a little peek at the birdwatcher,' grins Leif. 'Back before dark.'

'Just a minute,' calls Sigrid and trundles back into the shop, returning a few minutes later with a large brown paper parcel. 'You got bread and fish and cheese and a couple of bottles of beer. *Adjø.* Good luck.'

Anna sits in the prow with the dog beside her. Leif starts the engine with one sharp pull of the cord, and they putt-putt their way out of the harbour into the fjord and head north. The sun is bright, and the sea so smooth that she's tempted to slip off her gloves and trail her fingers in it as if they're out for a summer's day sail; but when she does the water is bitterly cold. She dries her hand on her jacket and turns to face Leif. He is leaning back against the tiller, one broad forearm controlling its sweep. Apparently he takes her change of position as a sign that she would like to talk. Settling himself comfortably against the gunwale, he says, 'Missus Larssen? You want to tell me who you think this guy is? Be sure of one thing, I won't say a word, not to anyone. Not even Sigrid, if you don't want me to.'

He is too direct. These are not easy memories, smooth from retelling. Anna shakes her head.

'No. Thank you.'

Leif gives a shrug and leans against the tiller once more, looking to the horizon, as if her past is of no concern to him.

For a long while the sea slides beneath them, blue opal beneath the boat. And then Anna, sitting in the prow with her knees drawn up to her chin, suddenly hears herself saying what she has only said once before in her life, 'I met Harry Quinn in Paris in April 1940, when I thought my husband was dead.'

She is looking past Leif, too, back in the direction they have come from, as she tells him about the garden of the Palais Royal and the two blissful months that followed, how on 15 June, with the Germans at the gates of Paris, news came that Vincent was alive. How, unhesitatingly, she collected her things from Harry's hotel room that same June afternoon and how, an hour later, she found herself standing inside a derelict freight-car in the north of Paris, waiting for her eyes to grow used to the gloom.

*

Vincent was lying in a corner under a pile of filthy blankets, his head covered in blood-soaked bandages. She recognized the tall, thickset man kneeling over him.

'They tortured him,' said Léon Carré over his shoulder, gently touching the moistened cloth to Vincent's face. 'Half drowned him; gave him electric shocks to his hands and feet and . . . body.' He handed her the bowl of water, and she held it while he wrung pink water out of the cloth. 'He'll be better now you're here.' And as if to prove him right, Vincent's eyelids fluttered open and he muttered something that might have been her name, then sank back down on to the pillow. Later, when Léon had gone, Anna sat by her husband weeping silently with shock and pity, and to her shame, despair.

Vincent slept on. Finally, exhausted, she lay down on a pile of dirty straw beside him. The last train south had left and Harry had gone with it, and there was nothing else to be done.

The following morning Vincent awoke early, and the fever had disappeared. Anna held his hand gently, avoiding the red, raw wounds. Shortly after nine Léon arrived with a bag of food, and the two men had a short, whispered conversation. When Léon left, Anna brought Vincent bread and a small glass of wine and set them down on the floor beside him. After a moment, he reached out and took her hand.

'I'm sorry.'

She took a breath. 'Don't. You went through . . . all that. All I had to do was wait.' Her throat constricted: even waiting had been beyond her, for after only a few weeks of widowhood she had met an American called Harry Quinn and had, hours later, gone happily, delightedly, to his bed.

She glanced down at Vincent's face. Perhaps it would be best to tell him now – a dressing ripped off quickly to avoid prolonging the hurt. Except this was her pain, not his, and he didn't deserve to share it.

'Here,' she said, handing him the wine and slipping her hand behind his head, 'drink this.'

Just before midnight Léon returned with a friend, Maurice. German troops were moving rapidly through the city, he told them. The railway yard was sure to be searched. They must move Vincent now.

'My place,' said Léon.

'No,' protested Vincent, 'it's not safe.'

Léon spread his palms. 'Where else is there? Not your apartment, they're probably already there. Just for a few days, then we'll find somewhere else. Come on.'

Together Léon and Maurice carried Vincent to a lorry parked at the edge of the tracks. He moaned softly as they bounced over rough ground and along potholed cobbled streets; by the time they arrived at Léon's door he was unconscious. The big man shouldered him like a side of beef and carried him over his shoulder up six flights of stairs.

German troops were everywhere in the city, and there were rumours of denunciations, searches, deportations, arrests. Through his old contacts in the police department Léon amassed a list of flats whose owners had fled or disappeared, and all that summer and into the autumn Vincent and Anna moved from one place to another, staying sometimes in empty, mildewed attics, and sometimes in spacious Right Bank apartments still full of their owners' possessions.

Vincent began organizing meetings with potential Resistants of every political persuasion. Within weeks he had spoken with supporters of de Gaulle, with renegade communists who had rejected the Party's official pro-German stance, with Polish, Czech and Norwegian refugees. Slowly, lines of communication were established between the different groups, couriers and messengers were trained, and the first 'pianists' set up their wireless links to London, and there was a brief feeling of optimism. But by the time winter came the situation had deteriorated again. Informers and collaborators were everywhere, and the Resistants, still largely isolated from each other, came to see that betrayal from within was almost as likely as discovery. Despite all Vincent's attempts to unite them, rival Resistance factions struggled for dominance. It was difficult to know who could be trusted. This time, when Anna asked to be trained as a courier, Vincent agreed and sent her to see Léon Carré.

'Les Perroquets is in a pretty seedy area, down near Place Pigalle,' said Vincent. 'You'll have to go there alone. Are you sure you want to go ahead with this?'

'Yes,' said Anna simply. 'I want to be of use.' And to respect myself again, she thought, and be worthy of you.

Vincent patted her shoulder. 'You'll be OK. Keep your head down and walk as if you know exactly where you're going. He's expecting you at five.'

At four thirty Anna emerged from the Métro at Pigalle, wearing a neat navy-blue suit and white blouse. She had studied the street map so that she would be able to get her bearings quickly and now set off confidently down the hill. On every corner there were scantily dressed girls. Some of them catcalled as she passed by. Half-way down the street she had to pause to let a van reverse slowly into an entrance, and one of the women nudged a friend and then stepped forward from a doorway and threw open her coat, revealing a shockingly thin bare body with a black triangle of hair and legs high-gartered in stockings.

'Hey, don't turn away. Take a good look, *chérie*,' she called after her, 'because that's what they all want, you know – the difference is they pay us for ours.' There was a screech of laughter from across the street and Anna hurried past, head down. As the cries and whistles multiplied she walked faster and faster, until she was almost running. At last she came to the junction of rue de Navarin and turned into a quiet side street lined with grimy shops and tall buildings. She slowed, pressing her hand to the stitch in her side. Most of the shop fronts were boarded up, with crude stars painted over the signs that had once proclaimed a kosher butcher, a shoemaker and a jeweller. On the other side of the street an elderly man in a ragged coat stood outside the window of a pawnshop clutching a brown paper parcel to his chest.

The café called Les Deux Perroquets was at the far end of the street.

Pinned to the door was the handwritten notice that Vincent had told her would mean that Léon was inside and expecting her: *Cherche Serveuse*. Half-a-dozen men fell silent as she entered and watched her as she walked hesitantly towards the empty bar. She realized she had no idea what to order. Rows of gaudily labelled bottles ran from wall to wall behind the counter. At one end, under a dusty glass cover, were two hard-boiled eggs and a dry croissant; at the other was a large birdcage containing a single green parrot. The floor around about it was littered with sunflower seeds and raisins.

Anna forced herself to walk through the café towards the cage as if greeting its occupant had been the sole purpose of her visit. The green parrot opened an eye.

'I thought there were t-two of you,' stammered Anna, poking her fingertip between the bars. 'Where's the other one?'

'Dead.'

The deep voice just behind her made her jump. 'And don't do that – he bites.' Léon was looking at her as if he had never seen her before. 'You're here for the waitressing job, eh? OK.' He nodded to a short stocky man lounging in the corner. 'Jean-Marc, take over for a while, OK? Now, you, *ma fille*, come on through to the back.'

Muffled laughter followed them through to the back of the bar. Anna followed the huge man down a corridor and out into a small cobbled yard with a stinking drain. At the far side a rusty metal staircase led up to a door. She gripped the handrail, which left brown stains across her palms, and climbed the steps.

'Here,' said Léon. He bent down and slid a key into the lock. There was a grating sound, and the door swung open.

They entered a large dusty room, empty apart from a cupboard, a table and two chairs. Old green paint peeled from the walls and lay in flakes upon the floor.

'This is it, Anaïs. Your schoolroom for the next few weeks.'

'Do we have to use codenames?' she murmured self-consciously. 'Is Léon yours?'

He raised his hand, 'Léon is all you need to know. No questions needed. If you're lucky, what I teach you will help keep you alive through whatever's coming. Just pay attention, and try not to waste my time.'

On the table something square and lumpy was hidden beneath a cloth. 'We'll begin', he said, lifting a wide grimy palm, 'by building up your memory.' He caught her surprised glance. 'Why? Because memory and observation can save your life, that's why. Look, this isn't a child's game,' he said abruptly. 'Concentrate. You've got ten seconds.'

He tweaked away the cloth and she was staring at a large tray. On it were thirty or forty ill-assorted objects: a tiny blue-glass vase, a watch, a shoe, a pencil, a beer mat, a pin, a match, a pipe, a domino. She stared at them blankly as Léon counted out the remaining seconds.

'Three, two, one. Stop.'

He replaced the cover.

'Now, tell me everything you saw.'

She could only manage to recall a dozen.

Léon shrugged. 'Again. This time, try to make a mental map of the tray, a link that takes you from one object to its neighbour, with everything in its place. See what I mean?'

She nodded and began again.

'Twenty. Not good enough.' Léon moved the objects around, swirling them and separating them. 'Now. Again.'

This time she managed thirty-two. Léon half smiled. 'A different game. Study the tray again carefully, Anaïs. Ready? Now, close your eyes. OK. What have I taken away?'

Anna peered intently at the tray and noticed the gap almost immediately. In her head was a picture as clear as a snapshot.

'The salt spoon.'

Léon grinned and unfolded his fist: the small tin spoon nestled in his palm.

'Very good. Again.'

After days of working with objects they moved outside. First he took her through the *quartier*, walking her through a set pattern of streets. Then she repeated it alone, and was made to report the tiniest tell-tale changes: a shutter closed instead of open, a policeman on the beat, an official car parked outside a certain house. He showed her how to rendezvous with a contact, passing in the street and then repassing when the coast was clear. He trained her to check her pockets each time she went out, so that she could be sure she wasn't carrying anything that might compromise a network. He taught her how to use a dead letter-box and a radio transmitter and how to write reports on thin onionskin paper that could easily (they said) be swallowed.

They rarely talked about personal matters. It appeared that Léon knew Vincent well, and he always referred to him with a mix of respect and gruffly paternal affection.

'He's a bright lad,' he said one afternoon. 'Brave and a lot of charm. When this is over, people are going to need heroes, Anaïs, and he will be one of them, mark my words.' And Anna nodded gravely, hiding a fierce, proprietorial pride.

Her training advanced rapidly, but even when Léon pronounced her ready Anna found she was given little to do. When she pressed Vincent to let her take messages, he refused, saying that there were more experienced couriers available whom he preferred to use. She could not decide if this masked concern for her safety or misgivings about her ability.

Over the next months she spent much time alone in the latest echoing apartment or wandering the streets, diligently practising her observation skills. The presence of the Germans was overpowering. On the *grands boulevards* armoured cars thundered down the tree-lined avenues and grey-uniformed soldiers were everywhere, swaggering along the pavements, singing raucously on the café terraces. Anna walked past them with her eyes lowered: in her shabby coat and with a tightly knotted headscarf over her hair she attracted little attention.

Occasionally she forced herself to walk through areas of the city she had visited with Harry, telling herself that this, too, was a kind of training and self-discipline. One morning she even walked through the shuttered arcades of the Palais Royal. The café was closed, and the bench where she had sat with Harry was empty, although green-necked pigeons still scrabbled in the dust. She walked on, resisting every spike of memory, until she felt she had exorcized him from her past.

But when one day the newspapers told how twenty refugees, including an American, had been captured in Marseilles and shot by the *milice*, she was shocked to find herself weeping uncontrollably.

Vincent laid the paper flat upon the table. 'Anna, stop it.'

She wiped her wet cheeks with the back of her hand. 'I'm sorry.'

He shook his head. 'It's war. There's no point agonizing about the death of strangers – it's a waste of energy. You must channel emotion into action, not self-indulgence.'

Her eyes filled again. 'But the American . . . I mean, every one of those men . . .'

Vincent interrupted her with a wave of his hand. 'If you are honest with yourself, the death of an individual American cannot be important to you.' He paused. 'Can it?'

It was not a question. Anna looked down at her hands. Vincent had never asked her what she had done in Paris during the months she had thought he was dead, and she had accepted that by delicate, unspoken consent the subject was to remain out of bounds. But even when his wounds had healed he remained distant from her, avoiding physical contact beyond a light goodnight kiss as he went to his single bed and she to hers. She wondered if his silence was a punishment and decided that, if it was, it was mild compared with what she deserved.

Now she stood. 'No, Vincent, it isn't important. I'm sorry. It won't happen again.'

*

It is nearly midday and Leif and Anna have reached the last headland before Sørvågen. Leif cuts the motor and lets the boat drift slowly on the current. He unwraps the brown paper parcel and hands her a piece of bread, some small pieces of dry stockfish and a slice of cheese. Anna takes off her gloves and drinks from the bottle of beer Leif opens for her and bites hungrily into the bread.

Leif chews slowly. Finally he says, 'It happened often in the war – not knowing whether someone was alive or dead. A friend of Sigrid's was told she was a widow and a year later she got engaged to an English naval officer; then news came that her husband was in a prison camp in Poland. No one's to blame.'

She doesn't answer.

'How old are you, Anna?' Leif asks suddenly.

She blushes. 'Forty-two.'

'No age. And you look younger.'

After a while she says, 'Do you ever think about people you used to know in the past, Leif, and wonder where and what they are now?'

He shifts his big body on the thwart. 'I guess the difference is I still see most of the people I knew way back. Toril Berglund, the first girl I loved, married a mainlander, a lorry driver. She has three kids now. I still see her sometimes on the quayside at Bodø: she's as big as a whale and cusses worse than a man.' He grins. 'I'd say I had a lucky escape there.' He holds the last piece of bread in both hands, peers intently at it.

'Then there was Ilse Hansen. She was a teacher over in Flakstad. Quiet sort of woman but with something about her all the same. We were close for a while. But then I went away to England to fight, and when I came back she'd married a friend of mine instead of me. I guess I try not to see her too much at all.' He shrugs. 'There have been a few others, over the years. Good women in the main.' He lifts the bread and bites deep into it.

Anna thinks about that for a while, occasionally tipping the cold bottle against her mouth.

When they have finished eating Leif rubs his hands down the side of his trousers and throws a last crust to the patient dog in the bows.

'Well, I guess it's time. Maybe you want to put this on?' He hands her a big yellow oilskin with a hood. 'Bulk yourself up a little, in case your man over there is doing a little bird watching of his own.' He draws the binoculars from their case. 'Get these focused, and we'll be off.'

He starts the engine, and they make for the tip of the headland. As they round it he says, 'Markusen's place is the red-and-white cabin right out at the left-hand edge of the village. There, see? No, don't turn quick, just move gradual, as if you're looking at the wildlife. Maybe train those glasses on the cliff, watch the sea birds for a while first, yes?'

Anna obeys, and the binoculars tremble over rocky outcrops padded with snow, where birds sit drying their wings in the sunlight. Slowly, she turns them towards the village.

'It's got a real tall chimney, see it now?' Leif has cut the engine and is assembling fishing lines and bait. 'Don't mind me, I'm just going to catch some supper while you have a look-see.'

Anna scans along the houses at the middle of the village, working her way out to the left. One house is empty, appears derelict; next to it is a blue façade, peeling paint. Then, a few yards further on, there is a red-painted cabin with a tall chimney at one side of the roof and a thin drift of smoke rising, grey against the white flank of the mountain. Against one wall stands a neat log-pile. As she watches, suddenly the door of the cabin swings open and a man steps out on to the platform.

Immediately, Anna jerks the glasses back towards the safety of the roosting sea birds, then, slowly, as if hypnotized, she brings them around and for a second has him in perfect clarity.

Harry Quinn is wearing a blue checked shirt and dark-blue jeans. He is older, stockier, his hair thinner and greyer, but his eyes are unchanged and looking across half a mile of water directly into hers.

Time changes everything and nothing at all.

A second later he disappears, and when Anna swivels the binoculars in search of him she finds him at the far end of the platform standing behind a tripod, swinging the large black barrel of a telescope in her direction. Panicking, she pulls the oilskin hood over her face and turns back towards Leif. The shaking binoculars focus on an innocent herring gull sailing over the mirror water behind them, trailing a ruffled, widening vee at its wake.

'OK, OK, hush. Stay calm now, Anna,' says Leif, as if speaking to a frightened animal. 'Won't look good if we run away as soon as he looks at us. And anyway,' he grins, 'I got a bite.'

Deftly he pulls in the line and scoops a large, struggling grey fish into the boat. 'Cod. Sigrid'll be pleased. Here, fill the bucket with seawater. No, no, keep facing me.' He kills the fish quickly and cleanly with a billet of timber and drops it into the bucket, looking up casually as he does so. 'Still there. He's got the telescope on us just now. You OK?'

Anna shakes her head, feeling Harry's gaze crawl over her like a spider.

Leif glances up. 'He's turning back to the cabin. I'm going to tidy up the fishing tackle for a moment. In the meantime you take a last look, just to be sure.'

Anna lifts the impossibly heavy binoculars and brings them slowly around. Harry Quinn, her lost Harry, stands framed in the doorway of the *rorbu*, hands on hips, staring out over the water. As she adjusts the focus once more she looks into his eyes and knows he is watching her watching him.

It's dark by the time they land back at Å. Anna declines Sigrid's invitation to share a supper of grilled fish and makes her way back around the headland to the cabin. The wind is rising and there are no stars.

In the cabin the stove has gone out and the house is dark and chill. Without taking off her jacket she lights the lamps, riddles the cold ash and rebuilds a fire. When she taps the barometer it falls dramatically: the brief lull in the winter weather is over.

By ten o'clock a gale is whistling around the cabin roof and waves are riding against the cliffs in battalions; she hears them as they crash their great weight against the rocks and roar back down the shelving shingle slopes. And there is a strange vibration coming up from the ground: beyond Hell Point the Maelstrom is stirring. Anna crawls into her bunk fully clothed and pulls the quilt up over her head.

But even though she eventually sleeps, she wakes in the middle of the night troubled by dreams and the wailing of the wind. As she sits in the bed, hugging her knees, the quilt pulled up around her shoulders, she remembers a story her father told her, of Draugen, the sea-ghost of a dead fisherman, who sails for ever in a half-wrecked boat and appears out of the gale amid funereal organ music to drag the living down with him into the deep.

# Eleven

In July 1941, following a series of coded messages from London, a French army officer arrived in Paris and made contact with the Resistance group. He had, he claimed, been sent by de Gaulle himself, with a personal message for Vincent Galland. Léon Carré was suspicious, but the major's credentials were faultless. When they had checked his story as far as they could, they drove him, blindfolded, to a safehouse where Vincent was waiting with Anna.

Léon, glowering signals of caution, untied the scarf, and the officer blinked, looked around the room and strode over to Vincent, his hand outstretched. 'I recognize you from your pictures. Major Antoine Desturbes, Free French Army.'

'Vincent Galland. And this is an associate of mine, Miss Anna Larssen.'

The major looked briefly at her and then enquiringly at Vincent. 'Mademoiselle. Obviously you have Monsieur Galland's confidence?' Vincent nodded, and Desturbes sat down and drew a silver cigarette case from the pocket of his overcoat. 'May I?'

His movements were rapid, nervous. Lighting the cigarette he inhaled deeply and said, 'Forgive me, Galland, but my time here is extremely limited, so I should like, if I may, to come straight to the point.'

Vincent nodded again.

The major crossed his long legs. 'We've heard excellent reports of your Resistance activities here, Galland. But a need has arisen for someone with your unique combination of operational and diplomatic skills.'

Vincent frowned. 'I'm no longer a diplomat, Major.'

'But you were once,' said Desturbes quickly, tapping ash into a saucer, 'and that makes you an ideal candidate for what we have in mind.' He paused. 'Perhaps you won't be aware, but although we're their allies the British keep us on a very short leash over there in London. The fact is we're almost powerless.' He grimaced wryly, '*Impuissants.* The British are doing everything they can to get America to join the war, but they monopolize all contact with them. And without a French perspective on the future of France,' he smiled thinly, 'who knows what these Anglo-Saxons will concoct between them?

'Major –' Vincent shifted impatiently in his chair.

Desturbes held up a hand for him to be patient. 'We believe there is a need for an intermediary, someone who can help win the Americans' trust and stimulate their interest in France, specifically. In other words, we want *you,* Galland.'

'Major –'

'No, please wait until I have finished. Conveniently for us, the British also feel the Americans may be impressed by a real live freedom fighter,' he smiled thinly, 'a *résistant de première heure,* to stiffen their resolve. And, on the practical side, you speak fluent English and have . . .', he turned to Anna, 'a beautiful Norwegian *wife,* who would tug at their heart-strings. *Enchanté*, Madame Galland.'

Léon looked from Vincent to Anna.

The Major shrugged and drew on his cigarette, 'We have common cause. There's surely no need for secrets between us, Monsieur Galland. As I said, a beautiful wife . . . and, as such, someone who must be in considerable danger here in Paris.'

Vincent was silent for a moment. 'How long would you expect this mission to last, Major?'

'Six months, a year? It's impossible to be precise.'

'And if I do this, I shall be free to return to France afterwards?'

'Of course.'

'And my wife may remain in America for the duration of hostilities?'

Anna laid a hand on his sleeve, but Vincent ignored her.

'Well?'

Desturbes nodded.

For a moment Vincent looked down at his hands and said softly, 'Then I accept.'

Desturbes returned the following day with detailed instructions. Vincent and Anna would travel south and cross into the Unoccupied Zone, where Vincent would have an opportunity to contact other groups in Lyons. They would then head on to Marseilles where they would take a boat for North Africa. From Casablanca they would take a plane to Lisbon, and from there travel to London and on to America. He handed over sets of false papers, travel permits and identities. Vincent's *alter ego* was Etienne Rousseau, an antiques dealer with a business in Antibes. Anna was Pauline Lescaut, his secretary. Together they memorized codenames, addresses and rendezvous points.

They set out in the first week of August, heading south, travelling sometimes by rail, sometimes on foot or by car and once in the back of a lorry. Vincent spoke for both of them whenever they were stopped and asked to produce papers. Anna's admiration grew as she watched him assume the personality of a fussy, prematurely ageing man, treating the German soldiers with just the right level of deference. The only time he appeared tense was when they crossed into the Unoccupied Zone and had to rely on the goodwill of Julien du Plessis, one of his old diplomatic acquaintances, whose estate straddled the frontier.

As they waited at dawn, luggage in hand, in a small grove of birch, to their left they could see the sun glinting on the binoculars of the soldiers in the village below. Birds sang, a chill breeze stirred the branches and the grass, heavy with dew, soaked their shoes. Their guide appeared out of nowhere: a thin, distinguished-looking man dressed in an ancient tweed hunting-jacket and polished brown boots. Without saying a word he beckoned them to follow, and the three of them walked in single file through the wood for half an hour. They emerged on the edge of a sunlit cornfield, where du Plessis stopped and pointed south.

'Your route is there, towards the far steeple. A kilometre further on you'll cross the railway line. Follow it along to the next village.'

Vincent nodded and began to thank him, but du Plessis cut him off.

'*C'est la dernière fois, vous comprenez? Jamais plus, Galland.*'

Vincent nodded, expressionless. '*Je comprends. Merci toutefois, mon ami. Adieu.*'

When they reached the town Vincent and Anna made their way to the railway station and, having bought their tickets, sat out of sight in the empty waiting-room.

'There are many men like him,' said Vincent quietly. 'He thinks he'll be safer if he plays both sides. So he helps the Resistance, just a little. He collaborates, just enough.' There was a long silence. 'He's a fool,' he said flatly.

It took them three days to reach Marseilles. Anna fell ill there, and it was late August by the time they sailed into Oran, where sympathizers offered them shelter in a small villa overlooking the sea.

Hungrily, that night they feasted on rice and mutton, ate nectarines and figs and drank sweet wine. Later, when their tactful hosts had disappeared, they climbed to the roof terrace and stood under the stars while a warm breeze from the desert passed through the garden, bringing them the perfume of flowers. To the east a red-gold moon was rising through pines. Anna leaned her head on Vincent's shoulder, and after a while his arm came to rest at her waist. They stood quiet and together for a long while.

Throughout the journey they had remained unfailingly tender and considerate towards each other, enquiring after each other's health each morning like an elderly married couple. But for Anna, safe and warm at her husband's side in the moonlight, the strain of staying aloof was suddenly unbearable.

Looking out over the garden, she said softly, 'Vincent, last summer, when I thought you were dead, something happened. I dearly want, please, to tell you about it. May I?'

There was a long silence, then she felt his finger trail along her forearm and tap gently on her wrist.

'No.'

He spoke gently but kept his profile turned away from her.

'No.'

The moon rose above the black pines, and the breeze sharpened. Vincent draped a wrap around her shoulders and led her inside.

Two days later they left the villa and began the last stage of their journey to Lisbon.

*

Anna had forgotten how beautiful Saint-Aubain-les-Eaux could be in the autumn: the hazy blueness in the morning air and the scent of blackberries that seemed to drift into the house from the woods; the drawing-in of nights and the lighting of fires.

Two days before Hal Keen was due to arrive she made up the guest bedroom at the far end of the house. It smelt damp and musty, so she opened the shutters, tied a scarf around her head and dusted the floor and polished the furniture like a good Norwegian housewife. Then she put freshly laundered linen on the bed and set a vase of dark-red chrysanthemums on the table by the window, so that their clean scent would spike the air.

Knowing the village's love of gossip, at lunchtime Anna had told Florence about Mr Keen's visit, and within hours the news went round that for the next few weeks Saint-Aubain-les-Eaux would have a resident *écrivain*. She had also been busy preparing the story of Vincent's life for public view. When he arrived Mr Keen, Hal, would find on the desk in Vincent's study a large box of cardboard files, all of which were neatly labelled: 'Prague, Childhood, 1908–24', 'Paris, Student Days, 1924–26', 'Madrid, Dublin, Berlin, London, Prague, 1927–33'. Two heavy dossiers, rich with detail, covered the war years.

When everything was ready Anna went out into the garden to calm her nerves. She raked the leaves into a rustling heap at the bottom of the garden and set fire to them. Then she made herself a cup of Earl Grey and carried it out to the terrace. She sat on the damp wooden seat, her chin tucked in the neck of one of Vincent's old sweaters, watching the afternoon sun flicker like fire through the trees and wondering if she would not be wiser to carry the files down the garden and feed them into the flames, one by one.

Or would that be a last, final betrayal?

There was no one to tell her.

As dusk crept up the lawn towards her, she shivered.

Mr Keen arrived promptly at the appointed hour. He unloaded from his car a large canvas duffel bag and a small case that she imagined contained his typewriter. He also had, hanging heavy from his shoulder as he walked up the path, a large leather satchel, apparently full of documents. He stood on the step, shifting his grip on the canvas bag.

'Hello again, Madame Galland. Thank you so much for letting me stay.'

'I did promise, Mr Keen.'

'I know. But thank you. And it's Hal, please?'

His easy informality was disconcerting.

Awkwardly she said, 'Would you like to look round?'

'I'd love to, if it's not too much trouble.'

They began in the drawing-room, with its tall windows and the fire burning in the hearth, moving through to the study where Mr Keen's eyes widened gratifyingly at the sight of all her neatly stacked files; then up the stairs and down the passageway to the guest-room, which he praised lavishly, especially impressed by the double windows which opened on to a tiny balcony above the terrace and the garden beyond. The American leaned over the railing, looking down on the terrace.

'Many happy evenings must have been spent down there,' he said, turning to look at her. 'With Vincent and friends?'

She went over to the railing and looked down into the darkening garden. Leaves were piled in drifts around the feet of the wooden table. They had sat there that last summer, she and Vincent and the Delamains. It had been a magical night – a slow-fading sunset, fireflies in the honeysuckle. They had drunk glasses of Muscat, tawny in the moonlight. She bent over further. The chairs stood in their accustomed places – for a moment she could almost hear Bertrand Delamain's growling voice and Astrid's throaty, excited laugh.

Vincent had been at unusually animated that evening, entertaining them with stories of political life in Paris. Relaxed, lightly and brilliantly satirical, he moved from one target to the next: Gaullists, Americans, British. Gradually the three of them had fallen silent under the spell of the amused, mocking voice.

And when the others had gone she and Vincent had sat on in silence, unwilling to leave the garden. Anna had been leaning back in her chair, watching the stars, and had felt Vincent's hand move over hers.

'Anna,' he murmured, 'dear Anna.'

It had been said with nostalgia, almost yearning. Like a man talking fondly of a country far away.

# Twelve

The letters of transit and the Lisbon plane took Vincent and Anna to London and from there, in time, to Liverpool and a ship bound for New York. The *Manx Star* was a grimy, wallowing cargo tub with a crew of gloomy Scots. The cabins for paying passengers were so cramped and noisy and stank so strongly of diesel and vomit that Anna was sick even before they left the harbour. Vincent spent the days on deck, ate with the crew and only came to the cabin when he could be reasonably sure that Anna would be asleep.

She wasn't, but she was grateful for the pretence.

When, on 4 December, the deafening thudding finally ceased, she came gingerly up on deck and stood at the rail watching dockyard workers loop hawsers around the great iron bollards on the quay. She gulped at the cold, hard air, seeing for the first time the serried grey skyscrapers of Harry Quinn's home city. Then, her nails driven punishingly deep into her palms, she followed her husband down the gangway on to the windswept jetty.

Although the British Embassy in Washington had been notified of their arrival there was no one to greet them. Anna shivered and pulled her thin coat around her. The cold was penetrating, the wind whistled in the metal fretwork of the towering cranes and made ripples on the puddles. Vincent was frowning across at the city as if blaming it for their predicament. Just as they were beginning to despair, from behind a warehouse bustled a familiar figure – a short, elegantly tailored man with trimmed grey moustache and little black eyes like olives.

'Vincent! Anna! I'm sorry I'm late. They told me eleven thirty.' Henri Richemont was out of breath but slapped Vincent's shoulders vigorously as he kissed him on both cheeks. 'Vincent. *Mon Dieu*, it's good to see you! Two years, man! But I've heard all about your work. You're enough to make a red-blooded Frenchman weep with pride. And especially me, because I make a royal living playing heroes like you in Hollywood films.'

He drew a breath and turned to face Anna. 'And the serene and beautiful Anna Larssen.' He kissed her hand. 'Or may I call you by your married name now? My dear, even more beautiful, but so pale and thin; Gisèle will want to whisk you away for pampering and tender loving care. Oh, of course, you haven't met Gisèle . . .'

He looked at the two tired faces, 'I'm talking too much. You must be exhausted. Come on.' He nodded to where a black limousine was waiting.

'Wait.'

The British had given Vincent the name of a hotel. Now, dazedly, he handed the address to Henri. The Frenchman looked at it, frowned and crumpled the note in his fist. 'You deserve better than that, my boy. I'll call the *rosbifs* and say you've made other arrangements. There's a room fit for heroes waiting for you at the Waldorf, *mon brave*.'

A chauffeur was already picking up the luggage and stowing it in the trunk of the car. Soon they were bumping their way out of the docks and into the canyons of Manhattan. Ten minutes later they came to a gentle halt outside a canopied hotel entrance and, trembling with fatigue, Anna stood by Vincent's side in the marble lobby while Henri saw to their room and their luggage.

When it was done, he turned to them. 'Now to the important things in life. Tomorrow night at seven – cocktails here with Gisèle and me. Just to prove to you refugees that there are still places in the world where such things exist. Now, rest well.' In a flurry of handshakes and kisses he was gone.

Henri Richemont's 'room fit for heroes' turned out to be a suite of vast pastel rooms, densely carpeted, with golden lamps, deep sofas and great cellophane-wrapped baskets of fruit and champagne. Beyond the salon was a white-tiled bathroom and beyond that a bedroom, with a bed as wide as a raft covered in a fall of shining satin.

Too tired even to comprehend what was happening, Vincent and Anna showered away a week's shipboard grime and crawled into bed. All that evening and on through the night they slept the deep, unconscious sleep of homeless people who have finally reached a place of safety.

It was morning when they awoke to a gentle knocking at the door and room service arriving with trays of hot rolls, butter, pancakes, coffee and freshly squeezed orange juice. The waiters opened the curtains, fussed with the napkins and flowers, arranged folded newspapers beside the plates, then smiled and bowed and left as quietly as they had arrived. When, finally, they were alone Anna and Vincent looked at each other and burst out laughing: it had taken all their self-control not to fall upon the food and cram handfuls into their mouths like ravenous children.

'My God, there are at least six different kinds of bread,' said Vincent wonderingly, lifting the corner of a starched napkin. 'And aren't those *pains aux raisins*?'

That breakfast at the Waldorf was the most delicious meal Anna had ever eaten. Her fingers smeared with butter, her upper lip frosted with sugar from pastries, her stomach warm and replete with coffee and hot milk, she sank back into the pillows and marvelled at how quickly the body could be restored.

At ten there was a phone call from reception to say that Mr Richemont had asked representatives from Goodman Bergdorf to call to take Monsieur and Madame Galland's measurements for a set of new clothes. Vincent started to protest, but even he could see that their meagre travel-stained wardrobe would not take them everywhere they needed to go in the city. Resignedly, he held out his arms and submitted to the tape.

At eleven they had another visitor. A polite Englishman introduced himself as Andrew Collings, from the British Consul's staff.

'Had a little trouble tracking you down,' he said, gazing around the room. 'I say, it obviously pays to have influential friends in New York.'

Vincent frowned. 'Obviously. Look, Collings, I've come a very long way for this. Could we please get down to business?'

Suddenly formal, the Englishman congratulated Vincent on his escape from the Nazis, welcomed him to America on behalf of the Free World and promised that as soon as he felt he was ready appropriate meetings would be arranged with senior figures in Washington.

It all sounded very vague, Anna thought, but Vincent nodded, and she was relieved to see his clenched fists open slightly.

At four o'clock the people from Bergdorf's returned, wheeling in a hanging rack of suits and dresses and carrying boxes of shirts, ties, blouses, shoes and underwear. On the instructions of their manager a young man and woman unwrapped and displayed each garment for approval.

'All this is for us?' said Anna incredulously.

The manager smiled. 'Certainly, madam. With Mr Richemont's compliments. If there's anything that doesn't suit we'd be more than happy to exchange it at the store. My card is on the box. Please just call. I'd be honoured to serve you personally.'

'We simply can't accept this,' began Vincent.

Anna put her hand on his arm, 'Darling, don't. Henri wants to do this. Don't hurt his feelings.'

Vincent turned away, leaving Anna to thank the sales assistants and shake the manager by the hand.

When, later, they changed into their new finery, they stood in front of the full-length mirror and saw themselves transformed: a tall, fine-featured man in a beautifully cut suit, and a pale, blonde woman in a figure-hugging black crêpe dress.

'You look beautiful, my dear,' said Vincent, bending to kiss her lightly on the neck. 'I, on the other hand, look like an American gigolo.'

'You don't. But even if you did,' said Anna firmly, straightening his tie, 'the moment you spoke, everyone would know you were a hero.'

His body was close to hers. She stroked his collar, stared up into his calm, smooth-skinned, weary face and wondered if at last he would close the last few inches between them. For a moment it seemed as though he would. He clasped her upper arms and drew her towards him. On tiptoe, Anna closed her eyes – and felt the brush of his lips against her forehead.

Gently, Vincent set her back on her feet. 'Time to go, I think.'

In the bar, Anna sat quietly at Vincent's side while he answered the Richemonts' questions about the war and life in Occupied France, giving tiny exclamations of disbelief. Vincent's long fingers were spread flat upon the table, and Anna saw Gisèle Richemont glance down and wince at the ruined nails.

At the end, Henri had tears in his eyes. 'Those bastards strutting down the Champs-Elysées as if they own the place. It's unthinkable. Impossible. Thank heaven there are a few like you who dare to fight back, eh?' He poured more champagne, 'To you, Vincent. To you, lad.' There was a catch in his voice, and Vincent looked embarrassed.

Gisèle leaned forward. 'And what is your mission here, Vincent, if one can ask?'

'The British say they have plans for me, and I meet with them tomorrow.' He tapped a cigarette against a gleaming ashtray. 'Of course, once my task here is done I hope they will permit me to return to France as soon as possible.'

'You'd go back so soon?' said Henri incredulously.

'Naturally.'

It was said so calmly, Anna thought. She glanced across at Henri, hoping he was not embarrassed, but the older man was watching his wife. Gisèle Richemont was considerably younger than her husband. Assured, glamorous, her dark blonde hair glossy and groomed, her lime-green chiffon gown plunging daringly down from her shoulders, she leaned forward. 'Surely they'll allow you a little respite, a little relaxation first?' she murmured.

'When the Germans relax, so will I,' said Vincent.

Gisèle turned to Anna and gave a brilliant smile.

'Anna, as his time with us is so short, may I ask your solemn hero to dance?'

Vincent was already rising to his feet.

Anna watched Vincent steer the woman on to the crowded dance floor. His hand rested in the hollow of her back as once Harry's had rested in the hollow of hers.

Turning away, she said to Henri Richemont. 'Your Gisèle is very beautiful.'

'As are you, my dear,' said Henri gallantly. 'Although perhaps a little pensive tonight. Still tired?' He reached across and touched her hand. 'What were you thinking about?'

'A little weary, I suppose, yes. And thinking . . . oh, just about how much we owe you . . .'

But Henri heard the pause in her voice and looked up at the wrong moment, and to her horror she heard herself say, 'And I was thinking about a man called Harry Quinn, who . . .' she hesitated, then finished quickly, '. . . who helped us get out of Lisbon.'

Henri raised his eyebrows and reached for the bottle of champagne.

'Anna, I'm an actor. True stories have a particular fascination for me. And I scent one here.' He refilled her glass, 'So. How intriguing. Tell me about him, this Harry Quinn.'

On the other side of the room Vincent's hand was still splayed against Gisèle's tiny waist.

Anna lifted her glass and filled her mouth with the tiny, kissing bubbles. 'I met him in Paris,' she said, breaking all her promises to herself, 'in spring last year, when I thought that Vincent was dead.'

'What a marvellous beginning,' said Henri delightedly. 'Paris in wartime, a beautiful young widow, a dead Resistance hero and a gallant Englishman. I can hardly wait. Tell me more.'

'Harry was American,' she said, then stopped. 'Henri, I've never told Vincent this.'

Henri filled her glass. 'But I'm a Frenchman, my dear, and totally unshockable in matters of love. Now, you weren't talking about Vincent, you were telling me about an intriguing character called Harry Quinn.'

Gisèle and Vincent were dancing in the centre of the crowded dance floor, their hands twined.

In the weeks and months of silence the tale had gathered its own momentum – now it spilled out, uncensored and unstoppable: the story of her love affair with Harry Quinn.

Music played, dancers danced. Anna blinked, suddenly aware that Henri was patting her hand sympathetically. What had she done? She'd said far more than she had meant to, that was for sure. She knew she had told him about Paris. She knew she had described Lisbon and the frantic search for exit visas and the introduction to the mysterious American who turned out to be Harry Quinn.

But surely she couldn't have told him what had happened the following afternoon; how when Harry had refused to sell the visas to Vincent she'd slipped out of the hotel and walked between the overhanging houses of the Alfama *barrio* towards Harry Quinn's apartment?

The music had stopped.

Gisèle and Vincent were making their way back to the table.

Henri leaned forward anxiously. 'Anna, my dear, don't cry.' He took her hand, 'This is all too recent, isn't it? I'm so sorry. Actors are fools – we forget the difference between movies and real life. Here.' He handed her a handkerchief and, after a moment, a cigarette. Anna inhaled, coughing as the smoke seared her throat, and watched nervously as Henri greeted Vincent and Gisèle, trying to detect from his manner whether she had also told him that for the last few weeks she had known herself pregnant with a child that could not possibly be her husband's.

# Thirteen

The following day, unaccustomed to New York late nights and champagne, Anna slept on. She heard Vincent leave for the consulate, but it was mid-afternoon before he returned. There was the jingle of a dropped room-key, and then she heard his voice, oddly slurred, swearing softly outside the door.

'Ah, still here, *darling*?' he drawled, throwing his coat down on a chair. 'I thought you might have decamped with your latest *bel ami*.'

He walked over to the drinks cabinet and poured himself a large glass of bourbon, swirling it around in the glass so that the liquid slopped over on to his fingers. He flicked drops on to the carpet. 'Well, don't you want to know how the meeting went?' he asked over his shoulder, taking a long deep draught.

'Of course.'

'Of *course*?' He turned, one eyebrow raised, and she saw that his face was white: emotion battened down under rage. 'Then you'll be interested to hear that my principal reason for being here was superseded at a stroke yesterday, by the Imperial Japanese Air Force, which had the temerity to attack the sitting-duck American Pacific fleet in Hawaii. Yes, while we were asleep every red-blooded American joined the war.' He slammed the empty glass down on the cabinet and poured another one.

'What do they want *you* to do?' said Anna carefully.

'Oh, me? Well, they think the best thing to do with me is to send me off on a whirlwind six-week *tour*,' he said, pronouncing the word as though he were spitting a fly from his mouth. 'They're working on the schedule as we speak: schools, concert halls and theatres. I'm to show the Great American People how right they are to join our noble cause.'

He dropped into an armchair and lit a cigarette. 'We should never have come. Collings's boss is in league with the Yanks and probably that phoney major we met in Paris. I doubt de Gaulle even knows I'm here.'

Anna knelt by the arm of his chair. 'What will you do, Vincent?'

He gave a bleak, unpleasant laugh 'Oh, I'll do what they want,' he said. 'What else is there?'

Anna hesitated. 'Henri Richemont says that the whole country is talking about the war. He says you could tell your story . . .'

'Do you really think I care about the opinion of some jumped-up French movie actor?' Vincent stood up. 'Story-telling. Movies. Fuck him.' He stared around at the pastel-peach opulence. 'And fuck his fucking capitalist hotel.'

He strode out of the room. Anna scrambled to her feet. The shock of the slamming door dislodged a small ornate mirror, which fell with a splintering crash. She crouched down, carefully picking up the shards from the marble floor

It took Andrew Collings four days to make arrangements. When everything was ready Anna and Vincent began a punishing round of receptions, conventions, interviews and conferences. Every evening, and some afternoons, Vincent stood on a new platform in a new city and spoke fluently, without notes. His voice had always had a mesmerizing, persuasive quality, and now, combined with his good looks and his heroic war record, it ensured him a warm reception. After each talk the host or chairman threw the meeting open to the public, but both Vincent and Anna came to dread the prurience of the questions which followed.

'Tell me, Mr Galland,' said a young, bright-eyed law student in Richmond, Virginia, 'were you ever actually *tortured* by the Gestapo?'

Vincent kept both hands on the lectern. 'Yes. And many of my comrades. Men and women.'

There was a thrilled murmur in the hall. The student persisted, waving aside an embarrassed neighbour, 'Forgive me for asking, sir, but what exactly did they do?'

Frowning now, Vincent said in his clipped English, 'They are people of great cruelty and limited imagination, need one say more than that?'

'So, did you tell them anything?'

Aghast, Anna half rose, but with a cutting gesture of his hand Vincent commanded her to sit.

'No, as it happens, I did not.'

There was scattered cheering and applause. Then a stocky man in a blue blazer, who had been lounging against the back wall of the hall, called out over the heads of the audience, 'Is it true there are communists in the French Resistance, Mr Galland?'

Calmly Vincent lit a cigarette. 'We welcome anyone opposed to the Nazis. When the German Army moved against Russia in June hundreds of French communists joined the fight.' Anna glanced at him. He did not add that he had accepted the comrades' shamefully late arrival in the Maquis without reproach.

A young man in the front row raised a hand, 'So, will you be here in America for the duration of the war, Mr Galland?'

'I intend to go back to Europe as soon as my work here is done,' he replied tersely. 'Next question.'

It was a few weeks before they began to recognize faces at the meetings. The man in the blazer appeared in a dark suit in Boston the following week and then in a sports jacket in Washington. On at least three different occasions Anna noticed a lean, grey-haired man in a raincoat listening intently at the back of the room. At the end of the Chicago conference Vincent pointed Blue Blazer out to a fellow Czech and whispered a question.

Jakob Gruber glanced around. 'Probably a government man. There's some sort of new secret security organization that's made up its mind we're all reds. They spy on us.'

'Well, let them spy on their allies if they've got nothing better to do,' said Vincent, glowering towards the back of the hall. 'We've nothing to hide.'

It was late February when Anna and Vincent walked wearily into the foyer of the Beverly Hills hotel.

Henri Richemont sprang out of his armchair and embraced them.

'*Mes amis*! Welcome to Hollywood! How has your tour been?'

'Most successful, if you believe the British,' said Vincent. 'Although we were never allowed to forget for one moment that we were foreigners.'

'Join the club,' said Henri blithely. 'This city's full of foreign actors, most of them Frenchmen like me, playing Germans in the movies. Now, how about a glass of champagne to celebrate your arrival?'

Vincent glanced at his watch. 'Henri, I'm sorry, but I have several calls to make. May I leave Anna in your care for a while?'

Henri nodded his bird-like head to one side. 'I'm always ready to look after beautiful women. Please, Vincent, go. Take all the time you need, although of course I can't promise that she will be here when you return.'

Anna closed her eyes.

'No?' said Vincent evenly. 'Well, I shall just have to take a chance on that, shan't I?'

'Anna, my dear,' said Henri, scowling melodramatically at Vincent's back, 'let me take you away from this tireless but unappreciative husband of yours and pour champagne into your slippers at once.'

He slipped a hand under her elbow and steered her through to a dimly lit bar, where deep leather chairs surrounded polished glass tables. She sank gratefully down and waited while Henri ordered a bottle of champagne.

'Well, what shall we drink to?' he asked, pressing a glass into her hand. 'Vincent? Love?' He glanced down at her waist. 'Or, if you permit me, may I say "the future"?'

'Oh,' she blushed, 'I didn't think . . .'

'I am a great observer of ladies' faces and figures,' said Henri smoothly, sipping his drink. 'And I see you blossoming. When is it due?'

'In August.'

'Vincent must be very proud.'

'Yes,' she said flatly. Every morning of their journey Vincent had asked how she was and insisted on bringing her a full American breakfast in bed – juice, eggs, bacon and toast – even though recently she had felt too sick to eat. She had also sensed him watching her these last two weeks as she struggled to fasten the waistband of her skirt; but he had never once referred to her swelling belly. There was nothing to be said, in any case. They had not slept together, even in Oran, and there was no possibility that the child was his.

Vincent strode back into the bar. 'I have an appointment in town tomorrow morning,' he said briefly.

'Then I hope you will let us entertain Anna in your absence,' said Henri. 'Although of course, in the happy circumstances,' he leaned forward and tapped Vincent's hand, 'we shall keep her programme suitably light and undemanding. Congratulations, both of you.'

Anna watched a mask slide down over Vincent's disciplined face. He raised his glass. 'Indeed. Thank you.'

He did not look at Anna. She kept her eyes firmly fixed on her glass, watching as tiny bubbles rose, desperately seeking the surface.

'So, Vincent, how do you feel about your first child being born an American?' asked Henri, digging his friend in the ribs.

'We couldn't be more pleased,' said Vincent mildly.

That evening, Anna lay on the bed and watched Vincent unpacking his case, hanging up suits, shirts and ties with his usual meticulous care. As he smoothed the creases from the last jacket he stepped back.

'Shall I do yours?' he asked, without looking at her.

Through a fierce headache brought on by champagne and utter weariness, Anna nodded. 'Yes please, Vincent.'

He took her dresses from the case and hung them up in the wardrobe, scooped underthings into a drawer and arranged shoes neatly at the bottom of the wardrobe. Anna watched him through half-closed eyes, the back of her wrist hard against her forehead. When Vincent had finished he disappeared into the bathroom and emerged carrying a moistened hand towel. With surprising gentleness he lifted her arm away from her face and laid the cool cloth over her temples.

'This is becoming too hard for you,' he said quietly.

'No. Really, Vincent, I'm fine,' she said. 'I'm just sorry. I know I'm holding you back. I don't mean to.'

Vincent sat on the edge of the bed, looking down at his hands. The confidence and arrogance of his public persona had disappeared.

'Anna, I . . .'

She kept very still.

'Anna, people may like to call me a hero, but we both know I'm not.'

She dug her elbows into the mattress, pushing herself up above the small swell of her belly, and watched the ruined hands twist the towel into a rope.

After a moment, he went on, 'If I were really brave I wouldn't feel like this.'

'Like what?' she whispered. She kept her eyes on his bent neck. 'Feel like *what*, Vincent?' she repeated.

He sighed and glanced sideways at her. 'Afraid. I'm afraid that if this . . . happens, I'll lose you. Even if we're together, I'll still lose you. And I live in dread of that.' His voice was cracking, and he closed his eyes.

Anna reached out a hand and laid it against his cheek. He had trusted her, even if he had never let her come close to the hidden, private core of his character. And in return she had betrayed him. Broken him.

Deliberately, Anna pushed the thought of Harry Quinn beneath the surface of her memory and held it there until it died.

'Vincent.' She knelt up on the bed. 'My darling, we will never let that happen.'

'Ah, my dear,' he sighed, and kissed her forehead with dry, courteous lips.

Four days later they were on another train, bound for San Francisco, the last city on the tour.

# Fourteen

Mr Keen remained in his room.

Anna prepared the supper and then went up to change. It had been a while since she had worn anything formal, and she tried and rejected three dresses before choosing a black silk skirt and a green blouse. Slowly, sitting in front of the dressing-table, she brushed her hair smooth and was struggling with the clasp of a pearl necklace when there was a knock at the door. Hal Keen stood outside, crisply turned out in a dark-grey suit, white shirt and navy-blue tie.

'Madame Galland, forgive me. I meant to give you this earlier. It's a little present, to say thank you for agreeing to have me here.'

There was an odd expression on his face as he held out a small, exquisitely wrapped box.

Anna murmured her thanks, and while Hal Keen watched she undid the expensive wrapping paper, beautifully trimmed with seals and tassels, and slid open a small blue coffret. On the label it said: 'Guerlain, Paris, L'Heure Bleue'. A stoppered bottle of memories.

Suddenly Anna's fingers were trembling so much that she almost dropped the box, and Hal's hand flashed out to steady it.

'Wrong choice?' he asked anxiously.

'No,' she said. 'It was my perfume, once. How did you know?'

'A lucky guess,' he said, briefly. 'Also, the Guerlain salesgirl at the Galeries Lafayette had very pretty red hair. Try it. Go on.'

Weakly she smiled, opened the bottle, tipped it against the pad of her ring finger and touched the perfume to her ears and wrists. The air filled with the hallucinatory scent of carnations and vanilla. Harry's fingers wandered across her bare shoulders, stroking down.

The American was staring, his eyes searching her face. Suddenly she wanted to tell the truth, to confess that a man called Harry Quinn had once given her the same pretty glass-topped bottle, a single drop of whose perfume now conjured up an entire city, an entire summer, like dried paper flowers unfurling in a dish of water.

She whispered, 'You're very kind, Mr Keen. Thank you.'

Satisfied, Hal Keen nodded and stepped back into the corridor.

Before Anna went downstairs she scrubbed her wrists and her ears like a schoolgirl, only to find that the scent of vanilla and carnation was somehow ingrained in the pores of her skin. It was still there when she went downstairs, floating around her side like a vengeful spirit.

She had left the original little blue box, Harry's gift, in room 16 of the Hôtel de Fleurie on the day Germans marched into Paris. Why had she left it? As a kind of sentimental talisman for him, a keepsake with the power to awaken memory of their time together. But later that same afternoon, as she bathed Vincent's forehead and rinsed the cloth stained pink with his blood, traitorous clouds of L'Heure Bleue had risen from her wrists to accuse her.

Oddly, since that day, she had only smelt the perfume twice: once at a glamorous presidential reception in Washington in 1953, when her eyes filled with tears before she recognized the scent for what it was; and once in the year Vincent died, when for some unaccountable reason L'Heure Bleue had been Astrid Delamain's favourite scent.

And now, of all the perfumes in Paris, Hal Keen had chosen this one.

On impulse, he said.

*

Waking early, Anna lies uneasily curled in the little wooden bed. She has dreamed of being pursued, of faces at windows, of doors slowly opening on darkness. To clear her head she dresses quickly and goes out, climbing the headland until she has a clear view northward along the grey, choppy seas of the Vestfjord.

No boats. No watchers.

Arriving back at the cabin, cheeks whipped scarlet, nose pinkly cold, she hunkers down in front of the stove, opens the damper and carefully feeds it wood, piece by piece, building a fire that will last. Then she fills the little stockpot with fish and onions and beans and potatoes and sets it to simmer. Soon the windows steam over, and the smell of cooking curls around the cabin, and everything is bright and solid and shining again. When the soup is ready she sits down to eat it, properly, at the table, with bowl and spoon and a thick slice of Sigrid's bread from the day before.

Afterwards, with her stomach warm and full, she pours a mug of coffee and drags the chair over to the stove. She props her feet against the rail and balances Kurt's new manuscript on her knees.

The cover is brown manila, with a typed label pasted on the front: '*The Janus File: A tale of the Cold War*. 90,000 words.'

Anna lets the manuscript fall to her lap. She does not really need to consult her dictionary of fable and myths, but she does anyway, just so there is no mistake.

> Janus: Roman deity, guardian of gates and doors, usually represented with two faces, looking forward and back. His temple doors were thrown open in times of war and closed in times of peace. His name is associated with two-facedness.

Slowly she opens the cover in search of the author's name.

*

Vincent never told her how he found the address of the eminently discreet gynaecologist who shared his time between clinics in San Francisco and the East Coast, nor did he ever explain how they could afford his charges. Anna made the appointment herself, in her maiden name and, although Vincent took her to the door of clinic, she went inside alone.

Dr Weldon's consulting room was bright with sunlight, pale wooden furniture and vases of fresh flowers. The doctor himself was short, tanned and balding, with gold-rimmed glasses and a sympathetic manner. He examined her and then sent the nurse from the room.

'Do sit, Miss Larssen, please. Now. Let's see. Well, you don't need me to tell you that you are in reasonably good physical shape overall – a little too thin perhaps – but then again there is often a little weight loss in the early months.' He looked at her over the top of the glasses, and Anna swallowed hard. 'But I understand you yourself have concerns about your condition.' He smiled, encouraging confidences; his teeth were impossibly white and even.

Her jaw was trembling. 'Y-yes,' she said, and then, louder. 'Yes.'

The doctor nodded and consulted his notes. 'Grave concerns?'

'Yes.'

'Please don't tell me if you'd rather not, but do I understand you're not about to marry the father of this child?'

Anna shook her head.

There was a silence. Dr Weldon was nodding, a frown making a concerned furrow in his smooth brown forehead. 'Well, Miss Larssen, I quite understand. Pregnancy can be a joyous thing, but it isn't always so, especially in wartime. No indeed. I quite understand.' He stopped frowning and consulted what appeared to be a list.

'If it suits you, Miss Larssen, why don't you come out to my clinic in the hills, and we'll run a few tests and see what we can do for you? Magda will give you details.'

He must have pressed a buzzer, for the receptionist came in carrying a clipboard.

'Magda, I'd like Miss Larssen to come to the Pines early next week, please. A two-day stay.' He stood. 'Mrs Arnold will give you all the details.' He was shaking her hand. 'I'm sure we shall be able to put your mind at rest.'

She stood in reception while the girl discussed the minutiae of appointment times, room sizes and fees. Only when everything was arranged was she free to go.

Anna pushed open the glass door and stepped out into the noise and heat and stupefying sunshine of the city street. For a moment she hesitated on the threshold, shielding her eyes with one hand and her belly with the other. Suddenly she was completely aware of the living presence inside her. Beneath her palm, beneath the smooth-stretched skin, beneath the swell of muscle, was a *child,* a living being. It was the first and only person in her life that had ever been completely dependent on *her*.

And she was about to destroy it.

For a moment she stood on the kerb, swaying. Then, eyes shut, she stepped out into the road.

There was a blaring horn, an angry shout and a blast of hot air as tons of glinting metal hurtled past her skin.

When she opened her eyes again the street was empty. On the far side Vincent was sitting on a low wall in the shade of a tree, his elbows propped on his knees, his hat in his hands. With his usual politeness he stood as he saw her walking towards him. When she reached him he held her at arm's length and looked into her face, then quickly stepped closer and wrapped his arms around her. She felt his breath, anxious against her hair.

'Everything all right, darling?'

'Yes,' she said, resting her head against him. 'Everything is fine. Just a few tests. On Monday.'

Vincent drove her out into the hills above San Francisco.

The Pines was a low white building surrounded by a high wall. Inside the gate Anna could see a paved courtyard with a single tall palm tree. Around it giant blue-fleshed cactuses twisted like starfish in the hot sun. A guard at the gate checked her name against a list. Vincent handed her case to the porter, and as Anna walked through the courtyard and into the house she heard the car turn and drive away. A blonde receptionist showed her to a small white room with a high, shiny metal-framed bed and told her that Dr Weldon would come and see her at eleven.

Anna lay in her white room with its views of pink hillsides and blue sky. Whatever was about to happen happened everywhere in nature, she told herself: accidents, nature protecting itself, or simple, inexplicable bad luck. It happened everywhere, all the time. Today was simply the day of *her* accident. It might have happened next week, on a train or in a shop or in a bathroom, but instead it would happen somewhere in this clean white building in the California hills.

She imagined all the other anxious women who had been in the room before her. Unthinkingly, she slid her hands down and for a moment let them spread over the gentle dome between her hip-bones. The gesture was too protective: she let her fists drop on to the coverlet and kept them there. After a while she turned her gaze back to the window.

The two nurses were impersonal, chatting across her prone body as they wheeled her down a corridor and into a small, brightly lit room. A green-masked man bent over her, his gold-rimmed glasses reflecting the white expanse of sheet.

'Miss Larssen, hello there. Now, you'll be under for just a short while. Nothing to worry about.'

Her mouth was dry, her tongue stuck to the roof of her mouth. For a moment she could only croak, then she managed to say, 'I'd like to see it. After. Just for a moment. Please.'

Dr Weldon shook his head. 'There will be nothing to see, Miss Larssen.'

Her head was swirling. Anna forced herself up on to one shaky elbow. 'I want to see it.' Then, louder, not caring now who heard, 'I want to see it? Do you understand? I want to see my baby.'

'Of course. Hush now. Relax please. Mr Henson? Dr Weldon beckoned to a gowned figure behind him who came closer and held a mask above Anna's face.

'I want . . .' Anna whispered, as ice rushed through her body and her mind closed down. 'I want . . .'

'Miss Larssen. Miss Larssen. Can you hear me?'

'She's bleeding quite a bit. Do you think they'll have to take her back down? What does the Wiz say?' A younger voice, this.

'He's gone, honey. Lunch with the bank president. Look, her blood pressure's OK. Pack that dressing in tight. Tighter. Miss Larssen, hey there, come on now, dear, you need to wake up. It's all over. Everything's just fine.'

Anna lay still, her eyes shut, and registered the dragging pain in her belly.

The younger voice said, 'Her colour's coming back a bit.'

'Uhuh. How's her pulse?'

A cool hand picked up her wrist and there was a silence. 'One-twenty.'

'She'll be fine. This your first time? You'll get used to it. They're always pale at first.'

There was a silence.

'She said she wanted to *see* it.'

'I heard. Crazy.' Someone tucked the sheets briskly under the corners of the bed. 'They're desperate to get rid of it, and then suddenly they're not so sure. Good old-fashioned guilt sets in.'

'I saw it,' said the young voice. 'In the sluice, after. A little boy. It wasn't what I expected, somehow. I mean you see a photo in a textbook, that's one thing. But this was, so small and, oh, I don't know, so . . . detailed, I guess. So *complete*.'

'Yeah. Well, now you know. Makes you think, huh?' Then, louder, 'Like this one'd better *think* next time, if she's got any sense. OK, she needs to wake up now. Hey there, Miss Larssen, *Miss Larssen*.'

A hand struck Anna's cheek, and in her shock she opened her eyes.

She moved her lips. She thought she said, aloud, 'His name is Michael.' But the two faces above her showed no reaction. Perhaps she hadn't spoken. Her eyelids closed again, and she slipped down gratefully beneath the surface.

Anna was discharged from the Pines and Vincent drove her to Henri and Gisèle's house in Bel Air. The car glided up the drive – a smooth rise between grey-blue cedars, a scent of flowers. Vincent helped her out, and she stood, hunched forward like an old woman. Henri Richemont ran lightly down the steps and hugged her.

'My poor girl. I'm so sorry.' He tucked his arm under hers and helped her up towards the front door. Of course, Vincent had simply told people that she had lost the baby. Which was true. At the top of the steps stood Gisèle, immaculate in white cotton, her dark blonde hair coiled and gleaming, tiny red toenails glinting.

'Anna, *chérie*.' She skimmed her cheek across Anna's, then stepped back and looked her up and down. 'Well, how are *you?* But, my dear, you're so *pale* . . . I hope they took good care of you?' Suddenly Anna wondered if it had been Henri's wife who had told Vincent about Dr Weldon. 'Now, what you need is a really good rest.' She offered Anna her arm and led her away up the curve of the marble stairs, whispering conspiratorially, 'And don't you worry about a thing, dear. We'll look after Vincent. You just concentrate on getting better.'

The following morning Anna woke up at five. She was feverishly hot and her stomach was cramping with pain. For a while she lay still, willing herself to endure it as some sort of penance. Then the room grew bright, the walls disappeared, and she was walking through the shimmering streets of a Californian town looking for a lost child. 'His name is Michael,' she said, clutching at the sleeves of passers-by. 'He's very small. Have you seen him?' No one had. She drifted through a narrow stone gateway and found the baby at last, lying small and blue and twisted on open ground.

A man in gold-rimmed glasses bent over her and took her arm.

'Swallow this,' said a voice.

'Is he dead?' Anna tried to say, through lips that were slack and numb. 'He is, isn't he?'

Weeping, she lay down on the soft earth beside the child and slept.

When she awoke it was, apparently, still morning.

Behind the partially lowered blind the window was open, and birdsong came in on the breeze. She was in a yellow room, wooden-floored with thick white rugs and dotted with dainty silk-covered chairs. The sheets of her bed were pure white, the borders embroidered with pale yellow flowers that blossomed in nubs and whorls beneath her fingertips.

A maid came in carrying a small tray with a glass of water and a small brown bottle and stopped when she saw Anna was awake.

'I fetch Señora Richemont,' she said and disappeared.

Gisèle came in twenty minutes later, dressed in a short tennis skirt and sleeveless white top.

She sat on the edge of the bed and took Anna's hand in hers.

'Anna. Back with us at last. You've given us all a nasty scare these last few days. How are you, *chérie?*'

She couldn't answer. From beneath closed eyelids tears poured down her cheeks. After a moment she felt Gisèle get up from the bed.

'You need a handkerchief,' she said. 'Here.' Gisèle patted her shoulder briskly. 'That's better. Now, Vincent is in town today, but he asked me to tell you that he'll be back this evening. He and Henri have been so worried about you, my dear. Men never understand women's problems, do they?' She smoothed the corner of the sheet. 'Now rest well and try to eat something. I'll send Antonia up again, and I'll be back later this afternoon.'

The door closed.

Anna ate the food that Antonia brought her and slept for a while. Then, in the quiet house, she got up and took a shower. For a long while she stood under the flow, her neck bent, letting the water drum all thought from her mind.

She studied her body as she dried it. The same long thin legs, the same small breasts, even the same slightly swollen belly, although that would now, she supposed, diminish. So little had changed, and yet she felt as if she had aged into another generation. Clutching the towel around her shoulders, she went back into the bedroom in search of a clean nightdress, then, exhausted by the effort, she made her way out on to the balcony and lowered herself into a deep-cushioned reclining chair.

She lay there all afternoon, watching the purple shadows of cedars spread slowly across the lawn towards the house.

It was early evening when Vincent returned. She heard feet running up the stairs, and then he was striding across the room. He was wearing a short-sleeved white polo shirt, and his skin glowed with health.

'Anna, how are you? My God, we were beginning to think you'd never wake.'

'I'm fine,' she said, 'absolutely fine.'

'Darling.' Vincent squeezed her hand and brushed her hair back from her face. His eyes were dancing. 'And today there's more good news.' He flung out his arms. 'They've finally agreed to let me go back.'

Anna stared at him.

'To New York?' she said slowly.

He laughed, 'No, darling, back to *France*. Well, London first. But after that France.'

'Oh.' Anna's eyes filled with convalescent tears. 'It's so soon. I didn't expect it to be quite so soon. When do we leave?'

'In four weeks.' He held her fingers, flexing them gently. 'Anna, I'm going back alone. You'll stay in here in America for a while. In New York.'

Once again it seemed that her future had been decided without her involvement. But she was too weary to care. Meekly she said, 'Where will they send you?'

Vincent smiled. 'I don't know yet. But *you*'ll be safe, and that's the important thing.'

She gripped his hand hard. 'Vincent, there must be so many ways you could help here. Please stay.'

Vincent peeled her fingers from his. 'I can't. Don't ask me to do that, Anna, because I can't.'

That night they dined with the Richemonts. Henri was all polite attention, adjusting a stole around Anna's shoulders, pressing her to eat and drink. But she hardly had the strength to slice the steak and picked listlessly at her salad.

Henri shook his head. 'Vincent, really, won't you reconsider moving to New York? Anna could stay on with us until she's fully recovered. We've sunshine and acres of room here: exactly what she needs. And even after that it would be a pleasure to have her with us.' His handsome face creased appealingly.

'I'm afraid it has to be New York,' said Vincent briefly. 'The British say they'll find us an apartment there, but if you know of anywhere that would be a great help.'

'Better leave it with us for a couple of days,' said Henri resignedly.

'Don't worry,' said Gisèle, 'I've already started asking around.'

# Fifteen

Anna is reading the *Janus* manuscript. As Kurt said, it is crudely written, but it is already clear that this is neither a biography nor a novel, rather a luridly fictionalized life of Vincent Galland. Although the author has changed the characters' names, their identities are barely disguised, and the content is so libellous that she doubts whether Messrs Manning and Blythe, whoever they may be, ever seriously intended to publish it in any language, let alone hers.

The early chapters contain lurid details of the 'hero's' youthful indiscretions. Victor Rothko, member of a Czech anarchist group, enters into a dubious friendship with a Russian diplomat during his teens, enjoys the high life and travels abroad without visible sources of income, marries a naïvely trusting Scandinavian girl called Else, flirts with communism and nationalism and then shams a commitment to wartime resistance while secretly promoting his own interests. She skims the next chapters. Rothko has numerous affairs, including one during a brief visit to America, where he seduces the wife of a close friend, a noted Hollywood actor. When Rothko and his wife return to France the political chameleon changes colour and attempts . . .

But there Anna closes the file. Now she replaces it carefully in its manilla envelope. She was meant, she guesses, to read it to the end. Choosing not to do so is a small but satisfying gesture. The book portrays Vincent as what he no doubt was, at various times in his life: womanizer, liar, hypocrite and traitor. It does not mention his intelligence, his consideration and his courage, apparently because the author cannot bear to acknowledge any positive qualities in a man he apparently detests to the point of obsession.

She remembers the conversation in the Grand Hotel with the young and earnest writer who called himself Hal Keen. He had said, 'Believe me, this book will be as accurate and true as I can make it.' How did she fail to see the heavy irony? And why did she not trust her instincts and see the shadowy, manipulative presence behind him?

At a practical level Anna has already decided that she will return the text to Kurt, saying that she does not feel that she can take it on. She will ask him if he has another job for her, but in the meantime her money will simply have to last – fortunately there is little here to spend it on. She reseals the envelope and sticks a return address label over the original, then sits and stares at it. For all her bravado the venomous spite of the book is disturbing.

Beyond the window the sky is darkening, but she decides to post the envelope at once: it has corrupted the atmosphere in the cabin, conjured up so many spectres that she almost has to shoulder them aside as she opens the door and steps out on to the platform.

Outside it is grey and windy and wild. Despite this, she decides to takes the upper track to Å. The cold, buffeting air jolts her awake, and when she reaches the highest point she leans against the gale, hands on hips, her lungs wheezing like ruptured bellows and knees hot and aching from the climb.

Far below, amid Å's huddle of red-and-white houses, life is going on as usual: woodsmoke is blowing in horizontal trails from chimneys, cod is drying on racks, seagulls are calling over the harbour and the snowmelt is swelling the streams that fall over sheer black cliffs into the sea. Anna is suddenly overwhelmed with fondness for the village, the island – this small, sturdy place that performs its everyday magic and restores her to herself, so that she becomes what before she could only dream of being: capable, self-sufficient, enduring as rock.

In a fit of sudden happy recklessness she decides to descend by the most direct route, the scree-slope. Choosing her spot, she slithers over the edge, legs extended, turning like a skier into the slope, using her gloved hands to steady herself. Half running, half falling now, she hurtles downward, her boots rattling over fine shale. On the last steep section above the track, yelling with childlike exhilaration, she leaps over a boulder, crouches for the landing and collides full pelt with Leif, dropping her parcel.

Leif staggers back against the cliff wall, winded by the impact. Anxious that she has hurt him, Anna puts a hand on his shoulders – and realizes he is shaking with laughter. 'You nearly killed me, Anna! Good thing you're light-footed – plenty of Lofoten boys have broken bones coming down that particular slope. Including me.' He stoops and picks up the parcel. 'Here.'

Anna, red-faced and panting, takes it from him. 'I know. I don't know what got into me. But', she looked back up the slope, 'it was fun. And no bones broken.' The smile transforms her face; the wind flicks tendrils of damp, pale hair around her head.

Leif grins back at her. 'I was on my way to see you.'

'Are the logs in? I was expecting them tomorrow.'

'No, your birdwatcher's on the move. He's been up in the hills here. Taking pictures.' He is watching her expression. 'Want me to take you up to Sørvågen again?'

She shakes her head vehemently. 'No. Thank you.'

'OK. So.' He hesitates, as if there is something else he wants to say, then shrugs, 'Well, I'll be getting back then. Blowy night ahead, by the look of it.'

For a while they walk on in silence, the only sounds the flapping of oilskins and the howling of the wind. As they round the last headland the afternoon light is fading into grey. They walk in single file down through a gully of bare-branched rowan and ash and emerge in the village. Lamps are being lit in the windows.

Leif turns and looks back where they have come from, at the red speck of the cabin half hidden in the gloom at the far side of the bay. 'You're pretty cut off out there,' Leif says.

'I like it,' she says defensively, and then, 'Do you miss Hell Cove?'

He shrugs. 'Sometimes.'

She thinks of two stocky figures toiling upward. 'Gunnar told me you and Sigrid walked over the mountains to get to school.'

The grin is back. 'We did.' He points to the dark-grey crags receding down the coast. 'Mannen, Torlinden and Hellsegga. We came through the passes. It was safer than the risking the Maelstrom to get to Å.' He looks out at the sea, which is graphite flecked with white, racing before a north wind.

Swiftly she says, 'Tell me what it was like growing up there.'

He rubs his chin and says slowly, 'Oh, it was pretty wonderful for us kids. We had whales spouting out beyond the bay, eagles circling overhead, sheep and cows in the low pasture behind the beach. In summer the sun shone all day and night, straight into the bay, and in winter there were the northern lights. You see them from here, sure, but not so clear. Out there they filled the sky: green, red, blue, white, glowing and fading, everywhere alight.'

They are almost at the water's edge now, and there is a steady lapping of waves against the pilings of the cabins. An elderly man is labouring up the slope towards them, bent under the weight of a large dripping sack. She sees Leif's face grow tense. '*Hei,* Harald.' The man pauses, nods back without looking Leif in the eye, hefts the sack higher on his shoulder and walks on.

Harald Ringstadt, she thinks. Harald Ringstadt whose son Lars was washed overboard and drowned in the Maelstrom. She looks up at Leif with sudden sympathy and sees his face harden. He shrugs and tugs his cap down over his eyes. 'I'll see you, then,' he calls gruffly, turning away from the sea.

She watches him reach the bend in the track. Perhaps she has pitied him too openly. Or, worse, perhaps she has used a kind-hearted man to help ward off her ghosts. She feels a sudden jab of impulse, like returning circulation in a long-frozen limb, and cupping her hand to her mouth calls to his receding back, 'Will you come to supper tomorrow? I'm expecting some wine on the boat and maybe even some French cheese.'

Leif stops, turns, stands looking at her. At last he calls, 'Sure. I'd like that. Long time since I tasted wine.'

'Seven?'

'OK. Seven. See you then.'

She watches as the dog runs out to meet him, the joyous barking echoing back from the mountains.

It's almost dark.

She'll need the torch for the return.

Swiftly she strides up the rise towards the glowing windows of the shop.

*

Vincent and Anna arrived back in New York in mid-April 1942. The official apartment provided by the British Consulate was predictably dilapidated, with greyish chintz and leaning standard lamps and a view of grimy rooftops and fire escapes. The following morning Vincent left for a series of meetings with diplomats and other men he didn't identify beyond the fact that they were 'military types'.

Anna stood at the window, looking down. It was time, apparently, to resume life. A week before they left California Dr Weldon had pronounced her fully fit and submitted a final bill which Vincent had paid without comment.

She opened the window. In the grid of streets below thousands of people were going purposefully off to their various destinations of work, family and friends. A faint sound of ships' whistles came from the river docks, reminding her of Oslo and the sea.

She was still at the window half an hour later when the telephone rang in the hallway.

'Is that the exquisite Anna Galland?'

'Oh. Hello, Henri.'

'Tell me that I have your undying gratitude. I think I've found you somewhere to live.'

She sat down on the creaky chair next to the phone table. 'Really? Where?'

'On the upper slopes of East Side luxury, my dear,' said Henri, obviously pleased with himself, '*chez* Peter and Helga Berghof. Peter's a businessman turned philanthropist; his wife's a writer, bit of an academic by all accounts. Anyway, I heard they'd decided to move to their estate in Argentina for the duration of hostilities, and when I called them they were in the process of shutting up what they like to call their "little town house" near the park. They positively jumped at the chance of having a nice Norwegian housekeeper looking after the place while they're away. Have you got a pencil and paper?'

'Henri, you're very kind . . .'

'I know, I know. Now, remember, when next we meet I shall expect nothing less than a share of the unqualified adoration you lavish on that gallant husband of yours.'

The following afternoon Anna rang the bell of an elegant three-storey house. A butler opened the door and showed her into a study that looked out over the tree-lined street. A few minutes later Peter Berghof entered.

He was a short balding man in his sixties, with pale, hooded eyes and a visible tremor in his hands. In heavily accented but formal English he said, 'Ah, Mrs Galland. Thank you for coming. Mr Richemont has explained your circumstances to us, but let me briefly explain our own.' In a rapid, breathy monotone he went on, 'Since I arrived here from Germany twenty-five years ago I have had the good fortune to build a very successful business enterprise. Today we still have friends in Germany and a number of financial ties but no desire to return there in the current . . . climate. 'Nor', the pale eyes glittered for a second under the heavy lids, 'do we wish to inflict any awkwardness or embarrassment on our American friends. At the end of this month we . . .' He took in a deep breath, and his hunched shoulders rose. 'Ah, good. Helga.'

A statuesque, grey-haired woman came into the room. She wore a black-and-white tweed suit, and gold bracelets collided gently as she held out her hand.

'Mrs Galland, I'm delighted to meet you. I've heard such marvellous things about your husband. Darling,' she turned to her husband, 'you have so much still to do. Let me show Mrs Galland – Anna? Anna – around the house.'

Taking her hand she led Anna gently away.

'My husband finds this situation very stressful,' she said quietly as they entered the hall. 'I am more philosophical or perhaps the truth is I simply have less imagination. Anyway,' she continued, her voice brisk again and with just a trace of the hard German 'w', 'I think we shall start at the bottom of the house and work up, yes?'

Anna followed her dutifully from room to room, awed by the elegant richness of the surroundings: oriental carpets, antique furniture and shelves of fragile porcelain. And paintings everywhere: Dutch landscapes, crowded allegorical scenes, intimate French interiors glowing like tiny jewels. By the time they reached the second floor she was open-mouthed.

'And here,' said Helga, throwing two tall doors wide open, 'the library.'

It was an immense galleried room running the whole width of the house. Tiers of shelves rose to the ceiling. Oak pillars, their surface carved into twining vines, supported a gallery; a green leather-covered desk sat beneath the window, and to its left a pair of club armchairs faced each other companionably across an open fireplace.

'Do you read?' asked Helga and then, quickly, 'As you can see, books are our passion. We have collections of German, American, Russian and English works, oh, and many French volumes, too, which may be of interest, since Henri tells us that you speak the language fluently. So, we would be so pleased if you would make use of the library during your time here.'

'Thank you, Mrs Berghof,' said Anna, 'I should love to.'

Their last days together in New York ran away quickly. Anna would have liked to explore the city streets with Vincent at her side, but during the day he was occupied and in the evenings he spent most of his time studying documents that he would not be able to take with him.

The night before he was due to leave they sat at the kitchen table, the remains of their meal in front of them. Vincent's open-shirted, relaxed Californian mood had disappeared, and instead he appeared uncharacteristically nervous and on edge. He drummed his fingers on the wood and looked around the cramped little kitchen.

'This is what I shall miss, Anna. This . . . normality. After a while you can't even imagine it. It's like a mirage, always floating just out of reach.' He glanced at her. 'In some ways I wish you were staying here, so I could think of you, sitting as you are now, with your elbow on the table and that glass cupboard door behind you. I would know exactly where you were.'

He stopped abruptly and reached for her hand.

In the last few days of their Californian stay they had at last begun sleeping together. Vincent had been considerate and tender: his fingers moved gently over her, as if he were trying to memorize every hollow and curve of her body – although once in the night she woke up to see him propped on one elbow, his eyes closed, his hand cupping the air above her breast, and knew he was imagining her with her lover.

They said their goodbyes on the platform at Grand Central Station. Vincent was to go to Washington for a final briefing before flying to London. Around them couples and families talked with forced confidence and over-bright smiles. Vincent thrust his hands deep in the pockets of his long tweed coat and scowled up and down the platform, peered at his watch and stared at other people, looking anywhere but directly at her. When the train was announced, with obvious relief he hugged her close.

'You'll be fine. And as soon as it's safe, you know I'll send for you.'

She nodded.

The woman next to them held a small boy up to his father, and the child thrashed plump legs in temper and turned his face away from the kiss.

Vincent frowned at the distraction and bent to embrace Anna, the brim of his hat lightly brushing against her hair. Then he turned and strode down the steam-filled platform, suitcase in hand, coat-tails billowing out behind him like a cloak.

She thought of that scene often in the years that followed. Over time it became her icon: a bright, enduring image she focused on whenever her faith in him began to waver: Vincent going off into unimaginable danger, with all those wonderful abstracts – resolve, courage, integrity – flying like glorious ensigns around him.

# Sixteen

By the time Anna came down for breakfast the following morning Hal Keen was already at work in the study, surrounded by open files. Then, late in the afternoon, she heard the first rapid pecking from the typewriter.

'Is it going well?' she asked him at supper as she watched him cut his steak into even pieces, then lay down his knife and use his fork as a spear.

Keen dabbed at the corner of his mouth with a napkin, 'Yes, thank you, I think so. There's a lot of original material in the files. And someone's done a good job of putting it all in order. Was that you?'

'Yes.' Her tidy Norwegian soul, she thought. Tidiness and punctuality and languages – the only things she had ever been good at. She refilled his glass.

'I thought I would invite an old friend of Vincent's to dinner on Friday. Have you heard of Bertrand Delamain?'

Keen frowned consideringly. 'He's one of the bosses of the PCF, isn't he?'

'Yes. They live on the other side of the village. They have a daughter, Isabelle. She must be about sixteen.'

Hal Keen was chewing, fast and distractedly. 'Yes, yes. Meeting some of the comrades would be a good idea, as long as you think they'll be prepared to speak to me.'

'Bertrand was one of Vincent's closest friends,' she said. 'I'm sure he'd be delighted.'

'Fine, fine.' Hal Keen speared a morsel of meat. 'I'd also like to see the letters soon, if that's possible.'

Anna stopped, her fork half-way to her mouth. 'Letters?'

'Vincent's personal correspondence. You have it all, don't you? That's what I've really been looking forward to. There must be hundreds of letters.'

Anna stared blankly. Letters. She was such a fool she hadn't noticed. But, of course, Hal was right, Vincent had been a prolific writer, and almost every morning there had been letters for him in the mail and others stamped and ready on the hall table. Yet there had been only a small number in the files themselves.

'Yes,' she said. 'The letters. Of course.' And as soon as the meal was over and she could decently escape, she went in search of them.

Vincent's clothes still hung in the wardrobe. Behind a pile of neatly boxed shoes Anna found an old attaché case, but it contained only yellowing theatre programmes, menu cards, photographs and books. In his cufflink drawer she found agendas for PCF receptions, drafts of speeches, and, at the bottom, an expensive bill from a Paris restaurant for two *couverts,* dated three years before. But there were no letters anywhere; none at all.

The following morning Anna telephoned the Delamains' house. Astrid sounded wary at first, then relaxed. Of course they would love to come and meet Vincent's biographer. Could they bring their daughter? Isabelle's English was in desperate need of improvement.

By Friday evening Anna was grateful that she and Hal Keen would not be alone for dinner. The American was polite and unfailingly curious about Vincent but otherwise had little conversation, and since they had few interests in common the evenings had begun to seem long.

Now she poured her guest a *porto* and told him what he wanted to know about the Delamains. Bertrand was a lifelong Party member, whose unwavering support for Moscow had made him an elder statesman of French Communism. He and Vincent had met in Paris in the last years of the war, and it was Bertrand who, after years of careful campaigning, had finally persuaded Vincent to join the Party in the early fifties. From that moment on, the two couples had grown close – it had been Bertrand who had found them La Verrerie, so conveniently near to the Delamains' own house in Saint-Aubain. After that, for several summers running, the Gallands and Delamains had holidayed together, sharing a rented villa in Antibes.

As she spoke she recalled how she had watched enviously as Astrid Delamain played in the pool with her young daughter. Anna and Vincent had never discussed children, and in some ways she had been glad. She had failed her husband and killed her unborn child and was not naïve enough to think that either crime could be expunged by the birth of a baby. (She had given her son the birthday he might have had at full term: 29 September 1942, the name day of the Archangels Gabriel, Raphael and Michael. For a long while she had found a certain sad comfort in counting off his imaginary years. That first summer in Provence Michael would have been eleven years old; little Isabelle Delamain was eight. This autumn of Hal Keen's visit to Saint-Aubain-les-Eaux he had just turned twenty.)

She realized that Keen was looking at her. Had they remained close to the Delamains? he asked carefully.

Anna thought for a moment before replying. The joint holidays had ceased, and there had perhaps been a perceptible cooling between Vincent and his old friend. But it had been to Bertrand Delamain that Anna had turned to identify the body found on the Breton beach and to the Delamain family that she turned now, even though since the funeral, like so many others, they had kept their distance.

Bertrand arrived punctually as usual. Wide-bellied and imposing, with his *coupe en brosse* and gold-rimmed glasses he had the air of a subversive company chairman. Hal Keen's hand disappeared into his fist and was shaken up and down with great force. Then Bertrand presented his daughter, and Anna saw the American take in the vision that was Isabelle Delamain: seventeen, green-eyed, swathed in a dress of bronze shot silk, her skin shining like a polished plum.

Astrid Delamain lingered behind her husband and daughter, and when she finally came forward into the light, hands outstretched, Anna was shocked. The beautiful high-cheeked face was almost gaunt, and the long black hair only accentuated the hollows under her eyes.

'Anna. This is kind of you. It's been far too long.'

Astrid's husky voice was flat-toned. The two women kissed, and Anna felt her friend's fine-grained cheek slide briefly and impersonally against hers.

Friends.

Was that what she and Astrid were, Anna wondered?

Despite the intimacy of those long, lazy holidays in Provence the two women had never grown close. Anna had been fascinated by Astrid's coolly confident beauty, had watched her as she performed the complicated rituals of her toilette – painting her lips and her flawless nails, brushing her hair, smoothing oil on to her long, smooth legs – yet in all that time the two of them had never shared intimate confidences or exchanged memories or even laughed together.

'She's a man's woman, that's all,' Vincent had said, and it was true. Astrid could spend hours in Anna's company without uttering more than a few bored phrases, yet when Bertrand or Vincent came into the room she would instantly become animated, vivacious and entrancing.

Watching Astrid greet Hal Keen now, Anna saw the familiar transformation: the widening of her eyes, the slow parting of the lips, the way her hand covered the American's and briefly imprisoned it between her own. And then she heard Vincent's voice, remembered from one of those nights in Provence, when in his sleep he had turned and murmured blindly into his pillow words that she knew were not meant for her.

'My God, you are so *beautiful*.'

A murmur of voices brought Anna back to her guests. Unused to entertaining on her own she had been dreading the chore of making polite small talk, but to her relief she saw that Bertrand was already making an effort to draw the young American out. Astrid had fixed a cigarette in an amber holder and was sitting back, seemingly content to leave Isabelle to chatter on to Anna about her summer holidays. Anna nodded and tried to look interested, but every few minutes she found her eyes drifting to Astrid's beautiful, expressionless face.

The meal itself was a success. The simple *potage au cerfeuil* was followed by gigot of lamb, cheese and salad, and for dessert Florence had made a *clafoutis*, on whose golden surface dark cherries sat like cabochon jewels on a shield.

When the table was cleared they returned to the salon for coffee, and Bertrand took on the host's task of pouring cognac.

With his back turned to the American, he growled, 'So. Monsieur Keen, do I take it you share your late hero's politics?'

Hal blushed. 'Well, yes, sir, I think my instinctive leanings are to the left.'

Bertrand turned, a tumbler in his hand. 'You *think* so? That's hardly a committed viewpoint, is it? By your age – what are you, twenty-six, twenty-seven? – most people at least know on which side of the Iron Curtain their loyalties lie.'

It was not said amiably, but Hal Keen failed to rise. 'Well then, I guess I'd have to confess to not being totally committed either way yet, sir.'

'And yet your publishers chose you to write Vincent Galland's biography. Touching display of faith, wouldn't you say?' Bertrand rolled a cigar between his fingers.

Astrid slowly turned to look at her husband.

Hal Keen said, 'I guess most publishing is an act of faith. I'm just grateful for the work and grateful to be able to write about somebody I genuinely admired.'

Bravo, Hal, thought Anna, as Isabelle Delamain, beautiful, bored and slightly tipsy, leaned across and tugged at the American's sleeve.

'Excuse me, but if Papa gets going on politics tonight I shall just *die*. What star sign are you, Monsieur Keen? I guess a Gemini.'

'I'm not sure,' he said, taken aback. And then, recovering himself, 'Actually, I was born in New York City on the 17th of April – what does that make me?'

Across the table Anna heard the date and froze.

'Old enough not to believe in astrology,' said Bertrand tartly. 'Isabelle, don't be silly.'

The girl pulled a face behind her father's back. 'Do you know French singers, Monsieur Keen? Johnny Halliday? Claude François?'

Hal, caught in a stifled mid-yawn, smiled. 'Sorry. Afraid not. Actually I prefer jazz to pop. In fact there's a great club in Paris, been going for years, called Le Hot. Do you know it?'

Isabelle edged forward, eager to find out more.

Bertrand turned to Anna and jerked the glowing tip of his cigar derisively towards the far end of the table. 'Christ. When I was their age I'd been a Party member for a decade. We fought a world war for this generation, and now politics bores them rigid'

Hal Keen overheard, straightened and looked distractedly at Isabelle.

'Ah, so, now you're awake, *mon brave*?' Bertrand grinned at no one in particular, emptied his glass of brandy with a flourish and poured himself another.

'I don't think I was actually ever asleep.' Hal Keen glanced at Anna.

Bertrand snorted. 'You and your whole bloody generation are

asleep, my friend; you shy away from political struggle, you're happy to live in a society that's intellectually and morally bankrupt. When you . . .' Bertrand suddenly swore softly.

Astrid, speaking to her husband but looking at Anna, said smoothly, '*Chéri,* it's late, and I think we and Monsieur Keen must have time to get to know each other a little better before we can discuss political generalities, don't you?'

Bertrand slammed his brandy glass down on the table. 'Politics aren't a generality. They're a necessity of life.'

'As is sleep, *chéri*,' said Astrid, smiling briefly, 'which is clearly what this poor young man needs right now.'

She stood and took Hal Keen's hands in hers. 'Welcome to Saint-Aubain-les-Eaux, Hal, and I hope you'll visit us very soon.'

To Anna she gave a light, dry touch of lips. '*Merci, ma chère. Une soirée merveilleuse. Comme autrefois, hein?*' but there was little warmth in her voice or her eyes.

Anna kissed Isabelle, and mother and daughter walked out into the hall to say goodbye to Hal Keen. Anna turned to face Bertrand, who had lingered behind them.

'*Merci, ma belle Anna*,' he whispered and suddenly took her face between his palms, kissing her firmly and deliberately, full on the lips. She smelt cigar smoke on his breath and felt the tip of his tongue slide between her teeth, flickering like a snake. She gagged and stepped back hurriedly, and Bertrand laughed and strode out to the hall.

Anna followed him, quietly wiping her mouth on her wrist.

Hal Keen, now visibly exhausted, made a half-hearted offer to help her clear up the dinner things but did not insist when Anna told him that she preferred to do it alone. He trailed wearily upstairs and she heard the door of his room open and close.

Anna moved around the kitchen, emptying ashtrays and washing traces of dark-red lipstick from the rims of glasses.

When finally everything was clean and dry and in its place she slipped off her shoes and walked noiselessly across the hall into the study.

Little had changed in the room. In the corner by the chaise-longue stood the record-player and, beside it, in their grey paper sleeves, were the old shellac discs Vincent loved to play as he wrote. The box of files stood on the side-table, and when she looked through them it was clear that Hal had kept them in order. But what she was looking for, now, with a sudden sense of urgency, was not files but letters.

She began the search in the obvious place, checking the drawers of the desk, but these contained only the familiar assortment of pens, pencils, erasers and unused envelopes, neatly arranged.

To the left of the desk was a low pointed doorway that led to a small side-chamber. Anna turned the key and swung back the heavy door, but the room was bare except for a pair of mahogany library steps.

She returned to the study and sat in Vincent's worn leather chair, revolving thoughtfully. Wherever the letters were, they were well hidden. Which meant that they hadn't simply been concealed from casual visitors; they had been hidden from *her,* too. Purposefully now, she stood and prowled around the room again. This time she took books down from the shelves, held the spines and fanned through the pages, releasing fine dust and a smell of dried, ageing paper. It took a long time to go through them all, and by the end she had discovered nothing more than a few pressed flowers. Then, just as she was going to abandon the search, she noticed, on a high shelf above the pointed door, half-a-dozen large, antique, leather-bound volumes.

Wincing at the noise, she trundled the library steps across to the doorway and climbed until her shoulders were level with the shelf. The nearest book was a handsome copy of *Plato's Republic.* She stretched out to take it down, hooking her finger into the top to pull it towards her. But the book didn't move. Puzzled, she reached to the back of the volume and yanked it forward, and at that moment six books slid forward at once. The Plato and its neighbours were empty spines, stuck on to the front of a deep wooden box. Testing its weight, and deciding it was heavy but manageable, Anna worked the box forward, scraped it over the edge of the shelf and took it out into her arms.

There were letters inside – at first sight forty or fifty bundles: letters, envelopes, postcards, small packets – some with stamps, some with neatly torn corners. On top of them was a single blue envelope, lying loose as if Vincent hadn't troubled to manhandle the box down off the shelf, and instead had simply dropped it in over the edge.

Something made her reluctant to hand the letters over to Hal Keen without having read them. If Vincent had taken so much trouble to hide his correspondence, surely he would have wanted it to be vetted before it was made public? For a moment Anna considered removing the wooden box entirely, but the empty space on the high shelf gaped like a missing front tooth. Instead, she slipped the tablecloth from the occasional table, spread it out on the floor and emptied all the letters on to it. Then she replaced the box on the shelf and surprised herself by remembering to move the library stairs back to their original position.

Up in her room she spread the letters out over the quilt. Many of the bundles had labels in Vincent's writing and were secured by rubber bands: 'Student Internationale 1952'; 'Veterans of the Resistance correspondence, 1947–1955'. All the famous acronyms were there: 'PCF 1952–'; 'CGT 1953–'. There was a slim bundle of postcards simply labelled 'Sartre'. Intrigued, she was about to unfasten this when another package caught her attention. A dozen letters, tied with emerald green ribbon. She undid the bow. The envelopes were luxurious and lined with green tissue paper; the first one whispered in astonishment as she opened it and drew out the two sheets of cream paper it contained.

At the other end of the house a door opened and closed. Footsteps came down the landing. Hastily, Anna put the green-ribbon bundle to one side and rewrapped the others in the cloth. She was just hiding it at the back of the wardrobe when there was a gentle tap at the bedroom door.

'Anna, I heard a noise downstairs. Is everything all right?'

The door handle angled down slightly, then, as she watched, it returned to the horizontal.

'Yes. Yes, thank you, I'm fine,' she called. 'I just got a glass of water. I had a bit of a headache, that's all. It feels better already.'

'That's good,' he said and after a pause, 'I enjoyed the meal. Delamain's quite a character, isn't he?' There was another pause. 'Well, see you in the morning, then, Anna?'

'Yes. Goodnight, Hal,' she said, and waited for his feet to move away from the door. Eventually, they did. Then for a long time she listened to the house, gently creaking to itself. When everything was silent she stood and walked over to the bed. The package of letters lay insolently on the coverlet, defying her to read.

# Seventeen

Indifference grows with invisible slowness across a marriage, like a cataract over an eye.

Anna knew that for years, out of consideration, or possibly something more, Vincent had taken care to conceal his infidelities. And out of similar consideration, and also jealousy, guilt and fear of loneliness, she herself had refused to see them. Like so many long-married couples they had played a polite, delicate game across the years. Its rules had become second nature and they had lived within the wary harmony it provided.

Had he ever loved her? Once, perhaps, in Paris, in those early days of the war. Yes, then he had loved her, she was sure of it. He had certainly cherished her and protected her – words which might sound lifeless now but which in her youth had been uplifting and intoxicating.

Even after the baby he had still loved her, although by then she understood that his love had become a self-willed demonstration, a proof of his generous spirit: by continuing to love her he showed her he could rise above her unfaithfulness. He had never thought it necessary to rise above his own.

Of course she had known whenever he was having an affair. Her finely tuned ear heard it in the altered timbre of his voice, the slight but unmistakable shift of his eyes.

She noted everything and said nothing. After all, they were small infidelities. They hurt, of course, but only a little, only for a short while: a bearable pain, like bee stings. And when each affair was over she and Vincent drew close again and mildly happy, as their relationship eased back into its habitual pattern.

So that she did not realize how unprepared she was when she slipped the first letter from its green-lined envelope and saw the bold handwriting on the cream paper and heard the imperious, passionate voice.

'My dearest, darling Vincent,' it began and ended, although by then her hand was trembling so violently that she could hardly read the sinuous characters, 'In love and desire always, Your adoring A.' And before she had time to prepare herself, to hold her breath against real pain, it had slid between her ribs with the force of a crossbow bolt.

For A, of course, was for Astrid.

*

When Vincent's train had pulled out of Grand Central Station Anna returned to the drab apartment, picked up her small suitcase and made her way to the Berghof house by the park. The couple had flown south and all the staff had gone: the elderly into retirement or service elsewhere, the young men to fight. Most of the rooms had been closed up: pictures had been taken down, linen sent into store and furniture shrouded in dust-sheets. Anna was to live in the few rooms that would remain heated: the kitchen, a south-facing salon, an attic bedroom and bathroom and the library.

It was quiet.

She went downstairs, across the black-and-white tiled floor and down the long corridor to the kitchen. The room was large, cream-walled and high-ceilinged, with a black range of monumental proportions running the length of one wall. At the far end someone had left a small electric hotplate, a toaster and a kettle. Beside the door a fridge the size of a wardrobe hummed peaceably. Anna made herself a supper of bread, milk and cheese and carried it over to the table, a great square of solid, scrubbed pine, large enough to sit a dozen people. Outside, traffic rumbled tranquilly up and down the street.

Afterwards she washed the dirty dishes and set them on the rack. One plate, one glass, one knife. There was comfort in this simplicity; being alone, which she had dreaded, was a balm. She was free to order her life as she wished, to let her mind go where it would.

And yet . . .

No.

She closed her eyes, clenched her fists under the water and waited until the memory dimmed and vanished. Then she dried the plate and knife and put them away, polished the glass until it shone and hung the damp cloth on the stove rail to dry.

And then, following a faint but discernible impulse, she made her way to the library, opened the tall double doors and breathed in the rich, welcoming perfume of books.

Life in the big house soon took on an established routine. In the morning Anna aired rooms, dusted mantelpieces and polished brass, silver and wood, and in the afternoon she read or went out to walk and buy food. In the space of a few weeks she came to recognize the doormen of the neighbouring apartment blocks, and they exchanged greetings. Each day she walked further away from the house, made herself stay out for longer, until she was no longer intimidated by the scale and noise and bustle of the city and was happy to be herself and explore.

In the evenings, after supper, she would curl up in one of the armchairs in the library. At first she chose books at random, as if she were picking chocolates from a box, sometimes attracted by a title, sometimes by an author or even the design or colour of a jacket. The idea that her father would have been horrified as much by her unscientific approach as by the novels themselves made her smile and only encouraged further experimentation.

Without a set plan she read widely, consuming, hungrily, Dickens, Hemingway, Jane Austen, Scott Fitzgerald, the Brontës, Graham Greene, Somerset Maugham, Thomas Hardy and Henry James. She became fascinated by the translated works, too, and sat with original and translated versions of Flaubert and Balzac and Proust open on the table in front of her. In the early days she kept a dictionary at her elbow in order to look up obscure English words, but soon she was flying along, the language transparent.

The dreaded months of loneliness sped past in quiet enjoyment. Curled in the library chair, she travelled, in the turn of a page, in the space of an evening, from eighteenth-century London to Great Egg in the 1920s, from a bleak green hillside in Dorset to the opulent mansions of Boston. Words resonated; images filled her mind like a sail.

But each morning brought news of the war. Crouched before the great rosewood wireless in the salon she often wondered whether reports of victories were in fact well-disguised disasters, but in any case they said little or nothing about individuals caught up in the fighting. She cut articles from the newspapers, especially anything that mentioned France and the Resistance. She tried to imagine Vincent in Paris, saw him walking through the shadows of the rue Saint-Denis on his way to visit Léon, his latest set of false papers tucked safely in his wallet.

And sometimes her will-power failed, and she thought of Harry Quinn and wondered where he was now. And whether, and what, he thought of her.

He had said to her, that last night in Lisbon, as she sat in exulted misery on the bed, 'Do you really despise yourself that much, Anna? Or is just me you loathe?' And later, angrily, 'Don't make the mistake of thinking that your husband is somehow superior to the rest of us. Because, I can assure you, Vincent Galland is a pretty unworthy hero from anyone's point of view, especially yours.' She had never forgotten the bitter, knowing tone of his voice. His contempt had been unbearable.

Her own attitude was more complex. It was easy to see Vincent's inconsistencies; more difficult to explain them away. Over time she found the answer was simply to blur one's focus; to say that one didn't know enough to judge, being woefully ignorant of politics and philosophy. Even when Vincent was denounced as a traitor by some of the causes he abandoned, Anna's first instinct was to defend him, to draw attention to his strengths rather than his weaknesses.

But now, in the cocoon of the empty house, she allowed his image to blur beyond recognition. In this new, fictional world of her imagination she allowed herself to think of Harry and Vincent as men who, if they had met, would almost certainly have become friends. After all, both of them had fought in Spain. Sometimes, if she closed down part of her mind entirely, she could imagine them as comrades in the International Brigade.

There they were, tense, unwashed, unshaven, red-eyed from lack of sleep, crouching behind the wall of a ruined building or hiding from Nationalist troops in a mountain cave. Shirt-sleeved on a sunlit morning, they posed for a photograph with other impossibly young men, guns slung over their shoulders, old-fashioned pistol belts around their hips. She closed her eyes and saw them so clearly: grimy, exhausted, yet laughing, their heads back, mouths open, eyes alight with friendship and trust and idealism.

Floating in the great porcelain tub, she imagined herself as their brave, loving, comrade-in-arms. On a hot morning in Granada she stood with them there on the steps, her arms around their waists, the sun in her face, laughing defiance at the camera . . .

She slipped down into the water until only her face was above the surface and dissolved into a black-and-white dream. Faced with great dangers, it would have been natural that she should be a little in love with them all, and they with her . . .

She awoke in cold water and a dark bathroom, shivering.

*

Sigrid has already put the two bottles and a small wicker parcel to one side, and Anna loads them carefully into the rucksack.

'That cheese smells like it could have flown here on its own,' calls Sigrid from the other side of the shop, where she is busy on the radio. 'If you hadn't come today I was going to drop it round to you.' Then, quickly, 'You setting off back so soon? It's getting dark out there.'

'I'll go by the sea. Don't want to break the bottles.'

'Got a torch?'

'Yes.'

Yes.

The wavefall on her left is slow and rhythmic. The air is still heavy, and there is a faint rumble like far-off thunder. Behind the black mass of the mountains the sky is flickering, alive with pink, gold and green. Anna cranes her head back and watches the air glow and fade and glow again, a cosmic display for the smallest of audiences. As the lights fade she trudges on, wondering if, up in Sørvågen, Harry Quinn is watching the same sky.

The following evening Leif arrives promptly at seven. He brings with him the smell of cold night air and a small, slightly bruised bunch of red and blue anemones.

'I got them in Bodø today.' He holds them out stiffly.

'They're pretty, Leif. It's ages since I've had flowers.' Anna fills a copper jug with water and puts it on the table. The colours glow like stained glass.

Leif looks around him. 'The old place looks good. Smells good, too.'

'Roast chicken', she says, 'and potatoes with herbs.' She has cooked everything slowly, carefully, enjoying the unaccustomed pleasure of preparing food for another person. The table is covered with a cloth, and two long-stemmed glasses sparkle in the candlelight. The bottle of burgundy stands open by the hearth.

Leif takes the beer she pours for him and sits in the armchair on the far side of the fireplace. He appears instantly at home, his big body comfortably relaxed, brown face alive with curiosity.

Anna smiles. 'So did you see your friend in Bodø, the lady with the big voice?'

Leif grins. 'Toril? *Ja.* She's expecting her fourth kid next month. She's enormous but still shifting fish boxes like a champion.' He stops and looks at her, seems about to ask a question, then apparently he changes his mind and nods over to the typewriter on the desk.

'You got some more work, too, I hear.'

'Nothing as hard as fish boxes. But, yes, I was supposed to start translating a book from English into Norwegian.'

'*Ja*? Famous writer is it?'

'No. Very poor. In fact it was so bad that I've refused to do it. I sent it back to America yesterday.'

There is a silence. Leif is watching her intently, and she shifts uneasily in her chair.

Suddenly he says, in the same easy voice as before, 'Why did you come here to Moskenes, Anna?'

She feels herself blush. 'Shall we eat? Everything's ready.'

But his eyes are still wide, curious. 'Was it to get away from that man Quinn?'

Now she wishes she had never invited him. She turns away. 'I hope you like garlic.'

But Leif persists. 'But then why did you . . . ?'

And for the first time in her life she loses her temper, wheeling around on him, hands on hips. 'Look. What I do and why I'm here is no one's business but mine.'

He blinks slowly, and it infuriates her.

'Some things are too bad to talk about – surely *you* can understand that.' Too late she hears herself – angry, eager to hurt.

Leif rises slowly to his feet; his tousled hair brushes the pine beams.

'Yes. Sure. I understand.' The great shoulders slope despondently. 'I'm sorry.'

Anna is contrite. 'Leif, it's me. I'm the one who's sorry. Truly. Please stay.'

His big face looks down. 'Better not.'

'Please?'

He lifts his head, looks at her warily, his hat in his hands. 'You still want me to?'

'I still want you to. Please.' She takes a breath. 'Will you pour the wine?'

Quietly he fills the glasses. The slender stems look impossibly fragile in his fists. She brings the brown oval dish to the table and spoons chicken, gravy and golden, aromatic potatoes on to the plates. Leif bows his head for a moment, but when he sees her pick up her fork he does the same, and they eat in an almost companionable silence.

Neither of them is used to the wine. It reddens their cheeks and makes their eyes glitter. Anna talks, and it is as if an ice wall is melting. She laughs over her obsession with the stove and the firewood and tells him about her climbs to the high peaks and is delighted when he knows their names. Leif talks of his early days as a boy on the Lofoten boats: sea storms, icebergs and nights in North Atlantic ports before the war.

'Fishermen,' he says with mock despair, 'they spend weeks at sea without saying hardly a word, but get them ashore, with food, drink, women and music, and suddenly even the old ones are singing or dancing around the room in their seaboots. With a beer or two inside him my father used to do this.' He stands and dances on the spot, humming loudly, his arms on his hips, knees out-bent in a galumphing, shambling hornpipe. Anna laughs, recognizing an old sea shanty her father used to sing, and joins in.

'That's it,' he says, reaching for her hands. 'Come on.'

Heady with wine they set off around the room, careening against the chairs, thudding out the beat with their heels on the wooden floor, dipping and turning in the four corners of the room. When the shanty ends with an emphatic triple stamp of heels, breathless with laughter and exertion they collapse back into their chairs, facing each other across the fireplace.

'Well, you dance pretty good for a dry-lander,' he pants.

'And I bet you're an ace at the polka.'

'Don't know, never tried.' He raises an eyebrow and gives her a first direct look. 'Teach me?'

Anna shakes her head, fanning herself with her hand. 'Not now, I'm too out of breath.'

'Here, I get the wine.'

She watches him shamble over to the table and pick up the glasses and the second bottle. He hands her hers, settles himself back comfortably and looks at her.

'Ah, there now,' he says, suddenly alert, 'you did it again.'

'Did what?'

'Changed colour.'

'I'm sure I'm red in the face,' she says, 'if that's what you mean.'

He smiles back. 'Yes, you are. Bright pink. But, no, I meant the colour of *you*.'

He takes a mouthful of wine and waves the glass at her. 'I tell you something few people know, Anna Larssen. When you work on the sea you learn to understand the signs, to see what the wind will be, what the sea and tide will do. Some people see these things clearer than others. I used to be pretty good myself, and people would ask me . . .' He broke off.

'Anyway, then one day I realized that it wasn't only weather I saw. I see things when I look at people. I see colours.'

She frowns. 'Colours?'

'Like a glow round people. Everyone is different. Sigrid has yellow all around her – yellow, like a daffodil; little Marika is a mauvey, nightfall shade – they'll have trouble with her, I think. Johan is red-brown, a kind of good, steady colour, and Gunnar is red-orange. When he stands by Sigrid they make fire.' He wagged a finger at her. 'Oh, I see you laugh, but it's true, I promise.' His face is creased in smiles.

She can't tell if he is teasing her and so frowns and tries to look sceptical. 'And what colour are you, then, Leif?'

To her surprise he reaches across and grasps her hand.

'Well now, Missus Anna Larssen, at this point every other lady I've ever told that story to flutters her eyelashes and says, "Ooh, Leif, and what colour am *I*?" '

Anna pulls her hand from his, but he is looking into her face and doesn't seem to notice.

'You didn't ask that, but I'll tell you anyway,' he says, his big head tilted slightly to one side. 'You're the colour of water.'

'Oh,' she says, suddenly sober and recognizing the truth of what he has said: that she is, has always been, the insubstantial, colourless space between solid things.

But Leif is smiling. 'It's rare – it took me a while to see exactly what it was – the colour *glas*.'

'I've never heard of it.' She is trying not to sound hurt.

Leif takes a sip of wine. 'I knew a Frenchman once, Jannou, a Breton fisherman. We met in Iceland. I used to teach him Norwegian words: *ship, fish, man, woman*, you know? And he taught me a little Breton. Then one day I looked out at the sea, and I said, "Jannou, what's the word for blue?" And he thought for a bit, and then he said, "Well now, Leif, there's no word in Breton for blue, only *glas*, which means blue and green and grey, all at once – the colour of the sea: the colour of water."

'The colour of water', he spreads his hands, 'is *glas*. And that's you.'

A year ago, she thinks, she would have wept, but now she settles herself back in her chair, rubbing her finger around the rim of her glass. 'I see. But you still haven't told me what *you* are.'

He is laughing at her now, and his eyes, deep in their net of lines, look like splinters of emerald caught in the light.

'Me? That's easy. I never change. I'm plain green, like seaweed. All the way through.'

# Eighteen

In New York the spring of 1942 was slow in coming. Even in April Anna still wore as many layers of clothing as she could and marched quickly through the streets to get her circulation moving. Despite her shyness she was getting to know the neighbourhood. She bought food from the little Italian grocery stores, aromatic with swaying hams; she sniffed the warm golden air of bakeries and lingered outside the brightly lit cafés, waiting for someone to open the door and send the aroma of freshly ground coffee rushing out into the street.

Most mornings she stopped at Antonio's Coffee House, where she had become friendly with one of the waitresses. Julie was a wiry, dark-haired girl of her own age, who spoke with a sing-song New York twang.

'Yeah, you gotta a tough break there, I think,' she said, setting down a milky coffee and slipping a sugar-coated biscuit under the saucer. 'Your husband off in Europe, you left to make your own way in the big city. Not easy, huh? I take my hat off to you.'

Anna smiled. She did not think that she was really 'making her own way'. Vincent had left most of his money in Lisbon, thinking that in the long term it would be safer and more accessible there than in America. The allowance he had arranged for her in New York covered food and necessities but little else, and the Berghofs' salary was a pittance: Anna guessed they thought she didn't need the money.

'You need a good job? You and me both. But they got no vacancies here,' Julie said quickly.

'No, I didn't mean . . .'

'Waitressing ain't for the likes of you, in any case.'

Anna wondered what the likes of her was.

'I bet if you think hard enough you'll think of something. You speak real good English. You do shorthand?'

Anna shook her head.

There was a shout from the far end of the restaurant. Julie grimaced.

'Anyhow. Stick with it, girl, you deserve a bit of luck.' She gave her a gentle, encouraging punch on the arm and sashayed off down the restaurant in her tight pink dress, flipping open her order pad as she went.

That afternoon Anna telephoned Andrew Collings and asked for his help in finding work. His secretary was brusque and dismissive, and it took her all her courage to insist on a meeting. Two days later she walked up the wide flight of steps to the British Consulate and the woman at reception directed her to the lifts. Nervous, Anna wrestled with the double cage doors. The only other passenger, an elderly mailman, reached across her and slid them shut.

'It ain't that difficult, honey.'

Mr Collings's office was on the third floor. A smartly dressed young woman sitting behind a desk looked Anna up and down. 'He'll see you for a moment,' she said. 'But he has a meeting at twelve.' With a show of languid disdain she walked over the door, opened it and announced, 'Mrs Galland, sir.'

Andrew Collings sat behind a cluttered desk dominated by two large filing trays, each containing a teetering heap of buff folders.

'Sit, please. Is there still some tea, Janice?'

'I'm afraid not.'

Collings pursed his lips and made a little 'not guilty' shrug. 'Another time. Now, Mrs Galland, do tell me how I can be of help to you.' His glance at his watch was brief but telling.

Twisting her gloves into a tight, sweaty rope, Anna explained why she had come.

The Englishman sank back into his chair with a sigh. 'Oh, I see. You're looking for *work*. Are you sure? We've nothing here unfortunately, but there is always voluntary work you could do, and the Wives, I'm sure, would be happy to take you under their wing.'

Anna cleared her throat. 'I need paid work, Mr Collings. I type, I speak several languages.'

He looked startled. 'Ah? Indeed. How interesting. Well, my dear Mrs Galland, leave it with me. I'll do what I can, of course, but I'm afraid things are desperately hectic at the moment. Was there anything else?' He picked up a file and began to scan the contents.

Clearly Anna was dismissed. She stood, red-faced, fiddling with the strap of her handbag. Mr Collings turned a page and then another. The only thing she could think was: If I stay here long enough, surely he will have to look up.

Still he sat, head bent, flipping through the folder, although she thought she noticed a growing pinkness about his cheeks. Seconds ticked by. She would have to leave empty-handed. It must, *must* be possible to speak, to say something. Suddenly she stepped up to the desk and leaned on it with both arms. Collings started in surprise, pushed his chair back and stared up at her.

Anna's thin face, framed by two wings of unfashionably straight blonde hair, quivered as she spoke. 'Mr Collings, my husband is quite a hero here in the United States. If the American press were to find out how shabbily you British are treating his wife it might be rather embarrassing, don't you think? So I shall telephone on Thursday. Please do what you can.'

It was a clumsy, desperate ploy, but at least it gave her a final line upon which she could exit with dignity. She walked quickly away down the corridor and then hid in the darkened stairwell for a long time, breathing deeply, while the caged lift whirred self-importantly up and down.

On Friday morning, having heard nothing, she telephoned the consulate again. The secretary was still offhand, but a man's voice, muffled, spoke sharply in the background, and when the woman came on the line again her voice was honeyed.

'I'm putting you through right now, Mrs Galland.'

'Ah good, yes, Mrs Galland,' said Andrew Collings. 'First things first: *mea culpa* for last Thursday. Truly. Didn't mean to offend, I assure you, just pressure of work, I hope you understand. Anyway, I'm really glad you called, because I've had a bit of luck. Any chance you could pop by later this afternoon?'

Anna arrived at the consulate ten minutes early for her appointment, and this time she managed the lift gates on her own.

Smiling appeasingly, Mr Collings offered her tea, asked after her health and then handed her a neatly typed note.

'This chap's got a good reputation among you linguists. Bit of a slave-driver, but quite a few of the European ex-pat community do odd jobs for him.'

Anna stared at the small piece of paper: 'Kurt Kirchener Translation'.

The address turned out to be an alleyway off Broadway: a narrow building with dimly lit landings giving on to a series of low-ceilinged mezzanine floors. On every level there was a constant clatter of typewriters and ringing of bells as the writers slammed their carriages back and forth.

Mr Kirchener's office was at the rear of the second floor. A woman in a purple blouse and skirt sat on guard outside it, her hair coiled in two grey plaits like earphones either side of her head. She was scoring a document with a proof-checker's blue pencil.

'Yes?'

'Mavis, is that her?' came a guttural shout from the room beyond.

The earphone lady looked up, tucking her pencil behind one ear. 'Mrs Galland?' She smiled. 'Go straight in,' she said, turning her attention back to the document whose borders, Anna could now see, were already heavily tapestried in blue.

The office was a largish room, lit by a green glass table-lamp that cast a bright cone of light upon the desk and plunged the rest of the room into a soft, underwater glow.

Behind the desk, busily revolving on his office chair, sat a short, wide man with long strands of white hair combed across a shining pink pate. His face was as round as a football, and beneath it a remarkable set of chins descended on to his chest and shoulders, like nested saucepans of gradually increasing size. He was wearing a brown knitted cardigan of great intricacy and a vividly patterned yellow tie.

Anna advanced into the room and then realized that the floor was covered with cardboard files, all piled on top of one another. Some of the untidy towers were three feet high, and as she picked her way around one she accidentally collided with another.

'Careful, careful, for pity's sake,' the man shouted. 'Now, sit.'

Anna looked around for a chair. The walls were lined with shelf after shelf of dictionaries; in one corner of the room stood a black and ancient stove, which threw a wall of heat out into the tiny room. There was no other chair. She eyed the nearest tower of documents, wondering if he meant her to use this as a perch.

'I said *sit down*,' barked the man, squinting up at her through horn-rimmed glasses.

She looked around her in panic and sank on to a low wooden stool in front of the desk. Kirchener leaned back in his chair, scrutinizing, she imagined, the top of her head, for that must have been all he could see.

'That idiot Collings says you have Norwegian, French, English, Swedish and German. How good is your Norwegian?' he bellowed.

'Not bad, Mr Kirchener,' she whispered.

He whistled through his teeth. 'What does that mean? Come on, come on. Be specific: is it poor, fair, good or excellent?'

This was no time for false modesty. 'Excellent, I suppose,' she said.

'And your English and French?'

'Um, both good,' she said, nervously. 'My mother was French. My husband and I speak both languages.'

He took off his horn rimmed spectacles and squinted at her. 'Vincent Galland is your husband, isn't he?'

Anna nodded. 'Do you know him?'

Kirchener put his glasses back on.

'Mavis! In here if you please. And bring the Eriksson manuscript.'

Mavis appeared in the doorway with a thick brown folder in her arms. She marched over to Kirchener's desk and placed it in front of him with a flounce. He flipped it open and studied the title page.

'We'll set you a little test. Go home and translate the first chapter of this into English. Don't worry too much, I can get it polished. But get the literal sense of it, OK? Do you type?'

Anna nodded.

'Got a typewriter?'

There was one in the Berghofs' study. 'Yes. But I haven't any paper, and I'm not sure . . .'

'Here,' Kirchener shot open one of the drawers of the desk and thumped a heavy packet on to the table. 'Ten pica margin, first line five pica indent, double space throughout, top copy plus a carbon. You'll need this.' He swivelled around at speed in the chair and selected a squat volume from the shelf. 'Dictionary. If you need more, then try the libraries. Come back in a week.'

'But what is it I'm to translate?' she asked, opening the brown folder.

'It came in last week. Per Eriksson, Norwegian poet and writer. He's just managed to smuggle out an account of the German Occupation. Should make interesting reading. Five dollars a thousand.'

'A thousand what?'

'Words, girl, words. Now, close the door on the way out; the damn stove is smoking again. *Mavis*!'

Anna stood with difficulty, piled the paper on top of the manuscript and the dictionary on top of that. Mavis came in and stood beside her.

'Has Delacourt returned that MS yet?' Kirchener said, without looking up.

'Not a word. But Erich Liebowitz is here.'

'Call the lazy Belgian and tell him I'll halve his rate unless he delivers by the end of the week. And show in my good friend, the one-armed Pole. You still here, Mrs Galland?'

Dazed, her arms already aching from their burden, Anna turned to run and collided with a bulky figure in the doorway.

'Oh my God, I'm so sorry,' she said, helping the man to his feet. He was in his forties, dark-haired; one arm of his coat was empty and pinned against his chest. With his other he picked up a file from the floor and tossed it cheerfully on to Kirchener's desk.

'No, my fault, I was in the way. Here, stop grumbling for once. Was this ogre shouting at you just then, Miss . . . ?'

'It's *Mrs* Galland, Erich, so mind your manners,' shouted Kirchener.

The Pole grinned.

'Now, one in, one out. *Goodbye*, Mrs Galland.'

With her first fee from Kirchener's Anna bought a blue woollen coat and a pair of leather gloves, proud that she was paying with money that she had earned herself.

'Not bad,' Kurt had said. 'But it took you twice as long as it should. You can *do* this. You don't have to worry about it so much. Get some confidence and *speed up*. Now, here's the rest of the Ericsson. Mavis will give you the money. Do you need an advance? Don't answer. I know you do. *Mavis*.'

Gradually Anna's visits to Kirchener's became a regular part of her life in New York, as it did for many of the translators who worked there. The agency was not only a place of work but a kind of international club for exiles. In the dilapidated sitting-room at the back of the second floor, on a winter's afternoon, she would meet Gurdinsky, who had been a senior civil servant under the Tsar, or the witty Jewish philosopher Iacomo Lappi, who had been smuggled out of Rome by friends, or Sven Bergman, a Dane who had had several novels published before the war, or two elderly Greek poets, Aleksis and Daphne Apostolis, or Erich Liebowitz, the one-armed Polish writer she had met on her first day.

Whatever the size of the gathering, Mavis Kirchener produced pots of tea, jugs of coffee and handed around plates of home-made cakes and pastries. The translators ate and talked, their English often as broken-backed as the armchairs in which they sat, and for the first time in her life Anna found herself a member of a group of friends and equals.

## Nineteen

'You like him?' says Sigrid, keeping her eyes firmly on the pile of papers she is franking.

'Of course,' says Anna. 'Leif is a very kind man.'

'Oh, yes, he's *kind* all right,' says Sigrid. She shuffles the papers, clips them together and picks up another pile. Bang, bang, bang. 'But he's lonely. Time he settled down.'

Anna has been expecting something of this nature ever since she stepped inside the post office and saw Sigrid's face. Sigrid whose colour is yellow, who makes a flame colour with her husband Gunnar and who would like everyone to enjoy the warming fires of coupledom.

'Sigrid, I . . .'

'You like him. He likes you. He takes you in his boat; you invite him to eat at your house; you know each other a year already. You're neither of you youngsters. Time passes, tick, tock.'

Bang, bang, bang.

Anna watches the sure-handed movements. Yes, beside you, Sigrid, she thinks sadly, I *am* transparent. The colour of water.

Sigrid slips the papers into an envelope and signs and seals it with a generous lick of her tongue. 'So, what's the problem? Is it this guy up in Sørvågen? Seems to me if he doesn't come to see you once in two weeks there's something wrong there. Yes? No?'

Anna opens her mouth, but all that emerges is a small distressed sound. She clears her throat. 'I don't know.'

Which isn't true, because of *course* it is wrong.

'He came in here yesterday,' Sigrid says sternly, her sleeves rolled up above the elbow exposing her solid, ham-like forearms. She nods. 'Your bird-watcher man. Oh, yes. Right in the shop. Stood where you're standing now.'

It must, Anna thinks, be possible to speak, to ask a simple question.

She waits for a moment, then says, casually, 'Really? What did he look like?'

Sigrid ponders. 'Not tall. Grey hair. Kind of hunched. Didn't smile much. Eyes a nice blue, though.' She opens a carton of cans and begins stacking them on the shelves. 'Sent one letter to France and one to America.'

It almost occurs to Anna to ask if she may see them, but she senses Sigrid will be offended. Instead, she remains silent, watching Sigrid's quick, regular movements as she fills the shelves with ordered rows of canned vegetables.

'So, do you think your so-called friend'll ever come and see *you?*' Sigrid completes a row of beans and goes on to the next.

Anna is certain, almost sure, that Leif has not told Sigrid anything. 'Mr Quinn isn't exactly a friend.'

Sigrid stands and turns, looking thoughtfully at Anna. 'Thought not.' She puts the last can down on the counter, surveying the thin face and pale hair of the woman who is slowly becoming a friend. 'You want to stay here for a while, Anna? We got room – Gunnar's away and Marika can share with me. It'd be no trouble.'

'Thank you, but no, Sigrid. I'd rather stay – I mean, I've got a mountain of work to do.'

Little Marika runs in, screaming. Marika whose colour is mauve, Leif said. Anna blurs her vision and looks at the child again, but all she can see is a damp red face under a tangle of pale blonde hair.

'Johan pulled my plaits. I hate him, Mama.'

Sigrid sighs. 'It's a beargarden. Marika, give me that ribbon, you crybaby, and come here.'

Anna watches Sigrid as she wipes her hands on her apron, takes gentle fistfuls of her daughter's hair and plaits it rapidly. Marika, all smiles, kisses her mother on the cheek and runs off shouting for her brother to come and play.

'If you want a bit of company you could take Leif's dog for a while,' says Sigrid, teasing long fine hairs out of the brush. 'He's away for a week now over in Bodø, and she's pining. She'd be good company, young Kersti.'

The brown-and-white dog is in a basket by the stove, her head resting dolefully on the rim. 'Yes, all right,' Anna hears herself say. 'Yes, I'll take her until he comes back.'

'There's a small sack of food behind the counter there and her lead's on the hook, but she generally runs free. Don't forget to give her plenty of water.'

'Kersti?' says Anna.

The dog opens one wary eye.

*

Vincent Galland was reported missing on 23 September 1962, a week after his sudden disappearance from Saint-Aubain-les-Eaux.

For two weeks the newspapers were full of false sightings and speculation.

Had the famous communist followed his English comrades, the elusive Burgess and Maclean, to Moscow? Had he been ill? In debt? The object of blackmail? Was he wandering somewhere in France, suffering from amnesia? The police put many of the same questions to the bewildered Madame Galland, who was pictured, fair-haired, thin and anxious, at the door of their country home.

Vincent's Parisian friends telephoned constantly, asking for news, everyone considerate but mystified. Local people wished Anna *bon courage* when they saw her out shopping. 'He'll be back, don't you worry,' said Jacques Flers, an ex-soldier and now manager of the bank in the main square. 'Its only natural after what they went through in the war, those lads. Sometimes it comes back to haunt them, even the bravest. When he's ready, he'll be back, trust me.'

But the two weeks lengthened to three, and still there was no news.

It was not until the middle of October that the police found a pile of weathered, rain-soaked clothes on the rocky Quiberon promontory in Brittany. Anna was driven out west the following day, and for five hours she sat staring out of the windows of the police car at ploughed fields, red, brown and umber, slick as recent wounds.

When she arrived, the chief inspector from Vannes, who had been briefed by the left-wing mayor, was gentle with her. She was shown into a small office with a high window and a harsh, metal-shaded light. Coffee was brought, sandwiches were offered and refused. Several police officers came in and stood around the walls. One sat at the table, ready to make notes.

They had packed the clothes in separate plastic bags, which somehow made them more difficult to recognize. White underwear and a pale-blue shirt could have belonged to any one of a million men. Florence had always ironed Vincent's clothing. She should be here, not me, thought Anna, staring stupidly at the label in the collar which identified the garment as couture-made. That morning there had been considerable ribald speculation among the junior officers, who had found it amusing that a leading member of the international proletariat should be so self-indulgent where fashion was concerned; but they had all secretly admired the hand-crafted brogues and the jacket of impeccable tweed.

Anna drew a silk necktie from a bag; it lay cold and damp in her hand. This, she knew, was Vincent's because she had bought it for his birthday the previous year: its pale-blue ground was conventionally striped with black and red, but she had been struck by the maker's delightfully florid name: Caron de Saint-Sulpice.

'Yes,' she said, 'this belongs to my husband.'

The chief inspector cleared his throat and thanked her deferentially. The note-taking officer stopped writing.

The newspapers that weekend were full of the news, drawing their own improbable conclusions about Vincent Galland's final hours and placing his photograph alongside a gloomy roll-call of the many *imprudents* who had died while swimming off the headlands of the Côte Sauvage. Some journalists speculated that, troubled by personal matters which remained obscure, the famous Monsieur Galland had chosen to take his own life on that most treacherous of coastlines, since he had chosen the time of the full moon and the equinox, the time of the biggest tides. All experts agreed that the body might never be recovered.

From Lorient to Vannes the gendarmes kept watch, but weeks passed before reports came in of a body washed up on a beach fifty miles north of Quiberon. The chief inspector was unwilling to recall Madame Galland to perform the grisly duty of identification and instead decided to approach a gentleman he understood to be a close friend, colleague and neighbour of the possible deceased. To his relief Bertrand Delamain consented to perform the task, and it was he who nodded silently from behind the glass partition when the morgue attendant drew back the sheet.

A few weeks later, in the absence of any note or compelling reason to conclude suicide, the examining magistrate returned a verdict of misadventure on Vincent Galland, member of the Légion d'Honneur and holder of the Croix de Guerre.

*

In the spring of 1944 two visitors came to the Berghof house on New York's Upper East Side.

The first was Henri Richemont. Bronzed, moustachioed and urbane, he arrived one sunlit evening, resplendent on the doorstep in a light-grey cashmere jacket and yellow silk tie.

'My God, Anna, this place gives me the shivers. It's not a house, it's a museum,' he said, looking around at the sheeted furniture in the hall.

'I've grown to like it,' she said. 'Come through into the kitchen, though: it's a little more homely.'

Henri blanched as he stepped into the echoing room and gave a dramatic shudder at the sight of the range.

'Well, I don't think homely is really the word and, what's worse, I'm beginning to doubt we have the makings of a good Martini here. The telephone, please?'

Anna laughed and pointed to the door.

Over cocktails at Sardi's Henri studied her with unashamed curiosity. She was wearing a rose-coloured skirt and white blouse; her hair had grown and she had tied it back. There was about her a quiet self-contained serenity that he had not seen before. He lit a cigarette and smiled at her through the smoke. 'Well, my dear, can it be that loneliness suits you? It's an idea that never struck me before, and if it's true it's a waste of a beautiful woman.'

'I'm not lonely,' said Anna, quickly. 'I have friends here now. Writers, and translators like me.'

'Ah yes, your work. I'd heard. That's good. Work is good, I mean. It helps . . .' He waved away the stalled remark, 'Anyway, *ma chère*, tell me all about your lovers.'

Anna smiled. 'That's easy – I don't have any.'

'So vehement. Why is that, I wonder? You have ink on your finger,' said Henri, leaning forward and lifting her hand.

'It's the typewriter ribbon. It jams.'

'Child.' He licked his finger and gently rubbed at the stain. 'And what news of Vincent?'

'Oh, a few letters. They don't say much.'

She had waited three months for the first one. When it came, the envelope was crumpled and dog-eared and looked as if it had passed through many hands, not all of them clean. Inside, some parts of the letter had been inked out by a censor and others had been cut out entirely with a scalpel. The remaining text was curiously impersonal, as if it had been dictated. She had read it through half-a-dozen times, searching for meaning.

'My dearest Anna,' it began, followed by a polite enquiry after her health. 'I am well and resting here in London after a period of activity.'

Resting? Activity? In her anxiety she decided that he meant he had been on a mission, had been wounded and was in hospital or convalescing.

> It feels good to be at the centre of things again. I know from your letter how much you would like to come over here, and of course I miss you, too, but the fact is that I am often away, and the North Atlantic crossing is too dangerous at present. Like so many others in this war, we shall simply have to accept that we may be apart for longer than we expected.

There were some curt comments on her decision to work, which appeared to puzzle him, and then he went on, 'Ironically, although the conflict often separates, it can also throw up remarkable coincidences. Of all people, last month in xxxxx [the word was heavily inked out] I met your friend [several words were cut out] who sent best wishes.'

Harry? Anna thought, leaping ahead to the last page. But there was no other reference to the mysterious meeting, just a short final paragraph. 'I miss you, and think about you every day. Perhaps you won't believe me, but I love you very much.'

She had wept a little at that: it was so like Vincent to write three emotionless pages and then add an ambiguous, heart-breaking sentiment at the very end.

Now she said to Henri, 'Last month he said he was well, but it was difficult to tell.'

'Do you miss him?'

She drew back in the chair. 'Of course.'

Henri's head tilted enquiringly, '*Un peu, beaucoup, passionnément, à la folie?*'

Anna smiled. 'And how is Gisèle?'

'My dear, such subtlety. I am suitably chastized. To answer your question, Gisèle is in perfect form, although unfortunately for me at the moment she prefers to drape her perfect form over Curtis Dunstan, one of the studio's new rising stars.'

'Oh,' said Anna.

'Please don't sympathize. Pity is far more demeaning than mere cuckoldry.'

For a moment they sipped their drinks in silence. Anna noted the sad, down-sloping lines around Henri's eyes, the self-mocking twist of the smile, and guessed why he had come. Grateful for the descending glow of gin she drained her glass.

'Two more please.' Henri sat for a long moment fiddling with the scalloped paper coaster. Suddenly he looked up.

'Forgive me for this, Anna. I was going to say it later, but . . . You have been on my mind a lot recently. And don't think,' he continued hurriedly, 'that I'm saying that because of the ineffable Curtis Dunstan. Truly not. No, in fact . . . ever since the day you arrived in New York. After Vincent left I longed to come and see you. And I would have done, except that I kept telling myself that visiting a friend's wife when he's fighting a heroic war thousands of miles away is hardly an honourable thing to do.'

Discreetly the barman set down two fresh mats and two Martinis. Henri watched him move out of earshot.

'So I stayed where I was. But I couldn't stop thinking of the night you told me about Harry Quinn and the child and of what that quack Weldon did to you afterwards. Oh, yes, Anna, I know. And I despise Vincent for it. No,' he waved her silent, 'please, let me say it. I am an acknowledged and self-confessed hypocrite, so at least allow me to recognize the same fault in others.'

He leaned forward, his tanned face serious, his eyes fixed on hers. 'You should let him go, Anna. If you stay you'll end up cold and alone in that marble shrine of his. You need someone constant and loving, not someone who worships you one day and betrays you the next.'

Anna looked up, her face scarlet.

'Vincent has never betrayed me.'

Henri shook his head. 'He has, darling, and he will again, believe me. Some men can't survive on single rations of fame and love. Their ego has great appetites: it is hungry for more. Vincent is like that. It's all there, obvious if only you look: the love of risk and danger, the pride, the womanizing and the lack of interest in other people.' His voice was becoming thick with emotion. 'Don't waste yourself on someone like that, Anna, someone *inhuman*.'

She pushed back her chair. Henri lunged across the table, grabbing her wrist just as she reached for her handbag.

'Anna, I didn't mean it. I planned everything so carefully, and now . . . Sit, please, let me at least finish.'

She sat, although he could feel the pull of her hand against his.

'This isn't about Gisèle and Vincent, either, believe me.'

Her hand slackened, and he caught the sudden blankness in her eyes.

'Ah, you didn't know,' he said softly. 'It's true. It even made Louella Parsons's column at the time.' He reached for his wallet and drew out a small square of yellowing paper: 'A little bird tells me that a certain *Mademoiselle from Our Bel Air* is finding Resistance irresistible . . . is all really quiet on the Richefront?'

His voice was breaking. She moved her hand out from under his and laid it gently on top of his. 'I'm so sorry, Henri.'

There was a pause.

'Sorry, but no?' His head was down.

'Sorry, but no.'

It was ten thirty when the limousine pulled up outside the big house. The meal had been awkward: they had said too much at the start of the evening and afterwards had talked incessantly to fill the silence that must elapse before it was over. Now Henri climbed wearily up to the front door, and took both her hands in his.

'I love her, you know.'

'I know.'

'And you, too, of course,' he said, with just a hint of the old panache, 'my Nordic ice-queen. But perhaps it's better for everyone that you turned me down tonight, eh?'

He kissed her lightly on the lips and turned away.

# Twenty

The dog is well mannered and obedient and settles in quickly. Anna makes a pile of old blankets on the floor beside the stove and Kersti curls up on it, one eye open and following Anna's every movement as she puts away the supplies. Throughout supper the dog sits politely to attention and afterwards gratefully accepts a plate to lick.

Just before midnight Anna opens the cabin, and as if this is a familiar routine Kersti bounds out into the darkness.

The moon is a spiny crescent in a skyful of stars. They wheel in great silence overhead: Orion, the Plough, her own little constellation of Cassiopeia. Anna smiles and gives the tiny shape a friendly wink, and then wonders why. Perhaps solitude eventually becomes a burden, and one seeks a familiar presence.

The dog has disappeared.

After a few minutes Anna calls her, but there is no response. Then, suddenly, from the foot of the cliff comes a flurry of loud, aggressive barking. Anna calls out again, and her voice bounces back in echo from the rocks. Then there is a scrabbling noise and the dog shoots up the steps on to the platform, agitated, her eyes rolling.

Anna kneels to stroke the panting animal.

'What was it, girl? Rats? Sheep? Eh? What was it then?'

Kersti nuzzles against her wrist, licking her palm, and whines.

Anna turns into the cabin, and tonight on impulse she shoots the bolt and draws the curtains tight. When, just before dawn, the dog begins to whine softly downstairs, she calls to her and makes room at the foot of the little bed. Perhaps Leif also does this some nights, for the dog curls gracefully into the smallest of spaces, rests her head on her paws and is soon fast asleep.

*

The spring weather in New York, which had begun unseasonably cold, had turned unseasonably warm by the time Anna's second visitor came to call. She recognized the military bearing of the tall, lanky figure on the step.

'Christian Desturbes, Madame Galland, delighted to see you again. Your husband is well, and sends his regards,' he said quickly, seeing her face.

'Ah. You'd better come in, Major,' said Anna, and showed him through to the little garden, with its arching foliage.

Desturbes looked around uneasily. 'Actually, it's Colonel now. Do you mind if we stay inside? I don't much care for the sun.'

'As you wish,' she said and showed him through into the salon. Desturbes sat on the sofa, ill at ease in his suit and tie and looking about curiously.

'Big place for one person.'

'I am caretaking. I only use part of it.'

He appeared about to say something, then lapsed into silence.

'You say Vincent is well,' she said, pouring cool lemonade into a tall glass.

'Very well, last time I saw him,'

'Where was that?'

'Last month, in France,' said Desturbes, laconically, tapping a cigarette on a slim silver case. He hesitated for a moment and then added, 'As you might expect, he's doing a tremendous job over there. Synchronized a whole programme of sabotage in May.' He smiled, stretching his top lip and its narrow dark moustache, 'Risky enterprise, but it paid off: drove the German military absolutely wild.'

'What do you mean?'

Desturbes drew on his cigarette. 'Well, there were some pretty awful reprisals – I'm afraid that's standard for the Boche these days. But the work the partisans are doing will almost certainly shorten the war. *Santé.*' He took a deep draught of the lemonade and set the glass down carefully on the table. 'But, actually, Madame Galland, that's not why I'm here, to talk about the war. Of course I promised Vincent I'd stop by and see how you were. Everything going OK? No worries? I understand you're working now.'

He put inverted commas around the word "working". Anna sighed and told him about the Kircheners, and Desturbes nodded, while his eyes darted from her to the room. When she stopped talking, he leaned back in his chair.

'Good to hear, good to hear. Now, the truth is, I need your help. First, can I ask you something in complete confidence?'

She was startled. 'Of course.'

'You met Vincent back in '38, didn't you? Knew him at the start of the war.'

'Yes. We met in Paris. He'd just got out of Prague ahead of the Nazis.'

'Quite, quite. And what would you say his political sympathies were at that time?'

'Political? He was anti-Nazi, of course. He feared Germany would . . .'

'Of course. And when the Soviet Union and Germany signed the non-aggression pact, can you remember, did it change his attitude at all?'

Anna thought back, remembering Vincent reading the newspaper headline, overturning a chair in his haste and despair.

'He was shocked, certainly.'

'Did it affect his commitment to the Resistance, would you say?'

She was genuinely surprised at the question. 'Of course not.'

'You understand, many communists refused to enter the conflict until much later on.'

Anna pushed her hair back behind her ears. 'But you know that wasn't true of Vincent. In 1940 he was imprisoned and tortured. In 1941 he came here on orders from de Gaulle himself. What is this all about, Colonel?'

The thin face grew tight and wary. 'Madame Galland, the tide of the war is turning. For my commander, General de Gaulle, who also faces the difficult task of working alongside his Anglo-Saxon allies, it is essential to have an accurate assessment of the emerging political influences and realities in his own country.'

Anna had forgotten the French love of abstracts. Baffled, she asked, 'How does this concern Vincent?'

Desturbes leaned forward. 'The communists are numerous within the Resistance, madame. It is the General's view that if they are unopposed, in the aftermath of war they will pose as great a threat to the stability of France as the occupying Germans. Already the battle lines are drawn, and one can say that the struggle for the future of France is only just beginning.'

'But I still don't see . . .'

'There is a political divide of enormous proportions between the two factions. Almost every member of the Resistance is on one side of it or the other, and their political views are no secret. But Vincent', he frowned, 'has a mixed past. He has a reputation for "looking both ways". He is, as they say, an enigma.'

'Have you asked him this yourself?'

Desturbes made a small movement of the hands. 'Sometimes the very act of asking such a question can precipitate an evasion or even an adverse reaction. We have preferred to speak only to a very few of his closest friends and associates, but still opinion is divided. And so,' he spread his hands, 'finding myself here in America, I naturally came to talk to you.'

'You want me to tell you whether Vincent is a communist or a Gaullist?'

The sudden directness from a mild-mannered woman was unsettling, and Desturbes flinched. 'You simplify, but yes. Exactly so.'

Anna was silent for a moment. 'Colonel, Vincent has never mentioned any political views in his letters.'

'I know, madame,' said Desturbes, and then flushed faintly. 'But you still know his heart better than anyone.'

And yet how little that is, thought Anna. She could hardly confess that despite having known someone intimately for three of the last five years, she still felt excluded from the innermost reaches of his nature. Whatever truth lay at the heart of Vincent he kept it inviolable, in a sealed room. Did he ever open it to others, she wondered? Had Gisèle Richemont been given the key? Hurriedly, she closed down this line of thought and concentrated on the Frenchman's question.

As always with Vincent, there was conflicting evidence. He had certainly been scornfully dismissive of the Comintern diehards in 1939. Yet when the Soviet pact failed he had welcomed the comrades unquestioningly when they threw themselves at long last behind the partisan movement. She had known him both as a patriotic Frenchman and a passionate Czech. And while, on occasion, he spoke critically of the

Soviet Union, culturally and politically he had little sympathy or affection for Britain or America. Where, given all these factors, would his loyalties lie if an autocratic, nationalistic, charismatic figure such as de Gaulle called on him to choose?

She said flatly, 'I'm afraid I can't help you, Colonel.'

Desturbes sighed. 'Trust me, you are not helping him by remaining silent, Madame Galland.'

'I realize that, but still the honest answer to your question is that I don't know.'

Desturbes stood, clearly battening down anger. 'Very well. I'd be obliged if you would not mention my visit to your husband. May I at least have your word on that?'

Anna nodded, and the colonel gripped her hand.

'*Au revoir*, Madame Galland.'

Anna watched him march off down the street and wondered what he would put in his report to his masters, whoever they were.

When news of the liberation of Paris came at the end of August Anna held a small party for her New York friends. Twenty ill-assorted people stood in the large expanse of the Berghof drawing-room, which for the first time in two years had emerged from its dust-sheets. Most of the guests were friends and associates from Kircheners, but some were from the neighbourhood: the doormen and shop-keepers who had become friends. Anna had wanted to invite Julie Abrahams, but she had left her job at Antonio's and no one had a forwarding address.

'I expect Vincent will send for you soon: you must be so excited, Anna,' said Mavis Kirchener, clutching her glass in two hands.

'The City of Light has just risen against its occupiers and all you can think of is that Anna's excited at the thought of seeing her husband again,' growled Kurt. 'Get a sense of perspective, woman.'

'And not everywhere is free yet,' said Erich Liebowitz sadly. 'The Nazis are destroying Warsaw and everyone in it. Where are the Russians?'

'Playing Stalin's war games,' whispered Kurt, gesturing in the direction of Gurdinsky. 'I hear they're sunbathing on the banks of the Vistula.'

'Where will you live when the war is over?' said Mavis, taking Anna aside.

Anna realized that she had not allowed herself any thought about the future. 'I suppose,' she said, 'I suppose it will rather depend on Vincent. He was a diplomat and a journalist before the war, although it's difficult to imagine him going back to that now. As to where we'll live, I don't know; I don't think Vincent will want to live in America.' She realized as she said it how sad she would be to leave New York, her job, her friends and her quiet, independent life of the past two years.

Anna Jakob shook her head. A thin, round-eyed Jewish woman of thirty-five, she had escaped Leipzig hours ahead of the Gestapo and during her four years in America had had no news of her father, mother and three younger sisters. Now she pulled her crocheted cardigan around her.

'How can we go back? They say that many cities have been bombed to the ground. And everyone believes Russia will expect half of Europe as her reward. It's foolish, but I almost dread the peace, you know? Here, we can imagine the best, but when go back we shall see for ourselves who and what has disappeared, and that will be the true heartbreak.'

*

Anna slid the last of Astrid Delamain's letters back into its whispering, green-lined envelope and let it fall on to the bedspread.

She had known. She had known even that first autumn, after the war. Of course there were awkwardnesses, distances: one expected these after such a long separation. But Vincent's rooms in London and in Paris had held the sense of a space recently vacated, the imprint of a female body in the air. And yet somehow she had forced herself to ignore the physical evidence: the black hairpin under the dressing-table, the tiny mother-of-pearl button in the pile of the bedside rug, the tangle of long, glossy black hairs blocking the trap of the washbasin.

Anna had cleaned and tidied and asked no questions, and for a while she and Vincent had been close again, even though later, in London, in New York, in Rome, in Saint-Aubain-les-Eaux, she knew there had been others.

Of course, she had never confided in anyone and, even if she had, what would they have said? French women friends would have raised a plucked eyebrow and remarked that such things were normal. Strains and distances occur between most men and their wives. Forget it, my dear, it will mend itself, you'll see. Go shopping; take a lover for your self-esteem, for your sensual pleasure and, if you wish it, for revenge. Why not?

But she did nothing.

Now, briskly, like a nurse inflicting brief pain, she swept the cream letters into a pile, shuffled them into date order and read them through, from last to first.

And by the end of her reading she had discovered . . . what?

That only a year before his death Vincent had told Astrid Delamain he loved her so much he could no longer live without her; that he had decided he must free himself, (of *me,* thought Anna); that Astrid would do the same; that, sealing this pact, they had made love together in this very bed a month before his disappearance.

Some letters showed her how much Astrid Delamain admired Vincent's integrity, his political commitment, his intelligent mind and his tenderness. Others told how she thrilled to his touch when his hands slid over her breasts or when his fingers slipped down the cleft of her buttocks; they described how she shuddered with unimaginable pleasure when he touched his tongue to her clitoris.

And from the last one, the oldest letter of all, a single sheet, dated 1945, Anna learned that for many years her marriage with Vincent had been a lie and a sham, because Isabelle Delamain was his daughter.

She ran to the bathroom and vomited into the lavatory bowl. Afterwards she laid her forehead against the icy porcelain, panting.

Isabelle, beautiful, vapid Isabelle, was Vincent's child.

As baby Michael had been hers.

Michael who would have been born, *should* have been born in the fullness of his time, on the 29 September 1942. Michael who this autumn morning would have been twenty and waking now in his bedroom under the eaves, hearing the same birdsong. And who instead, because of her own weakness, existed nowhere in the world except in her mind.

At some point she must have crawled back to bed, for she awoke at seven, and the first thing she saw as she raised herself on to one elbow was the slim pile of green-lined envelopes.

She had never been a violent person. As a child, on the few occasions

Gustav had thought it necessary to beat her, she had not fought back but screamed hysterically, panicked not so much by the pain itself as by his distorted face and the hissing, grunting noises he made as he wielded the cane and the pleasure he could not hide when he administered punishment. Even then, she realized, her virtues had been useless ones: timidity, compliance and restraint.

But now? Now she wanted to fly over the fields and into Astrid Delamain's bedroom; she wanted to grab a hank of that dark, sinuous hair and twist it until it tore loose from her scalp; she wanted to score the still-beautiful face with her nails and plunge her fingers up to the knuckles into the sockets of those green-lined eyes. With a cry, Anna seized the pile of envelopes and threw it against the wall where it flew apart like a bird caught in a turbine.

Her last conscious thought as she fell exhausted on the bed was to will all clocks to stop. But when, eventually, she awoke again time had ticked on unconcerned. It was eight, according to the little bedside alarm, and in the darkness she stared stupidly at the luminous hands, wondering if it was morning or evening. Morning, she decided. Her mouth was parched and her forehead thudded with headache and her teeth felt sharp and brittle, as if she'd been grinding her jaws together.

Kneeling down she picked up the cream envelopes and with trembling hands tied the green ribbon around them.

Hal Keen had wanted to tell the truth about Vincent. Well, here it was; his hero was a liar, a cheat.

She took the tablecloth from the wardrobe and untied it and threw Astrid's letters in with the others. Let him discover it for himself – and then let him try to make this man fit with the hero, the *homme du peuple* he had admired. She held the two ends of the tablecloth and tied them in a knot, then stood, head bent.

Except that Vincent had not betrayed 'the people'; he had only betrayed *her*.

And why?

Because she was unworthy of him: a woman such as she – quiet, insecure, insubstantial – how could she ever have hoped to keep a man like Vincent to herself? It was unreasonable. Unrealistic. And now that she knew it, was she, out of spite, going to bring him down?

He had hidden things as best he could from her. Not perfectly, but he had tried. And now he was dead, and this small, human transgression was history, nothing more.

His memory deserved better of her. Slowly she untied the cloth, picked out the cream envelopes and slid them beneath notepaper in the drawer of her bedside table. With the cloth bundle open in front of her she then examined every one of the remaining piles of letters, but there was nothing there that could not be handed over to Mr Keen.

With the bundle in her arms she paused, barefoot on the landing, to listen and then glided down the stairs to the study. Climbing up to the shelf above the door, she took down the false-fronted box and emptied the contents of the bundle into it: the packets of letters filled it almost to the brim. She left it on the desk, where he would be sure to find it.

# Twenty-One

It was October 1944 before Anna and hundreds of other exiled wives were allowed passage back to England.

At the port controller's office in Southampton a letter was waiting for her. Vincent had been posted to France. It was unclear, he said, when he would return.

'In the meantime an English naval officer called Richard Griffin has offered to settle you in and look after you. Lieutenant Griffin will be waiting at Waterloo Station, under the clock, at three p.m.'

They had been apart for two years, yet this last small, unexpected delay was too much to bear. Miserably Anna sat in the rattling carriage, looking out at green countryside that seemed largely unchanged, except for the brick pillboxes on every hill. But as the train reached the outskirts of London, damage inflicted by the blitz was everywhere. She gazed in horror at the shored, blackened buildings sprouting weeds and buddleia, the gaping shells of homes, their patterned wallpaper bared to the sky.

'Pretty bad, ain't it?' said a young woman opposite her, rubbing a clean patch on the window. 'My nan's house isn't far from here. Poor old biddy refused to go down to the Anderson shelter – said it was too damp for her bones and if a bomb had her name on it then too bad. They found her under a table with the whole bloody house on top of her, pardon my language. Well, life goes on.' The young woman pushed back curly brown hair and looked Anna up and down. 'Where you from then?'

Anna tried to think of an answer. 'Well, Norway originally, but I lived in Paris until the Occupation.' It sounded feeble. Hastily, she went on, 'My husband is with the Resistance in France.'

'Oh yes?' said the girl, 'I was in the WRNS, and my fiancé's still in the Navy. We're getting married in September, all being well. I'm saving my clothes coupons. Actually, Baby's on the way – although shouldn't say it, should I? Still, could be worse. Oops, here we are, Vauxhall. Waterloo's next stop, if you didn't know. Cheerio, then.' The girl leaped from the train while it was still slowing into the station and was gone.

Anna reached out and pulled the door shut. Other people's existences seemed to have so much more momentum than her own, she thought. They made plans, alone or together, changed their lives to suit. The train clanked out of Vauxhall and rattled over points. The Gothic spires of Westminster swayed into view, still remarkably intact, bordered by a surprising greenness of trees. And then, minutes later, they were entering Waterloo Station and juddering to a halt at the buffers.

A passing soldier helped Anna manhandle her suitcase down from the luggage rack. 'Where you bound for, darlin'? Fancy a night out on the town tonight?'

'No, no, thank you. I'm meeting my husband.'

'Too bad,' said the soldier, taking in the slender figure in the dark navy suit, 'You look as though you could do with cheering up. Here, I'll carry this for you anyway.'

At the ticket barrier she insisted on taking the suitcase herself. 'No, really, I'm fine, thank you. I can manage now, really.'

The soldier winked. 'Well, my love, if it doesn't work out with the old man, I'm at the Hammersmith Palais tonight. Just ask for Ray Evans – I'll leave a note behind the bar.' He gave a mock salute and disappeared into the crowd.

Above the milling heads Anna saw the great four-faced clock. She was half an hour late. She began to push her way against the tide of people heading for the trains, ignoring the muffled curses as her suitcase banged against hurrying travellers. When she reached the clearing of the meeting-space under the clock Richard Griffin was unmistakable – a tall, lean figure of about thirty, in the dark-blue uniform of a naval lieutenant. As he saw her coming towards him he swept off his white-topped cap and smiled handsomely.

'Mrs Galland, I presume. Delighted to meet you. Give me that heavy case. How was your journey? Come on, this way. I'll take you straight to the flat, shall I? Do you know London at all? Here, borrow my umbrella.'

Anna shook her head, dazed by the fusillade of questions and the drawling English accent. They crossed the rain-slicked station forecourt and joined the queue. 'South Kensington,' said Richard Griffin as a bus drew up. 'That's us. Your husband wangled a pretty good billet. Landlady's a bit of a character, though.'

Anna sat near the window. As they trundled through the streets Lieutenant Griffin leaned closer, pointing out the sights. Once, when she turned to say something, she caught him looking at her curiously. He gave a brief half-smile and resumed his commentary.

By the time they got off the bus the rain had stopped, but it was dark and there were no street lights. Anna walked beside Griffin, trying to adjust her steps to his pace. After ten minutes they turned into a small square of dingy, white-pillared houses and climbed a set of crooked steps to the front door. Griffin rang the bell, and Anna heard it sound in the depths of the house. There was a long silence then the door was flung open.

A tall, white-haired woman stood in the gloom, a cigarette pinched between two long, crooked fingers.

'Who's there?'

'Richard Griffin, ma'am, and Vincent Galland's wife. She arrived from America today.'

There was a silence. 'His wife?'

Griffin pushed Anna forward, and spoke loudly, 'Yes, Mrs Lepworth, Mrs Anna Galland, *Vincent's wife*.'

The cigarette end glowed red in the dark. 'Well, don't stand there letting all the cold air in. Come this way. What did you say her name was, Richard?'

Richard Griffin pulled a face behind the old woman's back but hurriedly suppressed it as a disembodied voice called back down the hall, 'Try not to be childish, Richard, there's a dear. It's high time you were out of your social and emotional short trousers. Show Anna to Vincent's flat and then pop by the kitchen and see me.'

Richard Griffin grunted softly under his breath. 'She wants her bottle of NAAFI scotch. A dram and a chat for Mrs Gwendoline Lepworth. Her husband was killed in the Civil War in Spain. She's had quite a life herself, but she doesn't get much opportunity to gossip these days, poor old thing. Anyway, here you are.' He stopped outside a doorway and took the key Anna handed him. '*Chez* Galland in all its glory. Not much really, despite its central location, I think old Gwen has a hard time making ends meet. Are you hungry?' he went on, as he showed her through into a dimly lit room. 'Vincent doesn't keep much food here. I thought we might go out to eat this evening, if that's all right with you.'

'That's fine, Lieutenant Griffin.'

'Oh, Richard, please.'

'Richard,' she said. 'I'll unpack and change.' She took the suitcase from him.

'Of course, take your time. Here, let me see to the blackout.' He fiddled with a large black blind. 'The bathroom's at the end of the corridor there. I'm afraid there probably won't be any hot water until this evening. Now, where's . . . ah.' He switched on the light.

Anna looked around her. Under the dim bulb she could see that the room was small and cheaply furnished but appeared neat and tidy.

'Here we are. Now you settle in while I go and see the old girl,' said Richard. 'Come and knock on her door when you're ready. Last one on the right in the main hall.' He patted the pocket of his naval greatcoat, and Anna saw she shape of a bottle. 'Give us quarter of an hour, eh? Then I'll need rescuing from her stories of London in the thirties, when gels were gels and every man was handsome and debonair. Sometimes I wish I hadn't been brought up to be so confoundedly polite.' He grinned and disappeared.

When he had gone Anna took a deep breath, but the room held no smell of cologne, in fact no trace at all of Vincent's recent presence. She looked at the sagging expanse of the double bed and after a moment's hesitation unfastened the suitcase and took piles of clothes over to the wardrobe and the chest of drawers, wondering if there would be enough space, but neither contained more than a few items of clothing. An alarm clock and telephone sat on a table at the side of the bed nearest the window. Anna arranged her books and photographs on the table at the other side, feeling like an intruder.

When everything was unpacked she slid the empty suitcase under the bed and stood. In the bathroom at the end of the corridor she did her best to wash off the grime of the journey with a sliver of foul-smelling soap. Her face in the spotted mirror looked pale and her hair was tangled and damp. She brushed it smooth, and the normality of the everyday gesture relaxed her.

The door of Vincent's room was warped, and it took all her strength to hold it shut while she turned the key. Timidly, she went down the hall and knocked at the last door on the right, heard Griffin's voice say, 'Don't worry, Gwen, I'll get it. Ah, good, yes, it's Anna.'

The landlady's flat smelt of cats and cigarettes, and Anna followed Richard down the passageway to a room lit with a strange orange glow. She stood on the threshold, taking in the surroundings. She was about to enter a large silk tent. Vast patterned hangings lined the walls; rugs and cushions covered the floor and the air was thick and heavy with tobacco and a sweet perfume, which appeared to be coming from a dish of smouldering pastilles in the corner.

'Oh,' said Anna, walking slowly forward, 'I've never seen a room like this.'

'Good,' came a dry voice from the other side of the room. 'When there's no one else to please there's not much point in over-conventional surroundings, is there? Well, Griffin here is dying to be off, so I'll see you later Mrs Galland.'

'Anna.'

'Anna.'

To her relief the restaurant was crowded. An elderly waiter showed them to a table and asked them what they would like to eat. 'The speciality of the day *was* venison, but I'm afraid it's off now.'

'What's good?' asked Griffin.

The waiter tucked his tray under his arm. 'Oh, well, I couldn't tell you that, sir, but we've got soup, rabbit, meatloaf, fish pie or cold meat salad.' He licked the end of a pencil, looking bored.

'I'll have the soup and the rabbit, please. Anna?'

'Just salad, please.'

'Beer?'

'No, no thank you.'

Richard Griffin said, 'I warn you, Anna, what they call wine won't be worth drinking.'

'Then I'll just have iced water, thank you.'

Griffin laughed. 'I can tell you've been in the States, my dear. Waiter? Ah, yes, thank you. A glass of your best tap water for the lady here. Food's diabolical everywhere at the moment, I'm afraid,' he said. 'Rationing is dire and some things are impossible to find.' He looked at a noisy table of GIs on the far side of the room. 'Unless you're American, of course.'

Anna, who had been enjoying the sound of the American voices, turned back to her companion. 'Have you been in London long, Richard?' she asked.

'Oh, quite a while. My war's been largely office-based, I'm afraid. Boring old desk jockey. Very dull, I don't get out much at all. But, since I speak the language, I've been working alongside your husband and his Free French colleagues, helping them out on this and that, keeping a watching brief, you know.'

He gave a brief smile, and she sensed he was being deliberately evasive. Perhaps his work was something secret. Certainly his eyes, watching her closely, were intelligent and enquiring. Just as she was about to ask him exactly what it was he did, the waiter returned with a bowl of brown soup, a bottle of beer and a tumbler of cloudy water. Making a face, Griffin chinked the glasses together. 'Cheers.'

'Cheers.'

She sipped the tepid water and watched him attack his soup with gusto.

'Richard, do you know when Vincent will be back?'

''Fraid not. Actually, despite what you might have heard, things haven't been that easy in Paris.' He lowered his voice so that it carried only across the width of the table. 'In August it was touch and go what would happen first, whether the Germans would blow up the city or the communists would try to stage an armed uprising before the Allied armies and the Free French arrived.'

'And what was Vincent doing?'

Lieutenant Griffin's spoonful of brown soup halted half-way to his mouth, and he looked at her with a strange, amused expression. 'Oh, picking his own way through the chaos, I suppose, as usual.'

Three weeks dragged past. Although she was now only a few hundred miles away from Vincent instead of thousands, it had made very little difference. Indeed, with no work to do, she was lonelier than she had been in the early days of New York. She had done her best with the flat, but for all its elegant proportions it was resolutely inhospitable, and she could do nothing about the threadbare carpets, the cracked basin or the long greenish stains under the taps.

One day, for something to do, she gathered Vincent's few clothes from the damp-smelling chest of drawers and washed them by hand in the sink, hanging them to dry on the old wooden clothes horse she found in the cupboard under the stairs. She was putting it back when a door at the end of the hall opened and Gwendoline Lepworth leaned unsteadily against the jamb.

'That you, *chérie?*' she called, slurring the words together. 'How come you don't pop in and talk French with your old *tante* Gwen these days? Izzat naughty Vincent keeping you all to himself?'

Anna stepped forward into the light. 'Vincent isn't here, Mrs Lepworth. He's still in France.'

Gwendoline put one hand to her dishevelled white hair. '*Is he?* Is he really, dear? Poor lamb. Now, you're his sister, aren't you?'

'No, Mrs Lepworth, I'm Anna Galland, Vincent's wife.'

There was a pause. 'Are you really? Well. Trick of the light. Don't mind me.' With one hand Gwendoline Lepworth politely suppressed a belch and with the other she waved a vague farewell. 'Byee. Pop in for a chat whenever you're feeling lonely, dear, and let me know the instant the brave boy's back.'

The capital was full of servicemen on leave: sailors with blank cap bands, soldiers in thick khaki, airmen in the light-blue jackets of the Royal Air Force, sailors in navy and white.

Anna wondered if Vincent wore a uniform when he was in London and found it hard to imagine. In fact she was finding it impossible to summon up his face, and the soft-focus photograph that she kept on her bedside table was now as unreal as one of the Arthurian knights in her childhood books.

One night, lonely and bored, she summoned up her courage and knocked on Gwendoline Lepworth's door.

The woman stood on the threshold, clutching a small Pekinese. She was wearing a long knitted cardigan and velvet skirt, with strings of beads in profusion over a silk blouse. Despite the white hair, she was, Anna decided, not as old as she had first thought, and her brown eyes were disconcertingly sharp.

She stood aside and nodded to Anna to enter. 'I thought you'd moved out. You creep in and out like a mouse. Would you like a splash? Of Scotch, dear,' she said patiently, seeing Anna's frown. 'You do drink, don't you?'

'Yes,' said Anna and watched the woman shuffle stiffly across the room to a glass-fronted cocktail cabinet, where she tucked the dog under one arm and slopped spirit into a glass and handed it to Anna. Carefully, she seated herself in her high-backed chair and raised the half-full tumbler at her elbow.

'Mud in your eye. So, tell me, how are you finding London?'

'Rather dark and dreary.'

'Your husband grew quite fond of the place but was always hankering to get back to Paris.' Gwendoline watched Anna sip minutely at her whisky. Suddenly she said, 'You were young when you married, I suppose. Well, of course you were; you're hardly ancient now.'

'I was nineteen.'

Gwendoline lounged back against red chenille cushions. 'I met Nigel Lepworth when I was eighteen, but I wouldn't marry him – Lord, no,' she laughed wickedly. 'Kept him dangling for five years after he came back from the war.'

Anna swallowed, shuddering involuntarily as the spirit burned the back of her throat. 'Why?'

'Because he was a gorgeous bully-boy, my dear, with an eye for the ladies. Irresistible, but he'd have walked all over me if he could. I wanted to find out what I was made of before I took the plunge.'

Anna put down her glass. 'And what were you made of?'

Gwendoline Lepworth laughed, a loud, husky guffaw. 'Strong stuff, as it turned out. Nigel got a good deal more than he bargained for.' She raised heavily pencilled eyebrows. 'And he gave me no trouble at all, the lamb. We were happy as babes.'

There was a silence, during which Anna looked around the room with its hangings and low divan and silk-covered cushions.

Gwendoline Lepworth smiled. 'You married quite a man, too, I think, didn't you, dear? Did you make a good choice? Happy together?'

Surprised, Anna heard herself say, 'In the last four years we've spent more time apart than together. And I didn't choose him. He chose me. I haven't the slightest idea why.'

'I see.'

Gwendoline Lepworth looked pityingly at the younger woman. 'You know, in my experience, men like your husband are devastatingly attractive and almost impossible to fathom. Sphinxes are an open book by comparison. The Vincents of this world have a mirror instead of a heart, a fact their lovers rarely understand – and so they suffer.'

Anna put her glass down. Gwendoline shook her head and the chains of beads chinked together. 'True, my love, even if you don't want to hear it.'

'But surely some men are worth suffering for?' said Anna. 'If what they do is important and demands so much of them?'

The older woman tilted her head. 'Perhaps. A few. But what if they don't understand the worth of the offering?'

'It doesn't matter.'

'Not if you value yourself so cheaply.'

An angry blush spread across Anna's face and neck. She rose to her feet and then stood, clasping the glass and twisting it in her hands.

'I'm sorry, I have to go now.'

Gwendoline picked up a newspaper and pen from the table beside her, 'And *I* have a crossword to finish. More than forty minutes today – I'm slipping. Age, I suppose. Let yourself out, will you, dear, but do come by again if you're at a loose end. Oh, and when you see him, tell that young Griffin that my stocks of single malt are getting alarmingly low.'

Richard Griffin called to see both women a few days later and, finding Anna huddled alone in her room, invited her out to dinner. In a large West End restaurant they danced on a tiny dance floor under a twinkling mirror ball.

Griffin said into her ear, 'Are you enjoying yourself, Anna? You don't have to say yes; I know the music's ropey. Most of these chaps are more at home playing marches than jazz.' He glanced around the crowded room. 'Ah well, one must enjoy it while one can. And I'm afraid I shan't be around for much longer. I've got my posting. I leave in two days' time.'

'Where are you going?'

'Oh, not far, but out of town for a while.'

Anna leaned back to look into his face. 'I thought it would be over by now.'

'The Germans are fighting all the way back to Berlin.' The music stopped and he led her back to the table. 'Will you be all right here in London on your own? I feel bad about leaving you – having promised Vincent, and all that.'

'Don't worry about me, I'll be just fine.'

It was nine o' clock on a chill January night when Anna finally heard a key turn in the lock. Standing at the end of the corridor, she saw framed in the doorway a man in a greatcoat, his hat sloped over his eyes, a battered suitcase in his hand.

'*Vincent!*'

She flung her arms around him.

'Hello, Anna.'

His voice was flat with weariness; even as he said the words he stifled a yawn.

'Ah, sorry, I've been travelling for thirty-six hours. The trains are in chaos.'

'Would you like a drink? I've got some Scotch. Courtesy of Richard Griffin.'

'Yes. God, I'm tired.' He took his coat off, dropped into one of the big chintz-covered armchairs, leaned his head back and closed his eyes. When she returned with the glass a few minutes later he was asleep. Anna looked around her, wondering whether to wake him and decided against it. Eventually, she settled herself into the armchair facing him, curled her legs up under her and watched him.

He was, despite the tiredness imprinted on his face, in good health, she thought, and had been looking after himself. His hair was neatly cut, his nails pink and trimmed, his face only lightly stubbled. She wondered when he would wake.

But at midnight he was still sleeping soundly, and she decided to go to bed. It was chilly in the flat, and she took one of the blankets from the bed and gently tucked it around Vincent's shoulders. His coat was still in the hall, where he had dropped it, and she carried it through to the bedroom and hung it on the hook behind the door. As she smoothed the lapels, a long black hair detached itself from the cloth and curled around her wrist. She pulled it taut and then with a slight shudder let it fall into the wastepaper bin.

When in the small hours of the morning Vincent came to bed she was asleep, and he must have taken pains not to wake her because in the morning she only knew he had been there when she found the sheets turned back on his side of the bed and the impression of his head on the pillow.

# Twenty-Two

Three days after the dinner party with the Delamains and the discovery of the letters the telephone rang at La Verrerie.

'Anna. Bertrand. Look, there's something important that I need to discuss with you, alone. Could you come over for a drink early this evening, say six?'

'What is it?'

'Not over the phone.'

Why was he being so mysterious? Would Astrid be there? she wondered. Her mind racing through possibilities, Anna said slowly, 'Well, I'm not sure I . . .'

His voice was loud, overbearing. 'It's imperative, Anna. You must come.'

'Then I'll be there, at six,' she said.

Slowly she replaced the receiver and walked back into the kitchen. Everything was calm and ordered and in its usual place: copper pans hung in rows; bunches of rosemary and thyme scented the air. A wooden chopping board lay on the table, worn concave over the years. Yet every object suddenly had an air of unreality about it, as if they had been assembled and placed there to dress a theatre set.

At five thirty Anna set out to walk to the Delamains'. The sun was low, slanting across the lane through trunks of beech and pine, so that she walked through a dazzling loom of orange light and indigo shadow.

The house was set back from the road. It was twice the size of the La Verrerie, although not as pretty, its stuccoed walls painted a daunting shade of ochre and its garden nothing more than a dull sweep of turf dotted with pieces of rusting iron sculpture that had been an enthusiasm of Astrid's some years before. The dacha, Bertrand called it: his country retreat.

There was a long delay after she rang the bell, and Anna was just beginning to wonder if the invitation had been a ploy after all and whether Bertrand was about to appear with a towel around his waist and a drink in his hand, his lips archly puckered for a welcome kiss, when to her relief he opened the door fully clothed, wearing a knitted cardigan and brown cord trousers.

'What have you done to your hair?' he asked as he kissed her more or less conventionally on the cheeks.

She had, deliberately, drawn it back from her face into a severe chignon.

'I felt like a change.'

'Hmm. Not sure it suits you, really. I prefer your hair loose. More feminine. More attractive.'

She followed him down the passage that led to the back of the house. He was, she thought, for sixty, an undeniably vigorous figure. From the back he could pass for a rugby player or a miner: a big square frame, with thin arms and legs stuck on at each corner of the torso like legs on a table.

They emerged into the salon, and Bertrand waved her towards the low armchair that stood to one side of the fireplace.

'Scotch?'

She nodded.

Bertrand brought the drink over to her, standing too close, his eyes staring into hers from under their grey eyebrow quiffs. She shrank back, but he made no attempt to touch her and after a few seconds he turned and settled himself in a green leather chair. For a long moment he scrutinized her in silence, looking, she thought, like a massive toad on a lily pad.

Brusquely, he said, 'Anna, my dear, I shall come straight to the point. What I'm about to say may shock you, but I assure you I'm telling you it for your own sake and for Vincent's.'

'Vincent's?' She took a deeper gulp of whisky.

'Yes. Very much so.' He commenced the familiar, lengthy process of choosing a cigar from the box at his elbow, then proceeded to cut and light it. Finally, when it was glowing, he spoke looking at the tip and not at her.

'You must understand something, Anna. For us in the Party Vincent was a powerful symbol – the modern-day Resistance fighter. When he joined the cause he came with that reputation ready-made: he had always been a hero. And, as we all know, a hero's reputation can endure and inspire, even after death. Provided always', he tapped a section of ash into the tray, 'that it is protected.'

Anna said nothing. It was almost dark outside now, and she could see their reflections in the glass of the window. Bertrand said her name, and she realized that he had spoken and that she hadn't heard him.

He frowned.

'I said that for some time now Astrid and I have been worried about you.'

'Why?'

'We are concerned that your . . . emotional health . . . is in rather a fragile state.' The brown liquid eyes bulged slightly. 'I don't mean that you need psychiatric help necessarily, but that you are finding life without Vincent . . . exceptionally difficult, and that consequently your judgement is becoming clouded.'

'Clouded?' Now she looked up, genuinely puzzled.

'I'm afraid so. Look, Anna, everyone understands that Vincent was a very powerful personality and you miss his support and his strength. We all do. But it is necessary to take responsibility and to . . .' He said abruptly, 'Anna, to put it bluntly, you're in danger of destroying Vincent's entire reputation.'

'In danger?' It was said on Hal's rising inflection.

Bertrand leaned forward. 'This young man we met at your house on Saturday . . . the man who is asking all these questions about Vincent and the past . . . the man you have rather naïvely taken at face value.'

'You mean *Hal?*'

For a moment Bertrand's busy hands stopped what they were doing and his eyes sharpened their focus on her.

'Perhaps,' he said, mysteriously.

Anna was suddenly aware that Bertrand's winged chair was a good six inches higher than her own and sensed this positioning was not accidental. She straightened her back and took a mouthful of malt. It made her fingertips tingle. Blinking, she said, 'I'm sorry, Bertrand, I don't quite understand. What exactly do you mean, "perhaps"?'

The grey quiffs twitched irritation at being questioned. 'I mean, Anna, that Hal Keen may not be who he seems.'

She knew from his portentous tone that she was meant to be

impressed but said nothing, merely sat still, rolling the cut-glass tumbler between her palms.

Bertrand continued. 'For a start, according to his passport he is James Carter.'

Now he *had* surprised her.

'His *passport*? How do you know what's in his passport, Bertrand?'

He shrugged, obviously enjoying himself.

'Oh, it's not that difficult if you know who to ask.' He leaned forward, jerking the cigar at her. 'The real question is, what do *you* know about him, Anna?'

'I know that he's a writer; that Vincent was his boyhood hero; that he's been commissioned to write a book.'

'By whom?'

'Henson's.' Then she remembered something else. 'Oh, yes, and I know he was born in New York City on 17 April – he told us that, didn't he?'

Bertrand frowned and reached across to a folder lying on a table beside him. He opened it and ran a thick knobbed forefinger down the first page.

'Oh dear. Not true, I'm afraid. James Carter was actually born in Boston, on 20 June 1938.'

Anna blinked stupidly. 'No, that's not right. No. He definitely told me New York and 17 April. I'm certain.'

The toad eyes blinked. 'Why do you remember the date?'

She could not tell him that 17 April meant sunshine after rain in the gardens of the Palais Royal, with the trees misted with green and an American voice saying, '*Hi, kid*.'

'No particular reason,' she said and heard the odd note in her voice.

Bertrand sniffed, considered the lit end of his cigar.

'Perhaps.'

He spoke as an indulgent adult waiting for a child to catch up, but in his expression there was something colder, more deliberate.

And suddenly she knew that Bertrand had planned everything: the sudden kiss on the night of the dinner, the low chair this evening, the trailing perhapses, were all designed to unsettle and control her. And yet, above the toad's eyes, his forehead was glistening; as she watched, a line of sweat ran down the side of his face.

'Where's Astrid?' she said suddenly.

Bertrand croaked in surprise. 'Astrid? We're not talking about Astrid, Anna, we're talking about Hal Keen and you and Vincent.'

'Is she here?'

'No.'

'When will she be back?'

Bertrand's face was dark as old blood. 'Anna, be quiet. Now, tell me this . . .'

She stood. 'Bertrand, I've told you what I know, and now I'd like to go.'

'Sit down. I haven't finished.'

'Don't give me orders,' she snapped and was amazed at herself.

For a second his face was comical with surprise, then he controlled himself and said almost cajolingly, 'Anna, Anna, my dear girl, calm down, please. I'm sorry if I was sharp with you. But there *is* something you should be aware of. Please. Sit down.'

She paused. Then she walked over to the chair and sat down again, pulling the hem of her skirt down over her knees.

'Very well. I'm listening.'

'Good.'

There was another long pause as Bertrand regained control of the situation. Then he said, 'I have to tell you that Mr James Alan Carter is in all probability an agent of the American Central Intelligence Agency.'

Anna clapped her hands over her mouth, but she wasn't quick enough to stop the laugh. It pealed out of her until she was spluttering. As her shoulders shook, ribbons of hair escaped the clasp of the chignon and fell either side of her face.

'*Bertrand*! Don't be *ridiculous*. I'm *nobody*. Why would anyone spy on *me*? That's just nonsense.'

Bertrand surged out of his chair. 'Don't you dare talk to me like that, you stupid woman. Listen to me. Your late husband was an internationally respected communist – a great rarity. Don't you realize how much the West would like to discredit his memory? Can't you *see* how serious this is?'

She laughed, hysterically, and he took two steps towards her and slapped her across the face.

Anna rubbed her smarting cheek and stared at him open-mouthed.

Was he right? Was Hal Keen a spy? The conversations of the past two weeks raced through her mind. She had said too much, revealed too much. The letters. She had almost given him Astrid's letters. What if he searched and found them? She would have betrayed Vincent all over again.

Wide-eyed, she stood.

'I'm going home.'

Bertrand gripped the back of his chair, his eyes bulging. With an effort, he controlled himself. 'Anna, please. I apologize. I shouldn't have done that. It was unforgivable. It's just that we're worried, I'm concerned . . . Look, I'll drive you back.'

'I prefer to walk, thank you.'

His voice was weary, almost toneless. 'Anna, it's cold and it's almost dark. Let me drive you home.'

Bertrand hunched over the wheel, scowling into the gathering gloom. When they arrived at La Verrerie he reached across her and swung the door open. Anna smelt stale cigar smoke on his breath as his hand reached for hers.

'Anna, I'm sorry about this evening, but we must discuss this again,' he said. 'I'll call you tomorrow. Will you be in?'

She pulled her hand away and climbed out of the car. 'Perhaps,' she said over her shoulder and then walked with almost perfect composure up to the door.

Behind her Bertrand reversed the car savagely and an accelerating departure sent gravel spitting over the steps. Before she could find her keys the front door opened.

Hal Keen watched Bertrand's car disappear around the bend of the lane.

'Is there a problem?' Innocent blue eyes held hers.

'No.' She brushed past him and steadied herself against the hall table, placing her gloves and bag by the telephone. The house was cold, the fire unlit. She shivered.

'I shall lie down for a while. Don't wait for me at supper.'

Aware of the American's gaze, she gripped the banister rail and climbed the stairs.

In the little cabinet drawer in her bedroom were twenty cream envelopes.

Anna knelt in front of the empty hearth. Carefully she drew out the last letter and tore it into small green-lined squares. Then she lit a match and watched the hundreds of little flakes flare, blacken and curl and float weightlessly up the chimney. She replaced the others in the drawer and lay down fully clothed on the bed.

It was just after dawn, and there was no sound from the American's room when Anna let herself quietly out of the house, and walked down the lane in the direction of the river. The countryside was shrouded in mist – great muslin swathes hung above the fields and the hedgerows smelt of rotting leaves and damp earth. She followed the path down to a narrow gravel beach at the river's edge, overhung by yellowing willows. Reeds and grasses rustled as a breeze rose and began to disperse the mist.

Seized by a sudden impulse, she walked out on the old wooden fishing jetty, where the river eddied and whirled around blackened, slimy timbers. Sitting on the damp decking, her knees hunched up against her chest, she thought about Hal Keen who was not what he seemed and Bertrand Delamain who was. And about Vincent and Astrid. Astrid, who was the mother of Isabelle, who had been Vincent's lover at the end of the war and again at Saint-Aubain-les-Eaux, who had passed her lover's child off as her husband's.

She was crying now, the tears running down her face and disappearing into the weave of her grey wool jacket.

All those years, and now even her memory of Vincent was vanishing on the air like the lifting mist. Nothing was certain, nothing known. Anything could happen.

Rocks dissolved, ghosts were real.

*Harry.*

The old reel of memories resumed its queasy, flickering sequence: the gardens of the Palais Royal, a thumb under her chin tilting it up to the light, a hotel room in Lisbon, music playing, cigarette smoke, vanilla and carnations.

She lifted her head and gazed across the grey swirling water of the river.

Rocks dissolved, ghosts were real.

L'Heure Bleue: a gift from a stranger who, of all the perfumes in the world, had somehow guessed it was her favourite. A stranger who smoked the same cigarettes as Harry Quinn and whose name was so beguilingly similar. A well-informed stranger who had told her his birthday was . . .

On the far side of the river something moved. Startled, a black, long-necked bird rose from the water and flapped effortfully up into the sky. Anna watched it until it was a crooked grey hyphen above the bare treetops.

On the far bank everything was suddenly still.

And then she knew.

He was there.

He had never left.

She had thought herself isolated and alone, and yet all the time he had been there, watching, across all the intervening years, keeping his distance.

Restraint beyond reason.

*Hi, kid.*

Across the fields to the river came the sound of a church bell striking. She stood, conscious of her chilled feet and hands and turned her back on the water. Then she walked, hurried and finally ran back up the path towards the house.

# Twenty-Three

The tenth arrondissement of Paris had always been a place of transit. Perhaps it was because of the two great railway stations that crouched on its summit and the web of tracks that spread out from them, heading north and east. As if its residents had also moved on, the streets were lined with dingy hotels and insalubrious bars, lifeless shops and abandoned offices. Only the covered market, like a prison behind its black railings, hinted at the hidden community of the faubourg Saint-Denis.

Anna had made terse excuses to Hal Keen and travelled to Paris by train. Now she emerged from the Métro at the Gare du Nord and walked down the street, counting. The number she was looking for was above an old stone archway. The doors were tall and heavy, with peeling green paint and the marks of many hands. She pressed the buzzer and the postern door swung inwards. She stepped over the threshold into a dark courtyard. The tenements leaned over on either side, washing hung from lines. A faded notice, which looked as if it had been there since the pre-Revolutionary days, forbade her to trot horses through the passageway.

She walked over the greasy cobbles, under a second arch and into a second courtyard and then into a third. It was dark and quiet: no children playing, no birds, no flowers, just smells of cabbage and drains and four numbered stairways, spiralling up into the buildings at each corner. And in the second one, on the first floor, was a door, with the name Guillot printed on a grimy card.

Her timid knock reverberated up and down the staircase.

At first there was no sound from within the apartment, but then there was a shuffling sound and a soft click. For a second she caught sight of a glint behind the spyhole in the door. After a moment, a deep, hoarse voice said quietly, '*Qui est-ce?*'

Anna took a breath and said, barely loud enough to be heard, '*C'est Anaïs. Tu me reconnais peut-être, Léon?*'

He was older, much older. The broad shoulders were lower and rounder, the hair and beard grey, and he walked with a pronounced limp, resting his weight on a stick. Only the brown eyes, now magnified behind glasses, were bright and lustrous.

Léon held out his free arm and pulled her into a bear hug. His sweater smelt of tobacco and garlic. 'Anaïs. Good God. It *is* you. Christ. Let me look at you.' He pulled her down a passageway into a small sitting-room full of birdsong and spun her around to face the light. 'Christ. Anaïs.'

'It's Anna. And you?'

He laughed, and when he replied she realized that the accent she had always failed to place was Breton.

'Jean-Yves. But maybe it's too late for us to change our names now, *hein*? Sit, sit, Anaïs. Coffee? Something stronger?'

'Is anything stronger than your coffee?'

'Nothing I know of.'

'Coffee then, please.'

He moved around the small kitchen like an acrobat, leaning at odd angles to rest his right leg.

'Were you wounded?' she asked.

He picked up the stick and brought it down with a resounding thwack against his lame leg. She winced and then realized that the sound was hollow like a tambour.

'Blown up,' he said, beaming, 'in a marshalling yard near Lyons, early in '44. Explosives were never my strong point.' He carried a battered blue enamel coffee-pot across to the table and lowered himself nimbly on to the chair. 'I was sorry to hear about . . . Vincent.'

Anna held the cup inches away from her mouth. 'Did you ever see him, after the war?'

The big man nodded. 'At first, but not after Hungary. I was at the Arc de Triomphe the year the Russian tanks were in the streets of Budapest. He was standing next to Delamain, and they both gave the clenched fist. After that, well . . .' he grimaced, 'well, it was time to go our different ways, I guess. He had his views and I had mine.'

As he said it he hauled himself to his feet, took a battered tin from the mantelpiece and limped over to the window to feed a pinch of seed to the cageful of canaries. No, she thought, after Hungary Léon and

Vincent would not have found it easy to remain friends, trading on worn-out comradely memories.

Anna straightened her shoulders. 'I came because I need some advice, Léon.'

He put down the cup with a thud, spilling coffee on the stained table.

'Advice? From me? *Ma petite,* I'm flattered, but it's been twenty years. More.'

'I know, but . . . can I just tell you, and then if you think I'm mad or a fool you can say so and I'll go away?'

Léon stared solemnly at her through the magnifying lenses. 'You weren't one to make a fuss about nothing, as I remember. And,' he glanced around the brown-walled room, 'as you can see, life is pretty dull compared with before. *Rasant.* Enough to make a big guy crazy.'

He pointed to a photograph on the mantelpiece. A black-haired woman with dark lipstick and close-set eyes. 'Do you remember Rachel? Codename "Léa"? We married after the war. Litzi was dead, died in Auschwitz a few months before the liberation. Anyway, Rachel and I got hitched and we ran the bar together. She put up with a lot: for a long time I wasn't very cheerful company, I guess. In the end she ran off with a garage mechanic from Courbevoie. Now our nineteen-year-old daughter looks in once a month and complains I'm letting myself go.'

He ran his big paws through his hair. 'Anyway, I'm talking too much. It's lack of practice. Sure, Anaïs. Ask away. I'm listening, for what it's worth.'

She took a breath.

'Léon, I think I'm being watched. Spied upon.'

'Watched? By whom? Why? You should go to the police.'

Predictably, even after all these years it was a policeman's response; perhaps the whole visit had been a bad idea . . .

'No. They wouldn't take it seriously. It's no more than a rag-bag of stuff. Just intuition, really.'

'I never underestimated intuition,' said Léon slowly. 'OK, *ma petite,* tell me everything.' He reached for a Gitane. 'And don't skimp the detail.'

It took quite a while to cover everything or, rather, those things she chose to tell Léon. He watched her intently as she spoke, inhaling smoke slowly and deeply and then releasing it in a silent sigh. When she came to a halt he raised his eyebrows.

'And . . . ?'

'That's it.'

He grunted, then glanced at his watch and fumbled for the cane. 'All right, come on.'

'Come on where?'

'Out. I'm hungry. *Sauté de veau* on Thursdays. Hurry up or we'll be late.' He was holding the door open and wagging his stick to urge her through.

'But I wanted to talk.'

'Over lunch. Out.'

Chez Armande was a bistro down a side street two blocks away. The elderly couple who ran it welcomed Léon and seated him at what was obviously his accustomed table. They greeted Anna smilingly and winked at Léon as they laid an extra place.

Anna sipped at a glass of red wine and waited for him to speak. But Léon was enjoying himself, and the banter with the proprietors went on throughout the meal of fatty veal, potatoes and salad.

When the cheese arrived he sat back in his chair and clasped his hands over his belly.

'Well?' he said.

'Well what?'

He looked her in the eye. 'You tell me the rest, girl. Or you go back to Saint-Aubain-les-Eaux and we call it quits.'

She was embarrassed. She thought she had covered her traces intelligently enough. Blushing, she stammered, 'What do you mean, "the rest"?'

Léon leaned over and speared a wedge of Roquefort. 'Who you wore L'Heure Bleue for. Who your lover was in Paris that summer in 1940. Why that old warhorse Delamain thinks he can put you under pressure.'

She cross-hatched a morsel of Camembert rind with her knife, trying to think quickly. When, after a long time, no clever plan came to mind she sighed and told him everything.

By the time she had finished they had paid the bill, walked through the streets and were sitting on a bench on the concourse of the Gare de l'Est.

Léon shook his head. 'My God, Anaïs, still waters, eh? I remember you so clearly that spring. You were like a young nun, on your two knees gazing up at Saint Vincent up on his martyr's pedestal.' He reached across the table and clasped her hand briefly. 'Welcome to the human race, *ma petite*. Now, let's think about who could be watching you. You say nobody knew about you and this Quinn guy at the time?'

'Vincent knew. Or he guessed. After Lisbon.'

'And Keen seems to know far too much?'

'Everything. It's uncanny.'

Léon lit a cigarette, stuck it in his mouth and leaned forward, resting his forearms on his knees and staring at the grimy table.

'OK, I think we need to ask a few people a few questions.'

Anna felt a jolt of panic.

Léon grinned. 'Don't worry. These are old friends. Some in high places, some in low. None of them will blab. Can you give me a week?'

She nodded.

'And in the meantime you see what you can find out about your young mystery man. Put him under a bit of scrutiny for a change. Without alerting him, of course.'

'Oh, but what if I . . . ?'

'You won't. You can do this. Relax, Anaïs. You were right to come.' He stood and took her arm in his, 'Now, walk me back home and on the way you can tell me how you're going to explain away today's little disappearance to the watchful Mr Keen.'

It was surprisingly easy to lie, she discovered.

Her sister-in-law had been taken ill, she said. She had paid a visit to rue Jacob and had discovered the poor woman suffering from a bad bout of tonsillitis. Mademoiselle Galland lived alone and Anna had done some shopping and cleaned the place up a little. She had promised to return in a few days.

Anna had expected spying to be more repugnant than lying, but when, a few days later, she had a chance to look around Hal Keen's bedroom at La Verrerie she found she had very few scruples left. As she had expected, his door was locked. From her pocket she took the old chatelaine's key ring, selected one and turned the lock.

The air inside the room smelt faintly of aftershave – but, although there was a packet of Lucky Strike on the dresser, oddly, there was no trace of tobacco smoke and the ashtrays were clean. Mr Keen only smoked in her presence, it seemed. The room itself was tidy, almost obsessively neat, as if the American had already departed and had wanted to leave everything pristine for the next occupant. His shoes marched two by two under the wardrobe, his jackets and shirts swung like a military parade in the wardrobe. She checked the pockets: all were empty.

The chest of drawers revealed more evidence of a tidy, well-disciplined mind: socks, pants, vests, all precisely and efficiently folded. With great care she felt underneath them and then replaced them exactly where she had found them. Having searched all the obvious hiding places, she turned her attention to the less obvious ones: the top of the wardrobe, under the mattress, behind the chest of drawers. She checked her watch. Two thirty: he would soon be back. And then she noticed an odd grey mark on the cream bedside rug. At first it looked like a stain, but then she glanced up and saw a matching square shadow in the cream alabaster bowl of the ceiling light. She moved the dressing-table stool underneath it, removed her shoes and stood on tiptoe to reach inside the dusty globe.

The square was a notebook: small and thinnish with a serviceable black oilskin cover. Its pages were numbered, with a perforation close to the spine. There were many stubs, and the first page in the book was number twenty-seven and blank. She turned the page this way and that, trying to read the indentations, but they were too shallow. She would have had to rub a pencil across them, and that would give her away.

She wiped the cover of the book and replaced it in the lampshade. Then she moved the stool back to its original position and quickly checked that she had not left any signs of her presence. As she locked the door behind her, she heard the sound of footsteps coming up the gravel path, but by the time Hal Keen entered the house she was safely back in her own room.

Four more days passed before Léon called.

'I found that article you wanted, Madame Galland,' he said, 'but I didn't buy it. I think you need to check it over before we go ahead.'

She replied, she thought, quite smoothly. 'If you think that would be best. I could come tomorrow.'

'Certainly. I shall have it waiting for you.' Then he spoke very quickly, 'Shall we say the macaws at midday?'

'Fine.'

She pressed the button to cut the connection and waited. The soft click Léon had told her to listen for came a few seconds later.

Les Deux Perroquets hadn't changed much in twenty years. The walls were perhaps a darker shade of caramel and the counter a more dented length of zinc. A single green macaw sat in a cage at the far end of the bar, and Anna walked over to it, wondering if it could possibly be the same bird.

A man with lank black hair was lounging against a shelf of bottles, languidly polishing glasses with a grubby cloth.

'He's through the back,' he said, an untipped cigarette hung from his bottom lip. 'Down the . . .'

'I know,' said Anna.

In the same big, dusty room, now half filled with large cardboard boxes, Léon stood and kissed her on both cheeks.

'Anyone follow you?'

'I don't think so.' On the station, in the Métro, in the street, she had tried to remember what he had taught her so long ago: dawdling, window-shopping, sudden changes of direction; but she had seen nothing – no one falling back, turning around.

'Then let's hope not. Sit, Anaïs. Like old times, yes?'

She perched on the edge of her chair. 'What have you found out?'

'First things first. What did you tell Keen today?'

'That I was going to look at a dictionary I had had my eye on and afterwards that I was going to check on Marie-Christine.'

'OK, after this you go and see her. Take her a gift or something.'

'Yes, yes,' she said, exasperated. 'Now, tell me.'

'Well, you were right. All this has something to do with Vincent.' Léon rubbed his hands together and glanced up at her from under his brows.

'Look, Anna, I'll tell you everything I know, but some of it relates to the past, and it's going to hurt. Some of it'll be just as bad as that day in 1940, remember? When we heard Vincent had been shot.'

'Léon, *please*, now you're frightening me.'

'OK, OK.'

He took a breath. 'Did you know that Vincent was planning to leave the Party?'

She shook her head slowly. No, she hadn't known that.

'Did you know that he had bought a house in America?'

'*America*? That's not true. Vincent would never do that. He could never have afforded it, for one thing.'

Léon shook his head. 'Not true.' He opened a notebook and flipped through the pages. 'He bought High Haven Farm in Virginia in March 1959. Or, rather, it was bought for him. It's got a hundred acres of pasture and woodland and a four-bedroomed farmhouse with outbuildings.' He looked up. 'There's a dovecote, too.'

'But . . .'

'Wait until you've heard everything, Anaïs. A fortnight before Vincent disappeared, he bought two airline tickets for America. And the name on the second ticket was . . . Well, you can probably guess the name,' he finished gently.

He went on slowly, looking her in the eye. 'Think it through, *ma petite*. Vincent knew everyone in the Party – he had links at the highest level in the Soviet Union. Those old men in the Kremlin drooled over him: he was a bloody flagship, his credentials were impeccable. Especially after Hungary. They'd lost so many intellectuals and public figures – thousands of them – but not Vincent. He was still there, still loyally raising the fist at every Internationale. Getting the comrades on their feet every time.'

Anna nodded, waiting.

'So when somehow they found out he was planning to defect, to betray the Party and steal Comrade Delamain's wife, for some of those guys it must have been like the Pope becoming Protestant. You understand, Anaïs,' he said awkwardly, 'Vincent's thing with . . . well, it was more than a passing affair. In the PCF it had been more or less common knowledge for years.'

She swallowed, staring hard at him.

'No one cared too much. This is France; people shrugged and life went on. But then suddenly Delamain refused to play ball any longer. He became unpredictable, threatened to confront Vincent and expose him as a traitor. It was clear to the old comrades that the whole thing was going to blow – with the Party facing serious political and social humiliation. Some of them said they should just cut Vincent loose, but of course they couldn't: Vincent was too high profile and he knew too much. The publicity would have been bad enough, but they couldn't stand the thought of undermining the Party.'

Anna managed to swallow. 'Léon, are you saying that Vincent's death was not suicide, not an accident?'

'There's no way of knowing for sure. All I can tell you is that around the time he disappeared certain people knew his intentions and certain people had a vested interest in stopping him.' Léon put a heavy arm around her shoulders. 'Anna, it proves nothing. Vincent could still have had a moment of depression, a moment when he realized what he was doing – to Bertrand, to the Party and to you – and decided he just couldn't face it.'

In her mind she thanked Léon for his kindness. It might even be true, she supposed.

She shook her head. 'And Hal Keen?'

Léon stiffened. 'Ah, now that's different. I can't tell you anything about him at all. Not a thing. It's as if he doesn't exist. He's not accredited to any newspaper, and Henson's first of all said they didn't know him, then called back all flustered to say that they did. Which makes me think he may be a spook of some sort. When I followed that up, a friend of mine in the Sûreté clammed up immediately – but then those guys are pretty paranoid types at the best of times. Look, Anna, you said your instincts told you Keen was a phoney – that he was there for a reason. Well, I'd say, trust them.'

She thought for a moment. 'But . . .' She stopped.

'What?'

'The Americans must have known that the communists might come after Vincent. Why didn't they do something to help him?'

'Well now, I have to say, that's been puzzling me, too.'

'Léon,' she said slowly, 'what if they *wanted* to let it happen?'

'So they could watch the PCF tear itself apart? Maybe. My contacts told me the comrades have been arguing behind closed doors ever since the funeral. Bertrand's feeling the cold, that's for sure. And now there's Keen.'

Keen.

She said quietly, 'Léon, I'm trapped in the middle. What am I going to do?'

As he watched, the sky above the glass roof of the station clouded over and her eyes changed from blue to green to grey. Marry me, he wanted to say, letting his imagination soar in one last, brief, glorious flight. Marry an elderly, crippled French ex-policeman and I'll take care of you without smothering you and we'll move south and find a house with a view and live a simple, unheroic, unbeholden life.

His big face creased into furrows, and he rested a heavy hand on her shoulder.

'Only you can decide. But as a friend I'd tell you to run, Anna. Go alone, quickly and quietly, and as far away as you can.'

# Twenty-Four

Marie-Christine's voice on the entry phone was chilly.

'You're late. I've been expecting you since this morning. Come up.'

Glad to be well rehearsed, Anna climbed the four flights of stairs and knocked on the glossy black-painted door. Marie-Christine, thinner than ever, pecked four air kisses around her head.

'Go on through. You smell of tobacco. Where've you been?'

And the lies poured out effortlessly. 'Sorry. I went shopping. A few little luxuries we don't find in the sticks. And I bought this for you.' She held out a small carrier bag. 'It's Royal Jelly.' ('A carefully chosen gift can help avoid awkward explanations,' Léon had said, pushing her gently out of the door with a knowledgeable wink.)

Vincent's sister ferreted inside the bag and pulled out a jar. She undid the lid, sniffed and turned it around to peer at the label. 'There was really no need. I have my own supply, you know. It comes from an apiary near Saint-Rémy.' She held the jar out, as if interrogating a naughty child. 'Where did you get this?'

'Samaritaine.'

'Good God, Anna. How much did it *cost*?' Marie-Christine looked at her beadily. She was wearing a faded purple blouse with a silver and amethyst brooch, and her grey pleated skirt was felted with cat's fur. To her shame Anna realized she had no idea how much income her sister-in-law had to live on.

'Oh, not that much. Anyway, I can always take it back if you don't like it.'

'Don't bother,' said Marie-Christine curtly. 'You'll disappear for another half-day. Come on, I'll make us some herbal tisane.'

At La Verrerie Mr Keen was hard at work when Anna got back. Florence sidled up to her outside the study door.

'The gentleman made a long telephone call, madame, to his publisher, he said. *In America,*' she whispered, scandalized. 'He said he would pay the cost personally.'

'Then I'm sure he will,' said Anna.

She strode to the door and flung it open.

Hal Keen leaped to his feet in a flailing of arms and legs, crashing the telephone back on to its stand.

'Ah, Madame Gal –'

'Anna. Please.'

'Madame Anna, I wasn't expecting you until later.'

'Really? I don't remember giving you a –'

He wasn't listening. 'I'm glad you're back,' he said, interrupting her breathlessly, 'because I'm really stuck on one particular section of the book.'

Anna looked at his damp face. 'Paris in 1940 or Lisbon?' she asked quietly.

The young man blushed. 'Oh, well, it's both, actually, but mainly Paris.'

She pretended to consider the matter and shook her head. 'I'm afraid I'm too tired just now, Mr Keen. We'll have to leave the past until tomorrow.'

In her bedroom nothing was out of place. Nothing at all, except for the nineteen cream envelopes in the drawer of the bedside cabinet. And she knew those had been moved because she had left a one-franc piece on the top one, exactly in the middle of Vincent's name, and now, when she unlocked the drawer and opened it out slowly and carefully, the coin was lying on the stamp and the single blonde hair which she had placed between two of the middle envelopes had disappeared completely.

She should have expected it.

Without rereading them she carried the letters the grate and burned them all one by one, using the poker to break each charred millefeuille into tiny unrecognizable crumbs.

That night she slept on the sofa by the window. The comfortable rosewood double bed mocked her, as did the photographs on the dresser and the pictures on the wall and everything she and Vincent had ever owned together. By morning she had made up her mind.

At nine Florence knocked at the bedroom door.

'Madame, it's late. Are you unwell?'

Lying to the old woman was difficult but necessary. Keeping her voice light and firm, Anna told her of a visit to a specialist in Paris who had confirmed an earlier diagnosis. 'There is a problem with one of the valves of my heart. They will need to operate within the next few weeks, and it is likely to take many months to recover.'

She watched the kindly woman's face wrinkle in sympathy and tried not to care.

'Sadly, I shall have to sell the house.'

'Oh.' Florence's eyes were suddenly brimming. 'Oh,' she said again.

Anna took her hand. 'I'm so sorry.' That much, at least, was true.

When she had gone Anna lay back on the pillows. Then she took out her pocketbook and leafed through it looking for the telephone number of Laforêt Dufour.

Dispatching Mr Keen was much easier, and she did it without compunction as they sat eating lunch.

'I'm afraid I lied to you about my whereabouts yesterday, Hal,' she said, carefully dissecting sole.

His eyebrows rose in amused disbelief. 'Lied? I can't imagine you telling a *lie*, Mrs Galland.'

'Really?' Anna put down her knife and fork. 'Well, I'm afraid I did. I didn't go to Paris to see a bookseller. I went to see . . . a specialist recommended by my doctor. You see, there's been a problem for some time. Only recently it has become more . . . pressing. A weakness here,' she laid her hand against her chest, 'in the valves of the heart.'

He was still staring. 'What do they say . . . ?'

She waited for a moment, as if collecting herself.

'That I shall need an operation. It is delicate, but the chances are fair to good. And afterwards there will be a long period of convalescence.'

'Where? When? How long for?'

He was almost indignant, like a man who knew he would have to explain to someone else.

'Soon,' she said. 'A clinic, in Switzerland.' It had seemed like a suitable place for an invalid and far enough away. 'I've no idea when, or if, I shall return to Saint-Aubain-les-Eaux, and the house will go on the market immediately.' She sipped the chilly wine. 'You're welcome to stay until Friday. And by all means take the files and letters with you when you go. If anything else comes to light when the house is cleared I shall have it sent on to you.'

He was gawping at her now, open-mouthed, like a fish.

'Clear the house?'

She said, patiently, 'Obviously, in the circumstances, we cannot continue working on the book.'

His face was red; he looked genuinely distressed. He was, she thought suddenly, very young to be doing this – they should have chosen someone older.

'Perhaps you need to make another telephone call, Hal,' she said gently.

'Yes, of course. Th-thank you,' he stammered, not noticing. 'Yes, I probably do.'

# Twenty-Five

It's 17 April 1964.

Harry Quinn comes to the cabin early.

She has been expecting him: when she hears the knock she knows who it is in the same way she used to know it was Vincent calling even before she picked up the phone. She is dressed and ready, in reassuringly normal sweater and woollen trousers.

The dog stands barking at the door. From the side of the window she can see a dark-green zipped jacket and a gloved hand hanging loosely open.

She pulls back the bolt and lifts the latch. Sunlight floods the cabin and there he is, standing on the platform, his back to the sea, silhouetted as on that morning long ago in the gardens of the Palais Royal. And now, as then, he knows that she cannot see his face, and so he stands aside and turns to the light.

He is the same man, and completely altered. His hair is cruelly short and dulled with grey at the sides. The eyes are still blue, but their gaze is fixed and immobile, and the face itself has undergone a subtle sea-change, its lines, grooves and planes now sloping downwards as if from habitual sadness, disappointment or bitterness.

'Anna.'

She takes a breath. 'Come in. Leave your boots by the door.'

He draws off his gloves and bends over to fiddle with double knotted laces. The hands that had once stroked softly down her back are gnarled and veined, the nails bitten back to the quick.

Between them is a vertiginous chasm of years. She no longer knows this man.

'Coffee?' she asks.

He pulls off the second boot and looks up.

'Yes.' And after a moment, bending again to the laces, says, 'It's cold out there.'

As if sensing tension, Leif's dog runs between them. Quinn reaches across to stroke her, but the dog flinches away from his touch and sits to attention, ears back and eyes wide.

He says, without looking up, 'She found me last night, on the cliff.'

'You were up there?' Anna remembers the clear sky, the thick rime of frost on the wooden rail, the dog barking in the darkness.

He rubs his hands together. 'I had a tent and a good sleeping bag. I'm used to it. '

He has been there in the darkness all night, watching her. Anna is suddenly aware that she's breathing too fast, that the incoming air is not going beyond her mouth.

'Sit down,' she gasps, still unwilling to use his name. 'Here, by the stove.'

'Thank you.'

She watches him straighten the little cushion before he sits down. Harry is now a man to whom neat edges are important.

'Anna?' he says.

She turns towards the stove and opens the door, fussing with the fire and the damper until the silence becomes oppressive. She sets the blue enamel coffee-pot to warm

'When did you arrive on Moskenes?'

There is another long pause.

'You know when.' His voice is low, timbreless.

She sees again the trained telescope, the muffled figure on the shore at Sørvågen.

'Yes. You'd sent the note. You telephoned Sigrid. Why didn't you come straight here?'

'We can discuss that later.' It is half command, half plea.

On a tray Anna places cups, spoons, saucers – fragments of a normal morning, which this is not. She wraps a cloth around the handle of the pot and pours hot black coffee.

'Sugar?' It is ridiculous. She doesn't remember whether Harry Quinn takes sugar.

'No thank you.'

'Milk?'

'No. Nothing. Thank you.'

She sits down in the chair. He is here, just a few feet away, the man who has come into her thoughts unbidden every day for the past twenty years.

Even as she thinks it, the usual memories fan out in their usual sequence.

But this isn't a memory or a dream. This sad-faced, morose man is real. So where has he been all this time? Is he married? Does he have children? Who are his friends? Who loves him? Every question is too vast and yet too banal.

Veined hands gripping the cup, Harry Quinn speaks.

'You're a translator.' He means it to be small talk, but the tone is wooden, like a policeman reading a statement.

'Yes. For a long time now.'

Another silence.

Then, with effort, he speaks again. 'Do you enjoy it?'

'It suits me, yes.'

'Good.'

The conversation is already running into shallows.

He is sitting immobile, as if by an act of will. In his face the only thing moving is a single small muscle beneath his eye. Mesmerized, she focuses on its minute, uncontrollable pulsing.

'So.'

'Well.'

They speak at the same time and smile at the sudden release of tension.

Anna nods. 'You go first.'

'No, you.'

He is used to being obeyed, she senses.

'I was wondering what you did now,' she says.

There is a wariness in his eyes now, and he is not smiling.

'What do *you* think I do?'

You play games, she thinks, shivering. And you watch me. Not watch *over* me, just *watch* me.

'Journalist?' she says aloud.

'Sometimes.' He bends over the coffee. As he drinks he makes a small, slurping noise. 'Try again.'

'Businessman ?'

'No. Third time lucky? Any prize on the top shelf if you get this one.'

His tone is light, and for the first time there is that small, remembered smile, and her heart almost stops. But even as she watches, the expression is deliberately extinguished, the self-control hideously visible, like the movement of a glass-walled engine.

Anna says, 'Harry, I think you work for the American intelligence service and have done for a very long time.'

The coffee-cup stops half-way to his mouth, then continues smoothly.

'Well, now, that's a little melodramatic, isn't it?'

He is taking control of the situation, as Vincent did, as Bertrand did, as he himself did in Paris and Lisbon so many years ago.

Calmly, Anna looks up. 'Is it?'

He stands and goes over to the window, keeping his back towards her. Instinctively she knows that for all his watching he hasn't been prepared for the living reality of her. He has to adjust and fine-tune whatever plan he is working to.

'This place is the end of nowhere,' he says, resting his head against the window frame and drawing a line in the condensation on the glass with a fingertip.

'Literally the end of the road,' she says. And then, to keep the talk going, 'In Norwegian, of course, Å is the last letter of the alphabet, not the first. I liked the idea of an end and a beginning in the same far-away place. And I thought no one would find me.' She lets her voice harden. 'But you did.'

'Oh, I have people who do that kind of thing,' he says, vaguely, the finger moving gently over the window.

'And are they paid to indulge your private investigations?'

He thinks for a moment. 'What makes you think this is my investigation?'

She ignores the question. 'I was only of interest to your employers because I was married to Vincent. Yet he's dead, and I am still under surveillance or whatever you call it.'

The line Harry is drawing on the windowpane becomes a square, then a barred cell. He glances around the room. 'I don't like confined spaces much. Could we go out for a while?'

Anna presses home what might be a temporary advantage. 'You mean now you're here you don't want to talk?'

He runs a hand across his short hair, and she sees a gleam of pink. 'It's not that. There are a great many things . . . we need to talk about. I just want some space . . . in between . . .' He sounds edgy, exasperated.

Anna stands and reaches her hat down from the peg. 'Come on

then. Kersti, here, girl. She belongs to a friend,' she says, as the dog bounds through the door. 'He's away at the moment.'

'Leif Pedersen. Used to be a fisherman.'

'And how on *earth* do you know that?'

Harry grins, and his face changes entirely. 'I'm rarely misinformed.'

'Is that so?'

Harry Quinn dominates and fills the tiny cabin in a way that Leif, a good foot taller and broader, never did. Turning her back on him, she walks outside into the open air.

From the shore comes the smell of ozone, seaweed and drying stockfish. Without waiting to see if he is following, Anna takes the cliff path and whistles up the dog to lead the way.

The climb is stiff but familiar, and she forces the pace, ignoring the initial pain in her lungs and the first protesting ache in her calf muscles. The dog bounds ahead, leaping from rock to rock, occasionally turning back to check she is following. When Anna reaches the high path above the scree, she looks back and sees Harry is only a few yards behind her. She leans against a rock and waits for him. His head is greyish in the daylight; he could be any middle-aged man out on a climb. Except that he comes on quickly up the slope, head down, shoulders set.

He keeps himself fit, she thinks. Perhaps it is a requirement of the job.

He stops beside her, looks out over the inlet. 'It's warmer than I expected.' There is a sly, sideways shift of his eyes towards her. 'Almost like a spring day in Paris.'

'Stop it, Harry,' she says. 'I'm tired of it.'

'Are you? So soon?'

That bloody interrogative lift.

'Yes, Harry, I am. You sent James Carter to Saint-Aubain-les-Eaux. You filled him full of little facts from our past – the perfume, the date we met. You even changed his name to remind me of you, didn't you?'

Again, Harry runs his hand over his thinning hair. 'No.'

There are tears of exasperation welling in her eyes now. 'You sent him to spy on me. Admit it.'

Again he shakes his head.

Then, after a moment, he says, 'James Carter was there to get close to someone else entirely. His role was to play you along, to see if we could destabilize the situation.'

'You're talking in riddles. Destabilize? What situation?'

'You don't need to know. And I'm not free to tell you. But you trust me, don't you?'

'Why should I? You've done nothing to make me trust you.'

He frowns and changes tack, and the process is somehow mechanical and obvious, like a grinding of gears.

'You know the truly amazing thing, Anna? In many ways you're just the same as you were in 1940 – same hair, same eyes, same voice.'

Green tissue paper whispers in her mind. A tiny form, twisted like a dying starfish, lies in a steel basin.

'I'm not, Harry. You know nothing about me now. Nothing at all.'

He sighs. 'On the contrary, Anna, I know a great deal. And about your late husband, too.' He is sure of himself now, leaning against the rock, smiling.

'Oh, really? Is that from your own observation or did you get these "people" of yours to do it?' Her voice is rising, 'I'm not your property, Harry. I could have been, but you didn't want me enough – in Lisbon you let me choose between you and Vincent, knowing exactly what I would do. And ever since then you've wasted your life spying on me as if I were some animal in your private zoo.'

He flinches slightly. 'I told you, Anna, *I* wasn't watching you. You just came within our wider focus, that's all.'

The wider focus that was Vincent.

'What did you do to him?' she asks abruptly.

Harry blinks. 'Nothing.' And now he understands. 'Ah no, you're wrong there, Anna. Vincent was important to us. We wouldn't have done anything to harm him, believe me.'

In Harry's world fiction and fact are joined like Siamese twins.

'I despise you,' she says calmly. 'I despise you people and all your absurd little Cold War games. You're trying to destroy whatever's left of Vincent because you can't bear the thought he was a hero.'

Anna walks away from him, down the track towards Å.

Harry calls after her. 'You read the Delamain woman's letters. He betrayed you.'

She stops, her back still towards him.

He shrugs and sticks his gloved hands deeper into his pockets. 'Anna, everyone in the Party knew about it. In fact every senior officer in Western intelligence knew about Vincent Galland and Astrid Delamain. It was a running joke.'

Over her shoulder she says, 'You collect information like a spider collects flies, don't you, Harry?'

'Gathering intelligence is my job, yes. Ever since the war. Even earlier. It's a chess game. You have to know your opponent.'

*Even earlier.* Anna is studying the scuffed toe of her boot. Slowly she says, 'You knew that Isabelle Delamain was Vincent's daughter?'

There was a silence. Then Harry cleared his throat. 'Astrid and he were together in '44 – right up until you came back from America.'

'And you knew it.'

He sounds exasperated. 'Yes, I knew it. Look, there were reports. Fellow Resistance members who didn't share his politics.'

'You knew Isabelle was Vincent's child.' Her stomach is knotted tight, and there is a crazy thudding at her temples, but she wants it clear.

'Yes.'

'*Stay where you are.*' She has heard his feet move on the loose stone and now turns on him.

'*And did you also know that when I left Lisbon I was pregnant with yours?*'

He has trained his face not to register emotion, and she almost misses the brief flicker of shock.

'Well, at last, something you didn't know. But even if you had it wouldn't have made any difference, Harry, would it? You'd just have written your report and left it at that. Because your job was just to watch, wasn't it, Harry? So that's all you do. Watch.'

Again he moves towards her.

'No. No.' She backs away, 'Don't come any nearer. Leave me *alone*.'

Then she is off, running directly down the slope, the path sliding away under her shoes. She runs straight down, faster and faster, until the stones are streaks of grey at her sides. Thirty feet above the path her flying foot strikes a rock and suddenly she is falling, headlong down the hillside amid a shower of sharp rocks.

'She's awake.'

A woman's voice. Sigrid's voice.

'Here, let me.' A man.

A cool cloth is pressed against her forehead and releases a flood of pain.

'Hush.'

'Harry?'

'Hush. No, it's Leif.'

She opens one eye and sees him kneeling beside her.

'What happened?'

'You fell down the scree slope.'

'Where's . . . ?'

Leif frowns and leans back. 'The American? He's gone.'

*Harry.*

'Drink this. You got a lump big as an egg on the side of your head, girl,' says Sigrid, bustling across the room with a glass of milk. 'Luckily for you there's no bones broken, although you left some skin up there on the rocks – fell on your knees and elbows, like Johan. Here.'

Anna stretches out a hand covered in scratches and bruises and takes the glass. Swallowing is an effort. From far away she hears Sigrid's voice.

'Can you stand?'

'Here, hold on to me.' Leif's arm goes around her waist.

'I'm fine,' she says curtly, flinching.

'Fine is good,' says Sigrid, 'but you were damn lucky not to kill yourself up there. Now, tonight you're going to stay here, end of argument.'

After supper Sigrid takes Anna up to Marika's room. She disappears for a moment and bustles back in bearing one of her own voluminous white nightshirts.

'Put this on. Your arms stiff? Here.'

Anna protests, but Sigrid has dressed and undressed too many children to stand for any nonsense.

'Lift up your arms. Lie back. There!' she says triumphantly and covers Anna with the quilt. 'Now, sleep.'

It's dawn when she wakes.

Under the pitched ceiling a shoal of blue wooden fish hover motionless in front of the window. Around the walls are Marika's paintings: fishing boats, higgledy-piggledy families, landscapes of sea and rocks. At her feet a small toy seal lies next to a teddy bear.

Anna stretches her fingers, feeling the stiffness of bruised joints, then runs her hands lightly over her body. Tender, roughened grazes on forearms and ribs. She draws up her legs, flexing a painful knee to its fullest extent.

Outside, herring gulls call into the wind and waves murmur against shingle. Downstairs there are the first sounds of Sigrid's household stirring.

When she wakes again Sigrid herself is standing at the bottom of the bed, a tray in her hands.

'Good morning. How are you?'

Anna eases herself into a sitting position. 'Well, I think, thanks to you.'

'That's good. I brought you breakfast. Porridge and honey. You eat it while it's hot, yes? OK?'

'Yes, I will.'

'When you've finished you better try to get up – otherwise you'll set stiff like a statue. Come down and see me. I'm on post office duty now. Boat's just been.'

The door bangs shut. Her footsteps, running down the wooden staircase, are surprisingly light for such a heavy woman.

Anna is hungry. Ravenous. With amazement she realizes it is twenty-four hours since she last ate. She unscrews the jar of honey, dips in a tiny wooden ladle and drizzles golden liquid all over the surface of the porridge. She eats slowly, tasting each mouthful. When she has finished she scrapes the bowl, wipes a finger around the rim and licks the spoon clean. When she swings her legs over the side of the bed and stands the vast nightdress billows around her. Ignoring the sudden warning thud from her forehead, she bends to the chair to retrieve her clothing.

She comes down the stairs one at a time, avoiding putting weight on her right leg. In the post office Sigrid is chatting with two women customers, who fall silent when she enters. The air is thick with the smells of damp raincoats, coffee and bread.

'I think I'll get some air,' she says and takes her jacket down from the hook. 'Try out this knee.'

'OK. Just don't go far,' says Sigrid and turns back to the two waiting women.

Anna walks slowly in the direction of the jetty. It has snowed in the night, and between the rocks are white, felted drifts. The snow squeaks beneath the cleats of her boots, sounding loud in the still air between the mountains and the sea. At the far side of the bay is the tiny red square of her *rorbu*. I am still here, she thinks. Still here.

At the end of the jetty Johan and Marika, muffled and gloved, are playing with a model boat.

'I want it,' says Marika. 'It's my turn.'

Johan shakes his head. 'Uncle Leif made it for me. You'll break it.'

'I won't.'

'You will.' Johan leans over the jetty, steadying the boat by its mast.

'I want it.' Marika reaches forward, half picks the boat out of the water, then loses her grip on the slippery hull. The small boat strikes the water bow first and spirals quickly down into the deep water alongside the jetty.

'*Marika!*'

In a flurry of curls, the girl is gone, racing along the quayside towards the cottages.

Johan kneels on the wet stone, gazing down into the glassy greyness of the fjord.

'She did it on purpose. She sank my boat.' The boy is holding back tears.

Stiffly, Anna crouches down beside him on the jetty. 'She didn't mean to, Johan. She just dropped it. Will it be there at low tide, do you think?'

Johan shrugs. 'I don't know. There's a strong current. What will Uncle Leif say if it's lost? It took him ages to build.'

'Your uncle isn't the kind of man to worry over things like that. I expect he'll build you another. Or more likely show you how to do it yourself. Now, do you think you can help me up?'

'When I'm grown up I want to be a fisherman,' says Johan gravely, hauling on her outstretched hand. 'You pull in the nets like this.'

Anna presses a hand gently against her bruised ribs. 'What does your uncle Leif think about that?'

The boy frowns, wiping his hands down the side of his trousers. 'He thinks I should go to college in Bodø. He doesn't think fishing is a good job for a young man.'

'But your father does, I suppose.'

'Yes. He says he'll take me with him as soon as I'm old enough.'

'And you, Johan, what do you want?'

Under the pale ash blond hair the boy's eyes are grave. 'I want to decide for myself.'

At midday they sit around the table, heads bent, while in Gunnar's absence Sigrid says grace. Marika's face is tear-stained, and Johan is grinning.

Anna counts places at the table. Four.

'Where's Leif?'

'Oh, round and about, I guess,' says Sigrid, ladling broth into bowls. 'He'll be back for supper.' Her tone is reassuring, but there is something odd about the way she fails to meet Anna's gaze.

'His boat's gone,' says Johan, keen to be of help.

'Eat, you,' says Sigrid.

Anna looks at her friend. 'Where is he?'

'How should I know?' This time the big woman is muttering into the bib of her apron.

'Sigrid, you might as well tell me.'

'Tell you what?'

Anna says, slowly, 'He's gone to Sørvågen, hasn't he? He's gone to see Harry Quinn.'

The children are staring at their mother, whose face is scarlet.

'No idea,' says Sigrid firmly, holding out a bowl. 'Bread?'

'Sigrid?'

Suddenly Sigrid bangs her fist on the table; bowls jump and soup slops over the brim. She reaches for a cloth and mops at it distractedly. 'Anna, if you really want to know where Leif is I'll tell you. Well, you're right. He went to Sørvågen. Happy now?'

Anna's chair makes a loud scraping noise as she pushes it back, 'But it's none of his business. It's nobody's business but mine.'

'Children, eat your soup in the shop. Right now. Here, take some bread.'

Marika and Johan look at each other and sidle unwillingly to the door.

'Anna,' says Sigrid quietly, once she is satisfied that the children are out of earshot, 'what makes you so different, heh? You think you're any better or worse than other people? He wants to help you.'

Anna runs both hands back through her hair. 'Sigrid, please. I came here because I was running away. It wasn't brave, but at least I did it. For once in my life, *I* chose. Å is the end or the beginning for me. I may swim or I may go under, but *I* decide.'

Sigrid stares at her from the other side of the table. 'I see, Anna,' she says quietly. 'Well, if you want to put your life in order you better get up to Sørvågen right now. After all,' she stands up, 'if Mr Harry Quinn is your problem there's no reason why Leif should get hurt trying to help, is there?'

'Hurt?'

'It was Quinn who brought you here yesterday. When he came back later he tried to take you away. Leif wouldn't let him. And Quinn told Leif to stop interfering. And they're two grown men shaping up to knock each other senseless, when Leif reminds him you're asleep upstairs and tells Quinn to get the hell out of there.

'Well, he went all right, but he said he'd be back. And then this morning Leif says he's been thinking about things and that he's going up to see Quinn and sort this thing out once and for all.'

'Oh God.'

'Don't say that.'

'Sorry.' Anna reaches across the table and takes the big woman's hands in hers. 'I am sorry, Sigrid. Truly. I didn't want any of this. I'll go up there. Now.'

Sigrid nods. 'Take my outboard. Sea's plenty calm enough at the moment – there's fuel to get you round to Sørvågen and back if you keep close in. Know how to start it?'

Anna nods.

'Get going, then. You got a good four hours before dark.'

Anna steps down into the dinghy, turns on the fuel and grips the starter cord. It takes just two pulls to start the motor, then she is easing the boat away from the jetty and out into the fjord.

To her left the mountains of Moskenes peer down on her, their sheer, grey peaks cauled with snow. As she passes the Tjind headland and heads north a freshening breeze blows into her face and frets the ebbing tide into little waves that slap noisily against the hull. Warily she turns towards the shore, keeping to the lee of each point for as long as she can. Here, under the sheer vertical rock, gulls wheel overhead, their calls echoing back from the cliffs, and the water slipping beneath the boat is black rippled glass.

# Twenty-Six

Leif's little fishing boat is moored at the end of Sørvågen jetty. Anna cuts the engine and lets the dinghy drift gently alongside until she reaches the mooring post. Awkwardly, she secures the boat and steps ashore. A few elderly fishermen mending nets look at her curiously as she walks past. One of them takes a pipe from his mouth and calls after her.

'You want the American, missus? He's at the old Markusen place, last on the left, brown walls, you can't miss it. You'll find young Leif Pedersen there, too. Arrived a couple of hours ago.'

'Thank you.'

She walks quickly up the unmade road out of the village. A dog rushes out in front of her, barking and barring her path, but is called to heel by a woman's voice from one of the doorways.

She is climbing now, past the derelict cabin and the blue house with its peeling paint, and now here at the tip of the rise is the brown house, set apart from the others, piles of logs stacked neatly against its wall.

Anna looks around her. Far below on the jetty the fishermen are bent over their nets. A few children are playing at the water's edge and someone in the distance is chopping wood. She knocks on the brown door. There is no answering stir from the cabin. She leans closer. There are no voices, no noise at all. Gingerly she lifts the latch of the *rorbu* and pushes the door open.

'Harry?'

The door swings closed behind her. It is dark in the cabin; the air is cold and smells of woodsmoke and something else she can't identify.

'Harry?'

She feels her way forward, aiming for the crack of light under the far window, but trips over something bulky lying on the floor. There is a moan. Quickly she turns back to the door and flings it open. In the long rectangle of daylight lies Leif Pedersen, and beneath his head is a small pool of black-red blood.

Anna drops to her knees beside him. The side of his head is glistening and blood has dried around his ear and the side of his jaw. She picks up his hand. Big, heavy and lifeless, it fills her two palms. She turns it over and feels for a pulse.

'Leif, what happened?'

He doesn't move.

'Did Harry do this to you?'

'*What do you think?*' says Harry Quinn.

He is sitting in an armchair in the far corner of the room, with a shotgun across his knees. As she darts back towards the door he moves to block her, and once again she is astonished at the speed of his reactions.

His voice is calm and friendly as he says, 'Hello, Anna. I knew you'd come. Sit there where I can see you. *Sit!*'

His shout startles her. Obediently she drops into the chair.

'There we are.' Harry's voice is amiable again. He leans the gun against the table, lights the paraffin lamp, adjusts its flame and sets it on the table, then turns to face her. His face, lit from below, is comically cavernous.

'I see you've recovered from your fall yesterday.'

Anna nods. 'It looked worse than it was.'

Harry jerks his head towards Leif. 'I thought so. Same with him. He's not dead, you know. I didn't want to kill him, just stop him.'

Apparently both had been options. 'Stop him from what?'

Harry reaches for a packet of Lucky Strike cigarettes. 'Seems he's taken a quite a shine to you, Anna. I hope you haven't been leading him on.'

It is best to stay calm. 'No, of course I haven't.'

Harry blows out smoke and laughs. 'Well, now, I remember that you were pretty good at sending out the red-hot signals when it suited you, kid. A certain night in Lisbon comes to mind.'

'Harry.' It comes out as a whisper, and she forces her voice louder, doing her best to control the tremor running through her body. 'You were wrong that night, you know. Vincent *had* to get to America, but if you'd asked me, Harry, I would have stayed.' She tries to put twenty years of regret into the last sentence but hears its hollowness even as she speaks the words.

Harry is drawing steadily on his cigarette. 'Oh, really? And what else would have happened in this Anna in Wonderland life if only I'd asked you to stay? I suppose you'd have divorced your Resistance hero, or perhaps he would have died conveniently in the war. And then you'd have married little old me from New York, New York, and we'd have had our baby and lived happily ever after?'

He juts his chin forward, revealing the stretched grey tendons of his throat 'You only took two decisions in your whole life, Anna, and both of them fucked me over.' He cocks his head to one side. 'You don't believe me? OK, let me tell you.

'I got married, too, in '47. Lisa was an actress: twenty-three, Swedish, ash-blonde hair and blue eyes; docile, sweet, aloof, a perfect ice queen.' He looks at her. 'See any similarities? Well, I didn't, not back then. I just told myself I loved her. But it only took me a few months to realize that she was no Scandinavian ice queen; she was just plain *dumb*.'

He smiles with his mouth only. 'In fact, she was so damn *stupid* that after a few years I could hardly bring myself to speak to the woman, she irritated me so much.'

He stubs out his cigarette and draws another one from the pack. 'You taking this in, Anna?'

She nods twice.

'Good. Oh, and I should add that by then we've got two little girls, Hannah and Laura, who are pretty enough as kids but clearly as dumb as their mother. And me? I'm working all hours, taking all the postings I can get, just to avoid seeing the three of them every day. There, that was my life after you.'

Anna stares at the thin, bitter mouth, the yellow-stained fingers forked around the cigarette. How long had the Harry of Paris and Lisbon lasted? she wonders. A year? Two? She has been dreaming of a ghost for twenty years.

'I'm sorry, Harry.'

Harry Quinn closes his eyes for a moment.

'I suppose that is just about *the* most inadequate thing you could have said at this point. Well, your apology is not acceptable. You'll sit there now and hear the rest of it. Because there's more, and I know some things you'll *really* be sorry to hear. *No, you sit there and listen.*'

His voice has moved in an instant from calm to snarl.

Anna sits back, her hands gripping the arms of the chair.

Harry tilts his head to one side. 'That's better. And don't worry about Leif the Unconscious down there. He'll be out for the count for a long while yet.' He props the gun against the chair and settles himself comfortably.

'So, where was I? Ah yes. By now it's the mid-fifties and my bosses are taking a close interest in what the European communist parties are up to. A lot of information starts coming across my desk, and guess who gets frequent mention in dispatches. One Vincent Galland. Oh yes, Mr Janus himself.'

*The Janus File.* She hears Myles Pilkington's voice across the years, describing the man she had just met: 'Chiefly known for looking both ways at once.'

Harry is unstoppable, the words pouring from him in savage, sardonic fluency.

'Oh yes, after flirting with the Gaullists, teasing the social democrats and being hailed by the United Nations as a force for World Peace our weathervane has finally ended up as a top dog at the PCF. What's more, he stays there, even in 1956, when every decent-thinking intellectual in France jumps ship.'

He flings her a gleeful, malicious look. 'Now for our Vincent such consistency is rare, wouldn't you say? Well, that's what we think, too. So, we begin to ask ourselves: Why does he stay? What's keeping him there? We look and look. We look so hard that one day we find out the truth.'

'And it's so mundane it's laughable: Vincent Galland is sleeping with his best comrade's wife. Not only that, but the inside story goes that he's been doing it since the war, and there's even a rumour that the lovely Isabelle Delamain, only daughter of the said best comrade, is actually Vincent Galland's bastard.'

He pauses and smiles, waving his cigarette in the air. 'Well, I tell you, that was just a *gift*, Anna. A *gift.* Suddenly we have a lever against the highest-profile communist in the West.'

He takes a last draw on the cigarette, bends over to stub it out and picks up the gun again, holding the barrel against his face, a dreamy expression in his eyes. 'It's then I make my move. I get myself put in charge of the Galland operation. We send people in, deep and close. We focus so close that by the end I can tell you what Vincent Galland had for breakfast on any given morning in that damn dacha of his. Any given morning.

'But they need more. Hell, *I* want more.' His voice softens. 'Now I'm close enough to see *you*, Anna. After all these years I can see you.' His eyes are fixed on her. 'And the weird thing is that you look just the same – lovely and pure, like a young girl. I watch you, and I can tell how you do it – you get through life by just drifting, pretending nothing is real.'

Anna closes her eyes. He sees through her. He invades her. She is riddled with him.

'Look.' Harry stands and picks up an attaché case by the side of the table. From it he draws an envelope containing a series of eight-by-ten black-and-white photo prints. He holds them out to Anna. 'Look.'

She looks. There, blurred through a long lens, but still recognizable, is the terrace at La Verrerie. At the far end of the table Vincent and Astrid are leaning towards each other, while Anna, half turned away, is looking down the garden in the direction of the invisible watcher. Another photograph: she sits alone while Vincent and Astrid sunbathe by a swimming-pool; in the shadow between their chairs she can see that their hands are touching.

Harry jabs a finger at the photograph. 'You're living *his* life, don't you see that? Not yours, *his*.'

But there is also a shot of her and Vincent together in Paris, walking side by side in an avenue that could be the Boulevard Saint-Germain. It is summer, not too long ago, and Vincent is wearing the light-grey suit she always liked.

With the tip of her finger Anna traces the side of her husband's face, his shoulder, his arm, the hand close to hers.

'You don't know that,' she says.

But Harry laughs. 'Oh, but I do. I even know why you came running up here a year ago.'

'Did your spy Keen read Astrid's letters?'

Harry sighs. 'Of course – before you did; and being a well-trained boy he photographed them, too, so you needn't think they were lost when you burned them.'

Anna closes her eyes.

'No more now, Harry. Let me go.'

He shakes his head. 'All in good time. You haven't heard the most interesting part of the story yet. So, very subtly, we start laying out bait for Comrade Galland and his mistress. And you know what? He takes it. Such belief in himself, Anna – it's sickening.

'Anyway, we tighten the noose. We make contact and tell him that he's got no future in France; we point out he's simply toeing the Party line he doesn't believe in and trapped in a dying marriage.'

'Thank you,' says Anna quietly. Harry doesn't even notice that she has spoken.

'But, we tell him, if he converts, if he sees the Western light, so to speak, then we can get him lionized in America like you wouldn't believe. Oh, and this appeals, Anna, this lights your Vincent's fire. Ah, he says, yes, and I'll take my lovely Astrid with me.'

Anna is staring at Harry Quinn. He is the Draugen, a sea-ghost risen up to steal her past away.

'But then, disaster. Right at the last moment the lovely Astrid's husband gets wind of this little plan. Now, your loyal comrade Delamain's gone along with the Party for years, keeping Vincent in the fold, see. But, suddenly, instead of lending his wife he's losing her. And the rest', Harry sighs, 'is so predictable. Someone, not us, feeds Vincent a line about changed departure arrangements, and one night on a deserted beach in Brittany he finds Bertrand Delamain waiting for him. *Et voilà*: tragic death of a communist hero.'

Anna sits very still.

Everywhere she looks in her past there are distorting mirrors, untruths, illusions. Perhaps Vincent did find his old cuckolded comrade waiting for him on the cliff at Quiberon. Or perhaps – she looks at the intent face opposite – perhaps he found Harry Quinn.

She swallows and says quietly, 'Have you finished?'

'Not quite. We won't let it end there.'

'We?'

'None of us. The West won't. The Agency won't. You and I won't.'

She talks straight at him, willing him to understand. 'Harry, I'm not playing this game.'

'Game? This isn't a game.'

'You don't want me. You can't, because you don't know me any more. All you want to do – all *they* want to do – is to discredit Vincent.'

For the first time Harry looks puzzled. 'No. You're going to do that,

Anna. You're going to tell the world what a fraud your husband was.'

Anna sees Vincent's elegant, ruined hands, the clever, European face alive with passionate certainty.

'No, Harry.'

'He betrayed you. He made you live a lie.'

'It doesn't matter now. Living out your revenge would be worse.'

Harry stands, the gun slack in his hands.

'It's for your own sake, Anna. Only you can do it. You have to do it. Come with me now.'

She swallows. 'Where?'

He's speaking rapidly now. 'Bodø. I've got a car there. We'll drive to Trondheim and catch a plane. I thought it through. I thought of everything. We'll have a head start on them. I've got it all worked out. Trust me.'

'Who are they? Is this you, Harry, or the Agency?'

Harry smiles. 'Doesn't matter. It's the same thing. Come on, Anna. Trust me.'

'No,' she says quietly, and the word hangs in the air between them, oscillating slowly in the silence. Anna looks into Harry's face: his eyes are flickering over thoughts she cannot imagine.

There is a faint groan, and the body on the floor stirs.

Suddenly released into action, Harry strides over and thuds his boot hard into Leif's ribs. He takes his foot back and aims again, this time at the head.

'No!' Anna's voice is commanding. She reaches out and grabs the back of Harry's jacket with all her strength, twisting him back to face her.

'No! Stop, Harry, or I won't come with you.'

Harry is staring at her, startled by the force in her voice.

'Leave him alone. He's nothing to do with this.'

Slowly, wearily, Harry Quinn lets the gun fall to his side.

'OK.' He shrugs. 'But you must come with me. Now.'

'Yes,' she says.

He picks up a rucksack by the door and slides his shotgun into a hunting case. 'Hurry,' he says, 'we need to get to Bodø before dark.'

He takes one last look around the cabin, then grips Anna's hand, and together they walk down the path to the village. A cold wind is blowing now. The road is empty and the fishermen have gone from the jetty. As he walks Harry is humming.

'It took me a while to find you,' he says, swinging her arm and his like a courting couple. 'That line you fed James had me worried. We wasted a lot of time checking out clinics in Switzerland. How is your health?'

'I'm fine,' she says, conscious of the strength in his fingers. She is thinking of Leif, lying on the cold wooden floor of the cabin. Ahead of them, north of the village, the sky is filling with purple-grey cloud.

'When we finally decided you weren't in Geneva or anywhere near we had to start over. We knew you had the money from the auction, but you were being very clever with that. Just as you were clever losing us when you went up to Paris those times. Someone taught you well, didn't they? In the war, I guessed.'

He cocks his head and gives a strange lopsided grin. 'But I thought it through. I decided that even if Anna had changed everything else about her life she might still be doing the translation work. So one night I went myself and took a good look around Kirchener's office in New York – oh, don't worry, I put everything back where it was, although that guy's got some pretty dubious commies on his books. Anyway, what do I find? I find I'm right. I know you too well, you see? There on the desk outside his office: big brown envelopes from Norway, postmarked Å in the Lofotens. Where your father came from. It was so simple, I kicked myself I'd been so stupid.' His eyes are red-rimmed and watering now in the wind.

Anna, looking down at the rock-strewn track, says carefully, 'Now you're saying "I", Harry. *Is* this something personal?'

The grip on her hand tightens. 'Of course it is. Vincent has always been the Agency's business, but between you and me, Anna, how could things be anything else but personal?'

She swallows. 'Does anyone from your office know you're here?'

He gives a sly smile. 'I told them I was on a fishing holiday. Got a few postcards sent from Bergen. I wanted time, Anna, time to talk to you like this, otherwise I knew you'd never come with me. I'd never get a chance to explain.' He shivers. 'It's taken longer than I expected, though. We need to move quickly. Keep ahead of them, give ourselves some space now we're together.'

There is a tremor in his voice now. Despite the cold, sweat trickles down his face from under the rim of his cap. The path is levelling out as they approach the jetty, but still there is no movement from behind the shuttered windows. Casually Harry takes a large jerrycan from a row by the harbourmaster's office, then makes his way unerringly to Sigrid's boat. With a last pleading look around at the closed houses she climbs down into the dinghy and sits on the thwart.

'We could head back to Å,' she says tentatively. 'I could pick up a few things.'

But Harry pats his rucksack. 'I've got everything we need right here. Even a passport for you as Mrs Harry Quinn. I thought of everything. We don't need to go back.'

'But this boat belongs to a friend of mine.'

'Sigrid Pedersen. I know. Don't worry, we'll tell the harbourmaster at Bodø.'

'Oh.'

'It's a straight course, couple of hours south-east. We should get there before dark. I got charts and extra fuel.' He stows his bag and the jerrycan in a locker in the stern. 'Here we go.' He stands and winds the starter cord around his gloved hand. After four or five attempts the motor coughs into life and they head out into the Vestfjord.

'Cold?'

Anna realizes she has been shivering. The wind is driving straight down the fjord from the north, and icy air is finding every gap between glove and cuff, hat and collar.

'There's an oilskin in the rucksack and a life-jacket. Here.' He opens the bag with one hand, fumbles for a moment and tosses her a tightly folded bundle. 'The hood'll keep out the draught.'

Anna undoes the tapes and shakes out the yellow oilskin; she tries to shelter it from the strengthening wind, but it beats like a giant bird trying to flap out of her grasp. She stuffs her arms down the clammy sleeves and fiddles with the zip. With the oilskin hood up and the life-jacket fastened she immediately feels warmer.

'Better?' He has put his own life-jacket on and is sitting smiling and relaxed against the tiller as if they're out for a Sunday picnic, except that his cheekbones are purple-red now, his lips pinched and blue. Anna watches him from inside her hood, trying to summon up a memory of the loving wartime Harry, the dream Harry who kept her company for so many years, but that man has vanished.

He sees her watching and gives her an odd, jaunty wave and shouts into the wind, 'Don't worry. We'll be fine.'

His concern is almost touching. And, of course, he has been watching over her for many years now. It has been love of a sort. Perhaps he deserves more from her than fear. And perhaps conversation is safer than silence.

'Harry?'

'Yes?'

She speaks loudly, above the sound of the engine. 'You know, in all the days since Lisbon, there was hardly one when I didn't think of you.' And it's true, she thinks. Like a starving woman she gnawed those few sensual, poignant memories to the bone. Yet even though they made everyday life easier to bear they had somehow reinforced her fear of change, of standing alone.

She tries to smile. 'I thought you ought to know.'

Harry's blue lips widen. He says vaguely, 'I always knew we'd meet again.'

A wave smacks the side of the boat and spray splashes across his face, and he blinks in puzzlement. 'Anna, I see you sitting there and I can't find the words. All these years I've dreamed about this moment and now I can't find the damn words.'

She takes pity on him. 'We're not in our twenties any more, Harry. We know too much.'

He cuts across her. 'Did I scare you back there? In the cabin, I mean.'

She swallows, remembering the gun, the black-red pool on the floor around Leif's head.

'Yes, you scared me, Harry.'

He is staring beyond her now, into the grey heaving seas of the Vestfjord. 'These days I frighten myself.'

After a while he says dully, 'They won't take me back after this. You were right, of course, about private investigations. I don't know how I got away with it for so long.'

The wind is rising. Anna leans forward to shout, 'What will you do?'

He shakes his head and shrugs, hunches down again over the tiller.

After a while she sits back and lets the wind beat against the back of the protecting jacket, and there is only the sound of the motor and the waves. The cloud overhead is thicker, so low she feels she could almost reach up and touch it. Minutes later heavy rain comes pattering down into the boat and drums on her oilskin hood.

They are scudding south down the fjord. Away to her right, through a gap in the swathe of rain, Anna glimpses the dark mass of Moskenes and a huddle of tiny red houses at the foot of black cliffs, their lit windows like sparks in the gloom. She wonders if one of those tiny pinpricks is the store and if Sigrid is staring out of the steamy windows, waiting for her and Leif to return.

The waves are higher now, and the boat is riding down into deeper troughs. On the crest of each wave the motor whines shrilly, propelling only air, then they are bucketing down the slope into the next valley. Some of the waves are tipped with white: a thin curl of eager foam rushing under them.

Up and down, up and down.

Behind every grey black-edged wave is another and another and another. She is cold now, cold and wet, and the monotony of the waves is hypnotic: staring ahead, she feels she has always been in the boat, will always be in the boat.

Her head nods forward.

Suddenly Harry is shouting. 'We're making good time.'

She looks about her. The peaks of Moskenes have disappeared in the mist. Now in every direction there is only sea. She cups her hand to her mouth. 'Do you know where we are?'

'The wind's carrying us straight over to the mainland. Don't worry.'

She turns back, but as she does so the prow corkscrews down and sideways, and she tumbles forward, grabbing for the wooden thwart with both hands. A big green-grey comber slops in over the right bow. The right bow. She cranes around. All the waves are coming at them at an angle instead of from behind them. Anna rubs the rain out of her eyelashes. She turns to Harry and points, shouting into the wind, 'We're heading west!'

Harry shakes his head, is shouting something. She cranes forward.

'Take the tiller.'

Anna crawls towards the back of the boat as Harry edges forward, still holding the end of the tiller. He hands it to her and they change places. Hunched on the thwart, Harry takes off his gloves. From his jacket pocket he pulls out a compass and a rectangle of chart in a plastic wallet. Anna watches him wiping the surface of the map and the compass glass, again and again.

She cups her hand to her mouth. 'We're heading in the wrong direction Harry. We should be heading east!' She points to where she thinks the mainland is, but the boat is rolling badly now, lying almost parallel to the waves.

And then she hears something else. Not Harry's voice, nor the sound of the wind, nor the waves. Coming from far ahead of them, beyond the endless march of grey waves, is a roaring noise, like a thundering waterfall.

Anna listens. Listens then screams at the top of her voice.

'Harry! It's the Maelstrom! We're too far south. We've got to turn back to Moskenes.'

Harry looks up, bewildered, the chart flapping uselessly in his hand.

With all her strength Anna pushes the tiller right around, across the pull of the current, back towards where the invisible island must be. For a moment the boat spins faster, then a wall of rain slaps against her face and she knows they are heading back into the wind. The sideways pull of the current slackens, but now the boat is struggling against the advancing waves. The wind lifts a slice of freezing spray from each oncoming crest and deposits it in the little boat.

'No!'

Harry is shouting. On his knees in front of her in the pitching boat, he is shuffling towards her. He cups his hand to his mouth. 'Head south-east. South-east.'

His hand reaches out to grab the tiller. Anna holds on with both hands. 'No! Harry, we've drifted too far south already. We have to turn back, before the current takes us.'

Harry's hands are cold and hard on her fingers, prising their grip away from the tiller. 'No,' he yells, 'we keep going. The wind will blow us straight into Bodø. Give it to me.'

He shoves her hard, and she loses her grip and slips off the bench into the water that is now three inches deep in the bottom of the boat. Somehow she still manages to keep hold of the end of the tiller.

'*Let go!*' Shouting hysterically he jerks the tiller out of her grip with such force that she feels her arms wrench deep in their sockets. She falls back into the well of the boat as it rises to meet her; icy saltwater rushes down over her shoulders like a waterfall. She cranes her head back. Above her is a twenty-foot wall of water – they are under the sheer, grey, combing face of a giant wave.

Anna opens her arms and throws herself into the prow. Her hands grab at the snaking bowline, catch it, and as they head into the toppling crest she takes two turns of rope around her palms. The boat is climbing so steeply now that it is almost upright: Anna is standing on the thwart, a great weight of seawater avalanching over her head, filling her nose and her mouth. Just below the crest the boat teeters and falls; the rope around her wrist jerks tight.

Then, miraculously, the wave wall has gone and the little boat surges forward and down, emptying seawater over the gunwales as it plunges.

Still clutching the rope, and laughing with terrified joy, Anna wheels around. Her hair is plastered against her forehead, her eyes raw with salt.

'We did it!' she shouts.

But the stern of the boat is empty, the untended tiller waving crazily from side to side like a compass needle vainly seeking north.

'*Harry!*'

Behind the boat the shoulders of the giant wave block out the horizon as it heads for the open sea.

Anna outscreams the wind.

'*Harry!*'

The boat is slipping sideways down the oncoming swell. She grabs at the flailing tiller, but the next crest shoulders the boat sideways and she falls heavily. For a moment she is winded, then struggles to the stern, and this time her outstretched hands close on the tiller. Leaning against it with all her weight, she drags the nose of the boat around into the wind again. Immediately the motion calms. She half stands, turns, cups one hand to her mouth and yells Harry's name back over the grey, regressing waves.

'*Harry!*'

Up the next wave and down.

'*Harry!*'

Nothing.

Up the next wave and down.

Nothing.

Harry Quinn is a mile away now, borne like flotsam on waves of terrifying height towards the Maelstrom itself. For a while he struggles, flailing against the ravening water. And then there is only darkness and the merciful, icy, lung-filling depths of the sea.

# Twenty-Seven

Anna is vomiting: into the boat, over the side, over the stern. Trails of saliva whip about her face.

She hugs the tiller into her body. It struggles against her like a living thing as the boat heads into the endlessly mesmerizing grey swell.

She is tired.

Bone weary.

Her feet shift in the water sloshing up and down the bottom of the boat. It's tepid now, like puddles on a summer beach at low tide. The rain from the north is soft, and the wind strokes her face like a comforting hand. All she has to do is close her eyes, relax down into warmth and drift away.

Torn from her slackened grip, the tiller swings out and hurtles back, smashing into her face. A terrible pain arcs across her cheekbone. Suddenly she is wide awake, cold and terrified, and blood is running into her mouth. Awkwardly she slides around to the other side of the stern where she can hold the tiller with the weight of her body. She peels off her glove and with frozen fingers feels the side of her face and inside her mouth. There is a painful swelling just below her temple and her teeth have torn the lining of her mouth.

But the pain revives her. The pain makes the cold and the wind real again. Keeping her weight against the tiller, she scoops a handful of salt water and rinses it around her mouth, whimpering at the pain. When she spits, skeins of red float across the water in the bottom of the boat. And then the engine gurgles, chokes and stops.

It's difficult to manoeuvre the jerrycan and even more difficult to remain steady and pour fuel into the empty tank. As the boat dips and sways beneath her knees, gouts of strong-smelling fuel miss the hole and soak her clothes, but gradually the jerrycan lightens until all its contents have disappeared.

Moaning with exhaustion she stands in the stern and takes the starter cord in both hands. The motor whirrs but refuses to catch. She lets in the cord again and pulls with all her strength. Another cough and whirr. Her face is throbbing badly and she is almost dizzy with effort. This time the wave crests just as she begins pulling and she falls backwards into the bottom of the boat, still holding the cord. And hears the engine start.

'Come on, come on.'

She is muttering now, encouraging herself, encouraging the motor and the boat. Taking up her slumped position against the tiller, she adjusts her direction against the face of the oncoming waves and gazes out blearily into the failing light. If the wind has changed or she has misjudged the course she may have missed Moskenes and be heading out into the Arctic Ocean, or she may still be drifting southwards on the tide. But, as she has no means of knowing, all she can do is approach each wave at the same angle, head on and slightly skewed to port, towards where she imagines the island to be.

Her legs are numb, bent beneath her. Folded around the soul for safekeeping, the fishermen said, curled in their narrow wooden beds.

Rise and fall, rise and fall. The waves process down on her endlessly, from some infinitely powerful and remote source. She wonders how far they have travelled, how far below the surface their influence stretches. How many fathoms would one have to sink before the ebb and flow became imperceptible, before one was floating peacefully down through dark cathedrals of water to a silent, waiting seabed?

She is very, very cold now: all feeling, all sensation, all consciousness centred and reduced to a single, small, regular pulse.

# Twenty-Eight

The lights save her: the saffron squares of windows, the orange beacon on the clifftop and the great ragged bonfire on the end of the jetty, sending sheaves of sparks high into the darkness. From the top of one wave, lurching with drunken weariness against the tiller, Anna catches a glimpse of this whole glorious galaxy, floating low above the sea.

The lights disappear, but as she tops the next wave they are there again: beautiful, beautiful lights. '*Here! Out here!*'

She is waving in the darkness. And then a thought struggles into her mind. This is Sigrid's boat, efficient, practical Sigrid's boat: somewhere there will be a flare. Keeping the tiller braced with her ribs, she bends down and fiddles with the locker catch. Inside is Harry's rucksack. She throws it into the bottom of the boat. Behind the bag is a tin, which escapes her grip and opens as it falls. Bandages, plasters and small bottles bob on the surface of the water and wash around her ankles.

She bends over further, and she feels something cold and hard wedged into a clip on the side wall of the locker. A pistol. She tries to hook her fingers around it, but they won't grip. Desperately, she hooks her boot under the pistol butt and feels the gun dislodge from its clip; as she slides down the next incline it washes out into her waiting palm. She braces the barrel against the transom, feels the flare click into place, but her fingers are cold and useless and refuse to wrap around the trigger. Quickly improvising, she takes the end of the starter cord, feeds it through the trigger guard, winds it around her hand, points the pistol to the sky and jerks her hand upward.

With a whump and a roar a red tracer shoots up, up, up.

As it explodes into light she sees a thousand black waves, each one frothed with crimson foam, sweeping towards her. It is a vision of hell, more terrifying than the dark.

Then, ahead, beyond the light, there is an answering rocket that tells her they have seen her.

Keeping on is all that is necessary now. The flare has extinguished and the black waves lift her invisibly, one after the other, as she keeps the tiller pointing at the same rigidly held angle.

And then, at last, there is a light: a big, round, searching beam, growing closer, swinging over the waves like a lighthouse. She stands then, bracing her legs wide, and the next time the light swings by it shines in all its dazzling, wonderful, blessed glory straight into her eyes.

In the pitching cabin of the fishing boat it is warm and peaceful. As if from a great distance Anna watches four oilskinned figures come and go through the swaying doorway, shouting silently. Someone kneels beside her, speaks loudly into her ear, 'Your face hurt?'

She knows the voice. Nodding is painful and takes great concentration.

'Anything else?'

Shake the head. More pain.

He is speaking again.

'Drink.'

She opens her mouth and a cold, fiery liquid rakes down her throat, so that she coughs and her eyes fill.

'Again.'

There are boots and yellow trousers clumping soundlessly all around her. A silent hornpipe, she thinks, as she slides gently but definitively into unconsciousness.

'Hey now, Anna.'

In her dream she is drifting down through the dark, lofty space between the surface and the seabed, and the ghosts of two drowned men are floating in the tide, their hair wafting in slow clouds around their heads, their pale faces turned up to watch her as she comes eddying down to join them.

'*Anna! Wake up. You hear me? It's all over now. All over. You're safe. You're back home in Å. Look.*'

Home.

In Å, which is the beginning and the end . . . of something.

She stops her downward drift and looks up, up to where pale blueness and links of sunlight are playing far above her. For another moment she floats, suspended between equal forces, then suddenly her lungs are filled with a rush of air and she kicks out, propelling herself upward, faster and faster, until she reaches the surface and soars into the light.

Sigrid's round, ruddy face hovers over her like a harvest moon.

Anna lifts her head from the pillow.

'Is the boat safe?' she says hoarsely.

Sigrid's broad grin widens still further. 'Don't worry. She's a sturdy old thing, that boat.'

The prow above her head, then falling away beneath her. A thousand advancing waves, red-plumed in the night.

'She got me out of the Maelstrom.'

'I think you pretty much got yourself out of there, girl.'

Sigrid sits back, as if waiting.

Anna's voice seems to have split in two. She croaks, 'Leif. What happened to Leif?'

Sigrid straightens the coverlet. 'Tommy Moller found him unconscious on the floor of the Markusen place, and he and a coupla fellers from Sørvågen brought him back here. He'd lost a lot of blood and he needs stitches in a gash, never mind what he says. They'll take him over to Reine later on, get some X-rays.'

She straightens the sheet and does not add that the only thing her brother talked about as she cleaned his wound was this blonde, deceptively slight middle-aged woman. Nor does she say that when she came back into the room after telephoning the doctor in Reine she found him gone and ran down to the quayside in time to see him clamber aboard Tommy Moller's boat just as the boys were casting off again and heading out to sea in search of the missing pair.

Now she says, matter-of-factly, 'Markusen's daughter says the American hasn't been back. It was her boy who saw you leaving yesterday afternoon, heading south. That was how we guessed where . . . Anyway, this morning some people said we should call the police in Bodø, but I thought we'd best wait until you woke.'

It takes Anna a while to tell what happened: the empty stern, the flailing tiller, the shoulders of the great wave heading on down towards the Maelstrom, blocking out the darkening sky.

Sigrid listens then leans across and takes Anna's shoulders in her big, capable hands. 'It could just as easily have been you, kid. That close to the Maelstrom, it's a miracle you got back at all.'

*Kid.*

Anna nods, winces.

Sigrid hauls herself to her feet. 'I thought at first the cheekbone was broken, but it's not – just a bad bruise. You look like you could do with a bit of nourishment, though. Think you can eat? There's eggs and fresh bread and coffee down in the kitchen. The clothes on the chairback should fit.'

In the doorway she turns. 'I'll tell Marika she can have her bed back tonight, eh?'

'Yes. Thank you, Sigrid.' For everything, she means.

Leif's sister grins.

'No problem, kid. See you downstairs.'

Leif is sitting at the table, a wide bloodstained bandage around his head. Kersti is at his feet, her head resting against his foot. As Anna enters Leif half stands then subsides into the chair.

'How are you?'

She stands opposite him, her hand to her face. She is wearing an outsized, red-checked flannel shirt and a pair of voluminous, cinched-in jeans. From the kitchen comes the sound of Sigrid banging dishes and calling to the children.

Leif's eyes are on the great purple weal that runs across her face from jaw to brow.

She has to say it again. 'How are you?'

'Oh, I'm good. Thick skull. Just need a few stitches.'

She sits, looks at him.

'You could have been killed,' she says.

Leif says calmly, 'He was too quick – I didn't see him coming. One minute we were arguing – then he turned away and next there's a great crunch on the side of my head. After that I don't remember much, although I thought I heard your voice.' His pale face constricts. 'I was about as much use as a dead man.'

There is silence in the room, silence in the kitchen beyond.

'But you still came looking for me.'

Leif keeps his hands clasped beneath the table to stop himself reaching across to touch her.

There is almost a smile.

'Yes, I came looking.'

The kitchen door swings open and Sigrid appears carrying two plates of eggs and bacon and fried potato.

'Enough talking,' she says firmly. 'Eat.'

When the meal is done Anna turns to Leif. 'He had a rucksack in the boat.'

'It's there.' He points into the corner.

She crouches down, fiddles with straps stiff with salt.

Inside are a dozen packages, all wrapped in clear plastic, meticulously taped.

'Here, let me.'

Leif draws a knife from his belt, slits each package so neatly that the plastic wadding peels away like flesh from a filleting blade. Anna makes a small, neat pile on the table. Bills, receipts, two passports, a thousand dollars in hundred-dollar bills, road maps, sea charts. And a black leather wallet, soft with wear, containing a dozen photographs. Anna in a New York street. Anna in Paris outside the Café de la Paix. A long-lens grainy shot of a woman on a riverbank.

From the bottom of the pile she draws a small, deckle-edged snapshot. A thin blonde girl sits alone on a bench under a budding tree. In the background is the shadow of a Renaissance colonnade, and on the reverse, in pencil, in a precise, disciplined hand: 'Palais Royal, 17 April 1940'.

There is a clatter of sea boots on the platform. Gunnar stands in the doorway, muffled in a jacket and scarf, blocking the light.

'Leif. We go to Reine now. No excuses, man.'

Leif holds up his hand.

'One minute.'

Anna stands and puts on her jacket. She runs her hand back through her hair, and to Leif it is as though she is separating shiny ribbons of kelp. The sunlit air is lively with dust motes, and, as he watches her, her eyes change steadily in the light.

'Anna?'

He holds his breath.

'Go on,' she says. 'They're waiting.'

When he still stands there, big and immobile, she takes his hand and leads him out to where Sigrid and Gunnar are waiting.

Minutes later she is walking at a pace up the cliff path, a freshening breeze at her back. As she climbs, pebbles squeak under the cleats of her boots and small startled birds take flight.

**Also from Peter Owen Publishers**

# Cassandra's Disk

Further praise for **Cassandra's Disk** by Angela Green

'An improper English tale of twin rivalry with a twist . . . Fabulous.'
– ***Kirkus Reviews***

'Altogether intimate and intriguing, with a deliciously dry sense of humour, this is a powerful first novel which will remain in the memory for a long time.'
– ***Noel Virtue***

'The melodramatic, salacious plot could have been lifted from a soap opera, but Green's assured voice gives this absorbing debut substance.'
– ***Publisher's Weekly***

'She's very, very good. An excellent novel. I'm always wanting to come across a new writer who completely engrosses with their art, and she is one.'
– ***Alan Sillitoe***

'Engaging and ingenious . . . The comic writing is highy accomplished, as are the more lyrical passages . . . The most incisive device of all is saved for the concluding Appendix, in the form of a letter . . . to say more would be to spoil one of the subtlest and most breath-catching conceits of this arresting novel.'
– ***London Magazine***

---